■ ■ ■ ■

BLOOD OATH

■ ■ ■ ■

NIGHT RIDERS

NIGHT RIDERS

Giff Cheshire

CHIVERS

British Library Cataloguing in Publication Data available

This Large Print edition published by AudioGO Ltd, Bath, 2013.
Published by arrangement with Golden West Literary Agency

U.K. Hardcover   ISBN   978 1 4713 2668 4
U.K. Softcover   ISBN   978 1 4713 2669 1

Printed and bound in Great Britain by
MPG Books Group Limited

TABLE OF CONTENTS

I

The street leading to the main part of town crossed a bridge over a slough. Caine was halfway over, thinking of breakfast, when he heard the sharp, light *crack* of a gun directly below him. Each tortured nerve in his body hauled tightly. Simultaneously a man came onto the bridge's far end.

Caine reeled to the bridge rail and supported himself there, chest heaving. He shut his eyes when the gun *cracked* again. His fingers clamped into the splintery railing wood as he realized it was the first time he had heard close gunfire since that day. He opened his eyes and looked down at the carpet of water lilies covering the pond.

A barefoot stripling in tattered overalls was down there. He had a .22 rifle, and Quincy Caine gritted his teeth and waited as it fired again. The kid was knocking the big waxy yellow flowers off their thick stems. Caine forced himself to endure yet another

9

shot. The man approaching came up beside him at the rail, took a look at the kid, and grinned loosely as his hand dropped to his holstered gun.

"Don't!" Caine gasped.

The man glanced at him owlishly but pulled the gun. He emptied it into the pond, each shot snipping a flower. He aimed close to the youngster, trying to scare him, and the boy bent and scurried clear. Caine saw this absently. Terror filled him and he felt it all again — gunfire erupting out of stillness, bullets piercing thin panels of wood, one in particular finding a small head beside him and carrying human blood and brains to splatter on his face. . . .

The man laughed, and it was this that drove Caine toward him. Savagely, with a red flash in his brain, came a mad urge to kill. He spun the man with his hand and smashed a fist against the heavy jaw. The man staggered back, saying: "Why, you damned gun-shy son-of-a-bitch!" And Caine was on him again. The fellow danced off, a lot of cockiness knocked out of him, fumbling at belt loops for loads, then trying to break open the gun.

"So we got a gun-shy pilgrim!" he roared. "Tenderfoot, I'll make you hop!"

A shrill voice yelped — "Leave him be,

Tige Haig!" — and Caine realized the boy had climbed up to the road. "You put them slugs close enough I could smell powder, damn' you! I hope he busts your ugly nose!"

"Shut your trap, Johnny Renshaw! I'll make him dance!"

It shook the panic out of Caine, but none of the rage Haig's taunts had engendered. This was the man who had spooked Laura Flanders's team on the high pass grade, the afternoon before, in an attempt to kill her.

Caine pinned the man against the opposite rail, forcing him to drop the gun. Haig was big, broad, and burly. He bounced off the rail and hammered Caine's face. Caine rode out the charge, switched it, and drove Haig half the distance to the bridge approach. The man was rough and tough but lacked science. Caine weathered another rush and took the offensive. He had blood streaming from Haig's nose, and deliberately he ground thick lips against heavy yellow teeth. He knew then he could stop it at will, but he had a depth of shame to vent. He drove Haig off the bridge to where a knot of spectators had formed. There, deliberately, he knocked him cold.

"Pretty good, stranger!" a man hollered. "Only don't let him get behind you with a gun!"

11

Caine turned without speaking and strode on, brushing his clothes as he walked.

By the time he'd finished breakfast, Caine knew he'd roll on with the next stage in the late afternoon. There was no peace for him; he had found none since that day two years ago. He walked south of town, along the creek whose backwash formed the slough. He was burned-out, corroded, restless again. It was no new mood, but one that always preceded a long period of travel. He yearned for wheels under him, for strange landscapes rolling past. It was a palliative although it never really helped.

Johnny Renshaw's mention of Haig's name had struck a responsive note in Caine. As he tasted the deflated reaction of his unreasoning battle with the man, Caine recalled the details.

The stage that had brought him to the Three Forks country, the day before, had been plodding monotonously up the far side of the mountain pass. Caine recalled how dust had ballooned ominously on a high turn, far up the switchbacks and across the void of a deep cañon. Caine had twisted on his seat beside the stage driver to cant a stern stare upward. Behind a madly lunging team, a buckboard careened close to the outer edge, then rocked crazily on. A figure bent low on its seat, tightly on the lines, sawing in rigid concentration.

"Runaway!" Caine gasped.

"And slamming straight at us, if it stays on the road!" The driver's bearded, tobacco-stained mouth had dropped slackly. He cracked his whip and swore, but the pitch was too great for speed. The driver groaned — "Can't beat it to the turnout, nohow!" — and pulled over against the high bank. He bawled to the insiders: "Pile out! All hell's a-coming with wild horses a-draggin' it! Shove yourselves in against the bank and say your prayers!"

Jumping down, Caine found his legs light and springy with tension. He felt it rising in him, the crowding anxiety from which he was rarely free. He fought it, shoving it away, concentrating on the scrambling passengers. The careening buckboard had disappeared behind brush on the far slant.

"There's another switchback afore it hits this stretch," the stage driver said. "Inside turn. If she's lucky, she'll pile up there."

"She?" Caine asked. "You mean she or it?"

"She. That there's a girl. Laura Flanders."

Caine found himself shoving hard upgrade. It had looked like a shaggy-haired

13

boy to him. He could hear the plunging vehicle. Rounding a curve, he caught sight of the big hairpin bend. A tight sickness rose in him. He shoved against the pitch, trying to run, hoping he might slow the horses and give the girl a chance to skin past the obstructing stage — if she made the corner.

He saw the scrambling team sweep into the bend and come nearly around. He saw the buckboard skid and tilt, and prayed it would go over. It did, rolling from the road, throwing the girl into a sailing spill, carrying horses and all from sight. The ensuing silence made Caine wince.

The buckboard wheels were uppermost, still spinning, as Caine came up. A horse staggered drunkenly up in a tangle of harness, but the other lay stunned. There was a sharp notch at the cañon's end, glaring with direct sun, the road graded to effect a smoother curve. The vehicle had hurtled hard into the narrow triangle on the upper side. Caine saw the figure stretched, small and still, beyond the wreckage and went toward it.

He turned her onto her back. Laura Flanders, the stage driver had said. Her arms were scraped and bleeding, and he saw she had protected her face as she hit. It was a pretty face, unlined, strongly shaped.

They had interpreted the situation below, and the stage tooled up. Its driver came down from the road with a canteen of water. He grumbled: "That's once this high-steppin' miss traveled a mite too fast. Them horses had more travel'n she figured on. They got away from her." He sloshed water onto her face.

"She live around here?" Caine asked.

"Her and her spineless brother've got 'em a spread back a piece. Up the Bear Creek Pass road. We come by the fork. Old Dan Flanders settled there thirty years ago. Real man, Dan. Girl's like him. But that hang-tail Fred . . . !"

Laura spoke in a whisper, opening her eyes: "Something scared the horses." She sat up, throwing off Caine's restraining hand, then climbed unsteadily to her feet. She felt of her face with the flat of her palms, then looked at her scraped arms. She turned to study the overturned buckboard and its bashed seat, and Caine sensed a deep disturbance in her. The passengers had got both horses up and were untangling the harness. The off animal bled from a cut shoulder, but both horses seemed able to travel.

"What scared them?" Caine asked.

"I don't know. I'd just come over the pass

15

summit. I heard something go *thip,* and the off horse jumped. They started to run, and I couldn't hold them. But I know somebody was in the brush above the road."

Maybe it was only shock and imagination, or maybe this girl was more frightened than Caine had ever seen a woman be before. Her guard was up suddenly and she turned away from him. The passengers got the buckboard straightened out and back onto the main road, and they patched up the seat so she could use it. The girl kept wetting her lips with her tongue and watching the grade above them. The stage driver motioned to his passengers to climb aboard.

Caine signaled them on. "I'll ride home with Miss Flanders, if she'll lend me a horse to get on into Three Forks."

"Oh, would you?" Laura said, showing bald relief.

When the stage had climbed out of sight, Caine walked thoughtfully to the summit. The bank above the road was heavily covered with low-growing chaparral and held an ominous note for him, even after what Laura had claimed. He found nothing revealing on the dusty road and bare, red-earthed bank. This gave him some relief until, just short of the summit, he found a bald patch in the thick brush. It was boot-tracked. A man had waited here, impatiently moving about. Caine saw a handful of pebbles that looked freshly dropped, covering one of the tracks. He saw that from this point he had an unobstructed view of a short stretch of the road below. He lifted an uneasy hand to stroke his jaw, then went back down the road to Laura.

He said: "Tracks and some pebbles. Would a thrown rock panic your team?"

Laura pondered the question. Her hair was still wet from the water the stage driver had sloshed over her, as was the upper part of her faded cotton shirt. She had managed to wipe most of the blood off her arms, and he saw that her elbows were painfully scraped.

"It wasn't thrown," she said. "That would be Tige Haig. Fancies himself with a slingshot. Or a gun. And he doesn't care much what he pots at."

"Starting a runaway on a high downgrade wouldn't be idle mischief, ma'am."

She met his eyes. "I've got a reputation for driving fast. If I'd rolled off the road, I'd probably never have lived to deny I was indulging the urge."

"Murder, eh?"

"Since it failed, let's call it idle mischief."

She didn't mean to say more, nor did she

17

during the hour it took them to reach a gate branded with a Bar F. At some distance toward the foothills stood the neat, small headquarters site of a cattle outfit. A young man closely resembling Laura came out to meet them. Caine knew it was the hang-tail brother the stage driver had mentioned. He looked the part now as he stared with worried eyes at the glaring signs of disaster.

"What in blue blazes?" he demanded.

"Just a little runaway coming down from the pass, Fred," Laura said. There was a biting tone in her voice. "Don't let it bother you." She introduced the men, but Fred Flanders withheld his hand.

He kept staring at Caine. "You a railroad man?"

"I'm a man with no connections, Flanders. Are they building a railroad hereabouts?"

"They're dickering for right of way."

"Gunning for it, wouldn't you say, Fred?" Laura asked. Caine liked her spunk. It was obvious that she had little use for this man, whatever their relationship. He saw Fred flinch, then the fellow turned back into the house.

It took Caine three hours to ride to the little cow town of Three Forks, but he was in no rush. He had no place to go, just as he had come from nowhere as far as memory was concerned. He found himself trying to fit together the pieces of a puzzle far too vast for him to understand. . . .

The hell with that, Caine told himself as he started back toward town. He'd get to hell going again on the afternoon stage. At a halting point on the upper creek he had washed away the remnants of his fight. Although Haig wouldn't realize it, that had at least been a payment on a lovely girl's account. He was glad of it, and from it he had also drawn a measure of restored self-respect. He was no coward but he couldn't stand gunfire. He wondered restlessly how any man could after what he had been through in his time.

He kept remembering Haig had tried to murder Laura and confronting the obvious sequel that the man would likely try it again. Well, she had a brother, even if patently of little account. It was not his worry, and what use would he be in a situation such as this thing suggested, anyway? He would roll out on the first Concord.

It was mid-morning, and the town was already baking hot. Caine was perspiring, even though he idled through the main section on his way back to his hotel. The night before, loitering here and there, he had learned that Three Forks was expecting a railroad. No seeds of conflict lay in that. It was a pleasant, orderly, prosperous town serving a large cattle range. It needed a railroad.

"A cuss named Ford Johnson's bucking us," a man had said, in response to Caine's questions. "But he's a fool to think he can swing it. You can't stop a railroad out of hate, mister, nor budge the way it's goin' to be built. That's Johnson's main reason. Been a sorehead ever since we throwed him outta this town."

Caine had pricked up his ears. "Who's Johnson?"

"Runs a stinking shebang on Bear Creek Pass road, now. Tried to get a hold on Three Forks, but we throwed him out, bag and baggage. Vain cuss. Took it personal. Swore he'd get even, and he tried to do it through the railroad. Tried to persuade 'em to run up Bear Creek Pass. That's south of here. It'd by-pass Three Forks and put his stinkin' little Johnsonville on the line."

"Did he get anywhere?"

"Worried us a mite, at first. Tried to lease right of way up Bear Creek Pass on his own account. Figured givin' right of way to the railroad might be enough to persuade 'em his way. That way's a little shorter, all right.

20

Promised 'em a new town at Johnsonville, serving the same country but bigger and better. The man kin talk. He got his right of way, too, except through Bar F. Laura Flanders up and told him to go plumb to blazes. Spunky chit. Had to go against her own brother to do it."

Caine had smiled. "So Johnson threw in the sponge."

"Far as anybody knows. Trains can't fly over the Bar F."

"Has the railroad committed itself to the Three Forks route?"

"Not yet. But they gotta. Did Johnson get a easement across Bar F, it might make a difference, though. Railroads'd ruther have a town come to them than go out of their way to a town. But Johnson's hate never got him nowhere. Reckon he's smart enough to give up." The man had grinned, shrugged, and left.

As Caine walked through the door of his hotel, his gaze settled in surprise on Laura Flanders. She rose from a lobby chair and came forward, wearing a skirt and long-sleeved blouse that covered her lacerated arms. The woman was tall and lithe and young. Recalling what the man had told him of her stand again Ford Johnson, Caine looked at her with new respect. Her brother

21

might be a coward but she had inherited courage enough for two from her pioneering father.

"May I go to your room with you?" Laura asked. "We've got to talk."

Caine nodded, concealing his surprise and picking up the key. He left his bedroom door ajar when they entered, but she turned and closed it. She refused the room's one chair and strode restlessly to the window, turned, and looked at him. "I could use your help," she said quickly.

"I'm going out on the afternoon stage," Caine said.

She nodded. "That's what I supposed. That's how you can help me."

"Then I'd be glad to."

Laura opened the bag she carried and from it pulled a long, folded paper. "I want to give this to you . . . in return for a dollar to make it a legal transaction. I made up my mind when I heard a while ago how you whipped Tige. He's Ford Johnson's man."

"I wondered," Caine said.

She looked surprised. "You know about Johnson?"

"I picked up the story last night. And I might say I admire your nerve, ma'am. They seem to be a bad pair."

"You don't know how bad, Caine. This

paper is a deed to a section of good land . . . six hundred forty acres. Is it worth a dollar to you? All I want to do is record it in your name. I don't care where you're going, so long as Johnson can't locate you before the railroad's built through Three Forks. In three months, say, you can deed the piece back to me."

"That's trusting me a long ways," Caine said. He took the deed she held out and glanced at it. Dry and legal, giving metes and bounds on a parcel of land. He'd seen many of them, and the feel of it brought back memories. He had come West to practice law, before a single moment changed everything. "What if I decided to hold onto it, standing on this deed? Or what if I go to Johnson and offer to sell the piece?"

"I just don't think you would do either."

Caine smiled. "I see you've done some smart thinking. I take it this section is the property that blocked Johnson's right of way. Deeded to a stranger whose whereabouts are unknown, he'd be stopped dead in his tracks. Does he want you out of the way because your brother would deal with him?"

Laura looked grave. "Unfortunately that's the case."

"And if I accept this property temporarily, I might be saving your life."

"Naturally I hope so. I aim to tell Johnson what I've done as soon as you're on your way again."

"Then I accept it," Caine said. "But why do you object so strongly to the Bear Creek route? A right of way through your property would probably enhance its value, if anything."

She came a step toward him and halted, her head lifted proudly. "My father was raising beef in this country when Three Forks got its first store. Johnson tried to get control of it a couple of years ago and didn't make it. If he manages to turn his stinking little Johnsonville into a railroad town, he'll kill this one. And he'll get control of the country. If my father was alive and had the same chance to stop that, he would. So it's what I'm doing."

It reached Caine, and that response lifted a strong sense of shame at his own lack of moral courage. The Caine who ran from himself, the Caine who couldn't endure his own memories, felt pretty damned small.

"Miss Flanders," he said, "supposing we put the deal through and I stick around."

"You'd simply draw what I've been getting. Underhanded scares, and some of

24

them something more than just scares, though not enough to go to the law about. The whole thing is for that key piece of property to belong to a man who cannot be located in months of searching."

"Or," said Caine, "a man who'll stand up to Johnson."

Laura met his eyes gravely. "I should warn you it would not be easy for you to stay here. Tige Haig's been telling it around that you're gun-shy."

"I am gun-shy," Caine said.

"Any particular reason?"

"My own reason."

"I don't think it would be wise for you to stick around, even if it would draw the trouble away from me."

"I want to stay."

She considered it for a long moment. "Very well, and you can live on your new property. There's a soddy on it. We use it for a line camp sometimes. Are you . . . ?" She hesitated.

"Financially solvent? Yes."

"The dugout's furnished. All you'll need is food. I'll leave the horse you borrowed at the stable for you. Don't bother about provisions. I'll bring some stuff over in the buckboard for you. I'll have the deed recorded and bring that, too. You turn south

25

at the forks, short of our place. You won't have any trouble finding it." She walked to the door, halted there, and for the first time smiled at him. "You owe me a dollar."

He grinned, and handed it to her. As she went out, he felt something lift in him that he had thought he would never feel again. Response to a woman. A thing he thought had died with Linda. . . .

For some reason he strode to the mirror above the pine washstand and looked into it. He saw that the face there was young, good-looking behind the haunting twists of bitterness. The soft black hair was untinged by gray. This seemed odd to him, for he felt old. Yet not so old, he discovered, as he had felt an hour before.

Laura Flanders was not at all like Linda, except in something deep that came from her, courage plus the warm and beautiful qualities that were a fine woman's. It was strange that he felt no disloyalty to the memory of Linda, his bride, with whom he had been honeymooning when the Blackfeet struck their stage. It had been his aim to find some growing frontier town and hang out his shingle. That had perished in the moment when a bullet found the life thread of Linda and snapped it, with her blood spattering him. The stage had escaped, beating the pursuit into the protection of a stonewalled stage station. But from that first moment Quincy Caine had not escaped.

II

II

Caine was walking thoughtfully to the livery where he had left the Bar F saddle horse when he saw Johnny Renshaw again. A burro and barrel cart were pulled in against the sidewalk, the little animal sour and droop-eared in the heat. The boy had a Chinaman's yoke slung across thin shoulders, with two punctured oil tins suspended from it by wires. He was sprinkling the deep, trash-littered dust on the street along the front of a store.

Caine halted. "That looks like heavy work, Johnny."

Johnny glanced up, recognized him, and grinned. "Man's got to eat, mister."

"You earn your own living?"

"What I get. Say, you sure set Tige Haig on his fancy britches this morning. A purty sight. But he swears he's going to get even. Say, what kind of a fit was you having there on the bridge, anyhow? What give him the

28

idea you're gun-shy?"

"I am, Johnny. I make no bones about it." Caine liked Johnny's unwashed looks. He doubted if the boy was over twelve. "Don't you have folks?"

Renshaw shook his head. "Not to speak of. Injuns. Pa settled a mite too far out on the prairie. Injuns got 'em both, but Ma hid me. Some neighbors come looking afterward and found me. Raised me . . . to get themselves a extra hand to work, I found out. The man beat the hell outta me, mister. I got a chance to scat when I was eight, and I sure did. Wound up here. It's a good town. Sure hope we get that railroad. Never seen a train."

"Sure hope you do, Johnny," Caine said. "You don't remember the Indian attack?"

"I was a baby. Mister, you oughta pack a gun. That Haig don't always give warning."

"Maybe I should. But they scare me."

"What happened?"

"Indians. But I remember."

Johnny looked at him thoughtfully. "Mister, there's one thing I've found out. Man gets the scaredest of what he can't get his hands on."

"The really frightening things're intangible, Johnny. I'm not actually afraid of guns. I'm afraid of what they make me

29

remember."

The boy nodded, a wisdom in his eyes beyond his years. "I been there, mister. And my advice to you is buy yourself a gun and live with it till it don't scare you any more. Men you can face. I seen you go after Tige Haig, who's got this country scared half to death. But me, I've got a dust storm to prevent. So long."

Caine walked on, aware he'd just been given a fatherly talk by a beardless boy. He went across the street, turned back a few doors, and entered a hardware store. When he came out, he wore a holstered Colt .44, slung from a belt about his middle. No one could have detected from his expression the tight tension it put in him. He could use the weapon if his nerves didn't freeze on him, just as he could ride a horse. Four years in the cavalry during the big war taught a man that. It taught him to face carnage and death, but it didn't teach him to see his bride die in a moment of apparent peacefulness, with her blood covering him.

He found the south fork line camp that proved to be a dugout set serenely in a saucer in the bare, low hills and bisected by the creek they called the Bear. Rimrock formed jaws at the lower edge, and he saw why this was a key piece in the right of way Ford Johnson wanted to secure for the railroad. Hills and scattered brakes made it the only approach to the mountain pass beyond. He rode into the section with a sense of possession, since in legal fact the land was his. He would make it his, he told himself, until the day came to turn it back to the Flanderses. He had a stake in the fight, a private stake, and this looked like a good place to make it.

There were springs near the dugout, and a grove of cool locusts growing in the sub-irrigated soil. In blossom now, they put a sweet, heady scent upon the still air. Caine picketed his horse in the heavy grass, in the shade of the grove. He inspected the soddy, which had a wall bunk and stove, a rough table, and two chairs. A coffee pot sat on the stove, a frying pan and two kettles hung from pegs on the wall. The poorest accommodations he had ever faced, Caine thought, yet he had a feeling he would like it here.

It was Fred Flanders, rather than Laura, who showed up in late afternoon with a buckboard load of provisions. He nodded a curt greeting and his face was truculent. He helped Caine unload the stuff and pack it into the dugout. Finally he pulled the deed from his pocket and handed it over.

"I don't like this, Caine," he announced. "I didn't like it even when we figured you were going to keep traveling. But it looked like a good way to get Johnson off our neck."

"What you don't like, then, is my staying here."

Flanders swung around and stared at him. "What's the idea? How do we know we'll ever get this piece back? How do we know what made you change your mind about going on? How do we know?"

Caine grinned at him. "Those're legitimate questions, Fred. But you'll admit that you took the initiative."

"My sister did."

"But you fell in with the original idea. Your signature's on this deed."

"That was before you decided to move out here. I don't like it, Caine. I don't trust you."

It was hard to feel sympathy for this man. Caine studied his face and found nothing there but indecision and fear and self-interest. "Yet you brought the deed over to me, Fred. Because you fear Johnson worse than you do me. I'll be his target instead of you now. You're safe on that score, at least. And you're weak enough so you have to do it, even if it forces you to do something you dislike, though not nearly as much."

The temper came up in Fred, and he turned it hotly on Caine. "Who're you to talk, you gun-shy. . . ."

He broke it off. Caine did not understand for a moment, for his ears were less tuned to range sounds than the other man's. Then he saw two riders break over a far rise and knew they had come up through the jaws of Bear Creek. They were heading toward the line camp.

Caine saw the raw fear come up in Flanders, who gasped: "God, it's Johnson and Haig. I'm getting out of here."

"Then get," Caine said calmly. But he felt his own scalp tighten. Fred's hand brushed the grips of his gun, and for a moment he seemed on the point of driving off at high speed. Something changed his mind and he slumped on the buckboard seat, waiting.

The riders disappeared for a time, then came up out of a nearby draw. Caine recognized Haig by his bulk and clothes, but the man with him was equally big. They rode in at a fast walk, guarded but confident, and halted their horses before the dugout. Johnson was younger than Caine had expected, although swart and heavy-featured. Like Haig, he had a touch of the dandy, but in his half-handsome face was more: a vanity and petulance that made good soil for the hatred he bore Three Forks for running him out. He sat his saddle tightly and he wore a gun.

"Fred," Johnson said, "we seen your rig heading this way. Got to wondering what interested you up here. Haig says he's already met up with this gun-shy pilgrim. What's he doing up here?"

Fred's jaw worked convulsively. "You lay off me, Johnson! We ain't got anything to do with this piece any more. Sis deeded it to Caine, here, this morning. Don't look at me like that! I didn't have a thing to do with it!"

"You're lying, Fred," Johnson grunted, but worry showed in his gimlet eyes.

"It's recorded. You can check at the courthouse. Johnson, you leave me alone! You got nothing to gain from us any more!" Fred picked up the lines, Caine understanding he had waited only to get that information across to Johnson, and the buckboard rattled away. The two mounted men made no effort to stop him.

Then Haig's hand moved toward his holster and came up with the gun. Caine had seen the motion, but the icy touch of the old panic had held him still. Haig lined the gun coolly, grinning without humor. "Drop your piece, Caine, and stand away from it."

Caine obeyed, feeling the sharp jerk of a muscle in his throat. Johnson swung down to pick up the dropped gun, and shoved it into his belt, then stepped into the clear.

"Maybe you'd like to sell this piece for twice what you paid for it, Caine," Johnson said. "It'd be worth it to me."

"That'd be two dollars, Johnson. Not enough."

"What do you want?"

"A lot more than you could ever muster. A decent break for Laura Flanders and the town and country she has the guts to protect. That's beyond you. You can kill me, but the property would still be in my name. I have heirs back East. Things would be in such a tangle the Three Forks depot would need repainting before you could find anybody to buy your right of way from." Caine spoke calmly, although the touch of ice was on his heart.

"Make him dance, Tige," Johnson said. "Then maybe he'll feel like dealing."

Caine nearly cried out in protest, but he choked the sound back. Haig's face still showed the marks of the fight, and they seemed more vivid suddenly. The man fired a deliberate shot, and the slug kicked up dirt between Caine's feet.

Caine stared down but didn't budge. He swallowed painfully and sweat broke out on his face. A muscle jerked sharply in his throat. But he had something new, a dignity that would not permit him to spread his feet, to jump or try to run. Haig fired again, and once again, the last shot nicking the sole of Caine's boot. The man looked baffled, and Johnson frowned.

"Cut it, Tige," he said suddenly.

"Whatever give you the idea this jigger's yellow? I got to admire guts, no matter who's got 'em. Caine, we want lease or title to a hundred-foot strip through your section. We aim to get it. You'd best deal."

"You can go to hell," Caine said.

They rode away. Caine stared at the scuffed-up ground. Johnson had taken his gun along. Caine suddenly wished for it hungrily. He could have shot them, even in the back, at that moment. But not until they had disappeared beyond the roll of land did he let go. Then he walked shakenly to the springs, fell flat there, and lay, still and trembling, for a long while.

Lengthening shadows finally roused him. He rose, drank cold water, and returned to the dugout. He unpacked the provisions

Flanders had brought. He arranged them neatly on the shelves, then made up his bunk and fetched a pail of water from the springs. Presently he made a fire, boiled coffee, and drank it sitting on the threshold of the dugout, smoking a cigarette. By that time, dusk was running in.

He nearly spilled the coffee when a mounted figure was highlighted for a moment on the south rim in the direction of Bar F. The rider came his way, and after a moment Laura Flanders's voice called out to him: "Caine!"

He answered, knowing it was Western custom to warn a residence before approaching it. Laura was dressed in Levi's and shirt again, with a flat hat resting on her shoulders, suspended by its cord about her neck. He rose as she swung down and strode toward her.

"I'm terribly ashamed," she said in greeting. "Fred heard the shooting and didn't have guts enough to turn back to see if they'd killed you. But I guessed what Haig was up to . . . the thing he tried to pull on you in town."

"There was nothing Fred could have done," Caine said.

Her voice was sharp. "Except to act the part of a man. Quincy Caine, I came over to release you from our bargain. Why should I ask you to run this danger when a Flanders rats out?"

Caine gave this long thought. "Would you like some coffee?" he asked. He was glad she had a sense of shame. It made him feel at ease with her.

"I would," Laura said, and they went inside.

He knew his lack of censure had eased her, and somehow the evening took on a quiet pleasantness. As darkness closed in, running softly and silently across the uplands, Caine lighted a lamp.

"It looks like you haven't eaten yet," Laura said. "I'll fix you something." He started to object but changed his mind. He helped her, awkward because he wasn't used to such work, closely watching what she did and for the first time seeing dignity in the simple skills that made people self-sufficient. They ate together, afterward sitting across the table from each other.

"I expect you've got the picture by now," Laura said. "A railroad trying to use Bear Creek Pass would have to come up the old water course left from the days of the big floods. It's pretty narrow in spots. This section lays across one such place. Ford Johnson has his leases to here. But they're not worth the paper until he can control this." She held up her coffee cup. "Here's to you."

"To us," Caine corrected, and somehow felt more lighthearted than he had a right to feel. He could look back with a degree of detachment upon the visit of Johnson and Haig. He knew Laura was curious about him but he had no wish to explain. He wanted to make this a test on the long odds that he could find the peace he sought.

Caine rode to the high ridge with Laura, an ease that she seemed to share filling him, and their talk was light. The high valley lay under a spilling moon, tipping black shadows from the scattered juniper. They said good night at a point where the sweep began to fall away again, and Caine turned back. It dawned on him that having a piece of ground he could call his headquarters, no matter how little his actual right to it, was having an effect.

A man's thoughts ranged naturally to what could be done with a piece of good land. It was beef country, and he knew little of raising it. But it impressed him as an interesting, wholesome, and not unprofitable business.

He had no wish for sleep, and the night was beautiful. Now and then a ragged cloud ran before the moon, mottling the countryside in soft mystery. The high air was cool and fresh, with the scent of desert flowers charging it. Good for a man long accustomed to hotels and stagecoaches and stuffy saloons. His horse was range bred, and Caine let it pick its own way. They followed the open crest of the land so that he could see a great distance on either hand.

His mind kept drifting to Johnson and Haig and the situation in which he had become involved. It had been free choice, and he had no desire to have it otherwise. A man had to make a stand and fight somewhere, even when his main enemy was himself. This was a good place for it, the best he had found.

It struck Caine that his horse had changed direction and was poking south, but he didn't haul it around. Presently the rough shapes of ranch structures rose in a small, partly wooded cup far below, and he knew it was Bar F headquarters. The buildings were dark, and he knew Laura had had time to reach home. He thought of her there in bed and liked the thought. Wheeling his mount, he headed downslope at an easy walk. He came to a rim, with no descent in evidence, and halted. The night around him was soft and sweetly scented.

Two quick punctures of sound touched

Caine's ears, and he stiffened in the saddle. They came from below, from the cup that was the Flanders headquarters site, and they were gunshots. Caine flung a glance along either reach of the rimrock, seeking a descent. He recalled that he was not armed, that Johnson had taken his new gun.

For a moment he thought he'd escape the old panic — but it edged in. He swung his horse to the right, seeking in motion to escape the feeling. It overtook him; it descended fully upon him. There was no more firing, and Caine was torn between the desire to investigate and to flee. He told himself that Johnson had nothing further to gain from Flanders, just as Fred had pointed out. Probably some four-footed prowler had roused somebody down there. But there *had* been shots, and he spurred his horse and headed for the dugout he was already thinking of as home. . . .

It was a sense of guilt that took Caine over to Bar F soon after daybreak. He had slept little, the old anxieties roiling in him, but stark fear took him as he rode into the Flanders place. There was no one in evidence, and, when he called, nobody responded. The kitchen door stood ajar, and he saw stains on the porch that made him

41

pause for a frozen moment. He swung down, investigated, and was sure they had been made by blood.

He skirted the stain and stepped into the kitchen. Nobody was in the house. A search of the barn and outside structures was fruitless. One horse gazed at him curiously from the day corral. The buckboard Fred had used to bring over provisions was gone.

Caine leaned against the water trough in the center of the compound, smoking and trying to figure it out. Wheel tracks showed the buckboard had stopped at the porch. Whoever had been hurt had been loaded and taken somewhere. There had been two shots. Caine ground out his cigarette, turned, and mounted. He followed the freshest wheel tracks out to the main road and north a distance, becoming certain they were rolling toward Three Forks. There was nothing he could do but wait until somebody showed up to explain, and he couldn't wait remaining still. He headed toward his own land.

He fixed and ate breakfast. To keep busy, he tidied up and brought in a pail of fresh water. He kept picking at the mystery at Bar F, but got nowhere.

The sun was high in the south when riders broke into view, coming from the direction of Bar F. Caine counted four. He watched their approach calmly picking out, as they loomed larger, the shapes of Laura Flanders, Ford Johnson, an unidentified man, and young Renshaw. He noted that the boy carried the .22 rifle with which he had been shooting at water lilies the morning before.

Caine identified a sheriff's badge on the unknown man's vest and he saw grave reserve on all faces. The party halted, Laura avoiding Caine's questioning eyes, and only the sheriff swung down.

"Caine," he said, "I'm Tom Engels. Got a few questions. What time did you get home last night?"

Caine stood silent for a moment. Then: "Why, I don't know. Midnight, possibly. I rode downcountry for quite a while."

"Where?"

"Along the ridge. To the south and back."

Engels nodded. "Bar F way?"

"I turned back at the rim just above there."

Tom Engels reached in his saddlebag and pulled out a gun. He held it out, close to Caine but keeping possession. "You ever see this before."

Caine smiled and shook his head. "It looks new."

"It is. Jenkins, the hardware man, says he sold it to you yesterday. Last night it killed Fred Flanders."

Caine swallowed. He flung a look of dismay and sympathy at Laura, but she wasn't watching. He saw that her face was white and strained. And more — bitter.

"The point is," Caine said, "you think I shot him."

"Somebody rapped on the Flanderses' back door last night. Fred went to answer. He got it twice, once in the chest and once in the belly. Miss Laura heard somebody scooting, fast. Not used to side-guns, I reckon. This seems to have bounced from his holster where he climbed aboard his horse. Now what have you got to say?"

Johnny Renshaw spoke up then. He still sat his saddle, studying Caine guardedly. He turned to the sheriff. "And that's where you're runnin' the wrong 'coon, Sheriff. Had I beefed a man that way, I'd've known it if I dropped a two, three pound gun. 'Less I wanted to plant it there."

It helped Caine. "Exactly. Had I done it, I don't think I'd have been that careless. It so happens that Ford Johnson took that gun away from me yesterday afternoon."

Johnson's face didn't change. "That's a bald-faced lie. I never saw this man before.

I know nothing whatsoever about him, except what Miss Laura says. Which looks bad. She was foolish enough to deed him a section of land I wanted. Fred objected to it violently. Caine was afraid Fred would make trouble about it. Caine wants to keep this land. He figured he could kill Fred and shove the blame off onto me. Maybe he dropped that gun on purpose, meaning to claim I'd taken it away from him. But it's not good enough, Engels. I can prove I was in a card game in Johnsonville, from dark last night to the wee hours."

Caine's legal mind was working fast. It was patently a frame-up but it didn't make sense. Of what value to Johnson would Fred's death be now? Fred was the weak one there, the one who would have dealt with him. Or had Johnson or his man hoped to get Laura? But that wouldn't have furthered their cause a whit, either, as far as Caine could see, and, if that had been the intent, the killer could have remained long enough to accomplish that, also.

"You don't believe that, Laura," Caine said.

She looked at him then, uncertain but tipped on the side of suspicion. "How do I know? It's true Fred was after me to get some sort of guarantee we'd get the land

45

back. I don't know what passed between you up here, yesterday afternoon. And you admit it's your gun. I picked it up myself. I took Fred's body in to the sheriff. I charged Johnson with murdering him. Coming back out, we stopped at Johnsonville. Three men swore Johnson wasn't away from there all last night, for what that's worth. And the sheriff had already found out it was your gun. The whole thing is . . . what reason would Johnson have for killing Fred now?"

There was a small smile on Johnson's face as he looked at Caine. "Arrest the man, Engels. If Miss Laura doesn't want to charge him, I will."

Tom Engels nodded. "Caine, I got to take you in." There seemed to be genuine regret in his eyes, a lingering doubt. "Get your stuff. Johnny, you go saddle his horse. Then you can go home with Miss Laura and help her out till she gets onto her feet."

Johnny rode his nag around the corner of the soddy, sober-faced, lost in thought. Ford Johnson's smile grew. Laura's thoughts were turned inward; she seemed to see no one, and Caine knew what the shock must have been to her. For all her concern, he could feel little sympathy for Fred. Her brother had been more than spineless; he had been truculent and head-strong and generally unpleasant. But as a sister, she was feeling his loss.

A prickling feeling ran up Caine's spine when he considered his own position. It seemed unbelievable that Johnson could make his frame-up work, but was it so unlikely? Quincy Caine was unknown in these parts. It was easy to prove that the gun that apparently had killed Fred Flanders was his, newly purchased by a man who, by common gossip, was gun-shy. Why would such a man want a gun? There was the deed to a valuable piece of property he had come by for $1. And how could he prove, from behind bars, that Johnson had any kind of a plausible motive? The panic began to crowd in upon Caine once again.

"You'll get your day in court, Caine," the sheriff said, not without kindness. "You'll get a fair shake."

"No, he won't!" Johnny Renshaw stepped around the corner of the dugout, holding the .22 in tight, grubby fists. "Sheriff, you and Johnson keep your hands away from your six-shooters. Caine and me're getting outta here."

"Don't, Johnny!" Laura gasped.

"Reckon you're upset, Miss Laura," Johnny answered, "or you wouldn't be such a fool. Don't know what it is, but Johnson

47

has cut hisself a cute caper. Me, I don't aim to see a good man hung to suit the schemes of a rotten one."

"You don't know what you're doing, Johnny," the sheriff insisted.

"Which of us don't?" Johnny snorted. "Caine, get their hardware. Then pack us some grub. Your horse's ready behind the soddy with mine."

Caine swung into motion, unthinking, wanting only to get away from there. He lifted the two men's guns, then stepped into the structure and, with trembling hands, threw together some of the provisions Fred Flanders had brought over. He placed them in a gunny sack, picked up his own bag, and stepped out. Johnny still stood on thin, spread legs, holding his small rifle on the party, his face grim.

Caine looked at Laura. "All I can say is . . . I didn't do it. You have all my sympathy and regard." When she didn't lift her eyes, he went to fetch the horses from behind.

Johnny forced the mounted ones to light down and enter the soddy. When he rode out with Caine, they led the animals, leaving the sheriff's party afoot. A mile away, Johnny turned them loose.

Caine had the calmness to think clearly

again. "The sheriff was right, Johnny," he said. "You're helping a man break arrest. That puts you outside the law."

"Not if law means justice," Johnny answered. "Johnson was sure fixing to put you on the end of a hang rope, mister."

"I appreciate that, my friend. But why?"

"You got two choices. You can try to find out, or you can scoot outta these parts. I know the country. I could get you through all right."

"Then where would you go?"

Johnny grinned. "With you, if you'll let me."

"I know of nobody I'd rather have along, Johnny."

"Whichever, we gotta hole up, and I know the place."

Johnny led the way and Caine followed without question. They climbed into the foothills, coming presently into the coolness of high pine timber. But Caine did not find himself put at ease by the distance they put between themselves and the sheriff's party. Something about Johnny's fierce, spunky decency kept putting a lump in his throat. The kid had had no thought of the consequences to himself. Regret rose in Caine, although it was too late to send the boy back. . . .

III

A day later they halted, high in the mountain wastes, after a twisting, confusing ride. "This is the place," Johnny said. "Was up here hunting once, with Tom Engels. Pretty soon we can work our way north through the mountains and come out where they never even heard of a telegraph."

"You were friends with the sheriff?" Caine asked.

"He let me sleep in the jail. Which is how come I got in on it. Woke up when Miss Laura brung Fred in the other night. Talked Tom into letting me come when I seen the thing was shaping up against you."

"Could we ever turn the tables on Johnson?"

"That," Johnny said, "would be a tough chunk to chaw. You're clear, and, if you ain't got nothing back there you care about, it'd be easier just to keep going."

Caine turned that over in his mind. For a

50

few short hours he had wondered if he hadn't found something to care about again. But the peaceful section of country he had liked was lost to him. A girl he had liked better had faltered in her belief in him. Why should they go back? It would only be to risk death.

They made camp in a ravine coursed by a cold mountain stream and overhung with thick pine. They could be approached only from either end of the hollow and there was distance enough to give them warning. Johnny had fish hooks stuck in the band of his battered hat, and he caught trout for supper. A lassitude was in Caine. He was washed out, inwardly corroded, no longer afraid now that escape lay ahead, but baffled and with a lingering sense of loss. If only Laura had shown some degree of faith . . . but that didn't matter now.

He knew they would go on, even though the uneasiness of guilt came to him as he contemplated it. Caine didn't sleep well that night. He roused time after time to make a cigarette and smoke in the moonlight. Johnny slept easily, but Caine knew the slightest sound foreign to the night would bring him awake. It seemed odd that a boy so immature should have developed such cunning. Yet in the experience of adversity,

Johnny was the older. From the start, he apparently had been obliged to fend for himself.

Whenever he managed to drop off, Caine's dreams were troubled. In the dawn, he thought: *I've been running ever since that day. But that wasn't my fault. Running out of this would be. I'll never sleep again if I run now. . . .*

The third dawn trouble came. Caine stumbled out of his blankets and walked the length of the little mountain grove. A rocky needle shoved sharply upward at the end. He noticed this, and now he climbed a distance over the rough, granite pedestal until he was above the surrounding terrain, the sable, wheeling heavens punctured only in places by pinpoints of twinkling light. On a broad ledge he flattened himself, and there he slept.

Daylight and cold combined to rouse him. He lowered himself, teeth chattering in the chill air. He flung an idle look in the direction of camp and noted that Johnny was slow in starting a breakfast fire this morning. He turned that way, somewhat relaxed and rested from his short sleep. He had no warning as he came out of the brush to see two men standing at the camp and no sign of Johnny.

Although they had the two guns they had taken from Engels and Johnson, Caine had not worn one. *Haig!* he realized. *Tige Haig!* It was too late to duck back, for they had seen him.

Haig stood by the ashes of last night's fire, a gun in his hand, watching Caine. A second man, ragged and with shaggy hair, stood at Haig's left, holding a rifle.

"Come in, Caine!" Haig called. "You can cook us some breakfast."

As he came up, Caine saw Johnny's body, still and flat, upon the littered earth.

"Had to wallop him," Haig said. "That little punk sure is a wildcat. Injun Jake, here, moved in on him like a cloud, but it woke Johnny up. Nearly got his gun working, too."

Caine swallowed, something pathetic in the still form hitting him harder than Haig's presence. Johnny had no stake in this, except a spontaneous feeling of friendship for Quincy Caine, a man worth not a good damn. He probably had faced death, only moments ago, and at the least had been battered senseless for that loyalty.

Hate came to Caine then that was above any fear. "You're the lowest kind of scum, Haig," he said. "You stink to heaven!"

The man only grinned. "Look who's calling who what. He done a pretty good job

53

fouling sign, getting you in here, Caine. But Ford Johnson wants you. Dead, that is. He remembered this Injun Jake. Jake's trapped this country, and he's got a bloodhound nose, anyhow. Located you last night. Figured to get the jump when you were asleep. You had us worried, moseyin' off the way you done. Didn't know that till we made our jump."

"Why," Caine asked, "does Johnson want me dead?"

"Johnson's got one thing eatin' his brain out like a maggot . . . that railroad deal. Once he thought he could ride Three Forks and this cow country with a Spanish bit. Plumb hurt his feelings when he got tossed out on his britches. But he figures, if he can make Johnsonville a railroad town, he'll still be high man in that country. And get fat and rich at it. Only thing is, railroad's apt to announce its route any day now, and Ford's in a sweat to hand 'em a nice long stretch of right of way."

"I'd heard that," Caine said. "How'll my dying help him?"

"Start us some breakfast," Haig answered. "If you make a funny move, you get it through the head. Johnny, too. Our orders, Caine, is to leave you two up here. For keeps."

"I have no doubt that you'll carry them out."

"With pleasure. I don't cotton to taking a whupping offen a gun-shy pilgrim."

Caine knew the man wouldn't explain the enigma. He started a fire, sliced bacon, and ground a double handful of coffee beans on a rock. Johnny stirred and almost instantly shoved himself to a sitting position. His eyes went to Caine, then appraised Haig with smoldering eyes.

"Don't believe in giving a man a chance, do you, Haig?"

Haig shrugged. "Why should I? And don't get sassy, button. Jake 'n' me aim to rest a spell. We'll start down around noon. Alone."

"Beefing us first, you mean?" Johnny said.

"That's the caper."

They ate, and afterward Haig rose. He pulled something from his pocket that looked like a slingshot, and Caine remembered it had been Laura's theory that he had used it to start her team's runaway. Haig got some pebbles from the creek and began to amuse himself by knocking a tomato tin off a rock.

Injun Jake looked like a half-breed, and he sat always with his rifle across his knees, his face stolid. If he had any personal interest in the situation, he didn't reveal it.

Caine saw no sign of Johnny's .22 or the two six-guns. Hate suddenly welled and choked him, and he hungered to get his hands on Haig again. It struck him suddenly that he *did* have something to hold him in this country, to make him fight for the right. Johnny. The waif who had given everything to a man he had simply liked.

Johnny Renshaw had chosen this country for his home, and relinquished it without question. But he deserved to live here, to grow here. He had ought to be spared the uncertainties and emptiness of constant rambling, particularly with the smirch of broken law behind. Caine turned this in his thoughts, and decision came to him.

That Johnny had an aching head was obvious, for at times he blinked his eyes and shook his head sharply. He kept watching Injun Jake, and Caine feared he'd tackle the half-breed. Caine warned Johnny with his eyes and got a brooding look in return.

Haig motioned to Caine. "Pilgrim," he said, when Caine walked down to the edge of the creek, "you stewed long enough?"

"How do you mean?"

"You had long enough to think about dealing your way out?"

"Ah," Caine said. "You're still after that."

"Sure. Hard trip up here, fellow."

Caine moistened his lips. The man was clever, making his cool threats of merciless death and letting them work a while before offering a compromise. "What's the deal?" Caine asked.

"Fred Flanders upset the apple cart. He mustered hisself a set of guts right at the last. Me and Johnson was coming over to see you that night, Caine. We seen Laura heading your way. Figured Fred was home alone, so we went over to see him, instead. He was. We saw him. But bedamned if he didn't turn ringy on us. Johnson pegged the cuss one notch too low, I reckon. Figured Fred'd go for anything that'd save his own lousy hide. But the man wouldn't set in on a deal that had to do with beefing his sister."

"What?" Caine asked sharply.

Haig grinned at him. "Sort of like that filly, don't you? Proposition Johnson made was to beef her and get you hung for it. She always held Fred in. Run things. Despised him. We figured Fred'd go for getting things in his own hands and shed of that. We figured he'd give Johnson his right of way. Damn me, if Fred didn't throw down on us and order us offen the spread. Fixed hisself, though, when he threatened to tell the sheriff about that offer."

"So you shot him?"

"Not then. Not with a wild man holding a gun on us. But we come back later."

"Now what?" Caine asked.

"You still hold that property in your name. You're charged with murder and on the dodge, and mebbe we could get the court to set that deed aside. But it'd take time, which is what Johnson is short of. I got a quitclaim in my pocket you can sign. We'll mail it from somewheres across the mountains, so it'll look like you done it."

"And if I sign it, I don't get shot. Nor Johnny?"

"Nor Johnny. Good deal for you, pilgrim. That Laura sort of took to you, too, it looks like. With her brother dead and you *ki-yi-ing* for yonder, don't reckon she'll have the heart to hold out any longer."

"But if she does?" Caine asked.

Haig shrugged. "If she's fool enough, things'll keep happening to her. Comes a time when anybody's nerve busts like a banjo string. She's about there. Fred's getting it sure shook her up. Halfway thinkin' you done it ain't helping any. You sign this quitclaim, and it's in the bag for Ford Johnson. And will I be glad? The man ain't been fit to live with the last two, three days."

"Why don't I deed the section direct to Johnson?"

"Stink too bad when he tried to record it. Other way looks better. Which you want, Caine? You gonna sign or you want a slug in your belly . . . mebbe after seeing one tear through Johnny's."

"Let's see the quitclaim," Caine said.

Grinning again, Haig fumbled with the button on his shirt pocket. Caine used that second, bending and scooping sand into his fingers that he hurled fully into Haig's eyes. The man cursed, shoving hands to his face, and Caine drove in. He had shaped a desperate plan in the last two hours, one that might go hard with himself but that might save Johnny. Tige Haig was the key. Injun Jake apparently had been hired mainly to serve as a tracker. With Haig out of it suddenly, it was doubtful that the half-breed would want to go ahead with murder on his own hook. He'd be more apt to strike out to get away from there.

But Injun Jake had a rifle. To keep him from using it, Caine caught Haig, who was trying to shove into the clear. The man was still nearly blinded, still cursing foully. "Plug the son-of-a-bitch, Jake!" he screeched. He kicked and swung desperately to keep at a distance. But the man's effort was futile.

Caine drove in under Haig's arms, getting the man's chest in his grasp. He heaved, lifting his burden in dead weight, instantly realizing his folly. The rifle hammered. The half-breed had fired at his legs, trying to cripple him. Caine brought Haig down in a powered smash, landing on top of him. He heard an explosive grunt, and for an instant Haig was still. Caine landed flat on him and shoved his fingers to Haig's throat. All the hatred he had felt for this man welled out of him. He gripped with all his power and at the same time kept slamming Haig's head against the rocky earth.

He was astonished that Jake hadn't fired again. He rolled off of Haig on the far side, breath ripping through his nostrils. He saw the grips of Haig's gun and got his fingers on it. He heard Johnny's .22 spit out and looked across Haig's body. Johnny fired another shot into the brush above them, which must have been at the half-breed who was not in evidence. There was no more firing.

Johnny hurried toward Caine, relief on his face. "That skunk sure got hungry for home when he seen you down Haig, mister! Didn't figure it was his business to put up a lone-handed scrap over something he don't know much about. I seen where they hid our shooting irons and sure jumped for them when Jake ran. I never hit him, but I figured I might mebbe cement that runnin' notion."

Caine got to his feet, rocking, his chest heaving.

"We got us a prisoner," Johnny said, nudging Haig's still form with a toe. "What we going to do with him?"

"Take him in," Caine said. "Johnny, we're going back to face the music."

The boy's face broke into a grin. "Mister, I sure hoped you'd say that. But it'll be risky. Haig'll swear him and the 'breed only tracked us trying to help the law."

"It might not be worth much," Caine said, "but he's given us a card. That quitclaim he brought out here and tried to force me to sign. That'll be hard to explain. And he admitted to me that they killed Flanders. The sheriff looked square. Given a reasonable doubt about me being guilty, and he might be able to dig up some better evidence against Johnson's outfit."

"Engels is honest. But what will Johnson be doing to you while Tom's at it?"

"I defied Johnson once. I'm willing to do it again."

Reaction was seeping into Caine. After trussing the unconscious Haig with his belt, Caine turned down to the creek, scrubbed face and hands, and walked slowly back.

Johnny had removed Haig's gun belt. He handed it to Caine, and Caine buckled it on and shoved the gun back into place. Hereafter he'd be ready for a fight when it came, and he knew he was moving into a hot one by returning to the Bear Creek country.

Haig came to and lay filling the mountain air with profanity. Caine and Johnny paid no attention, fixing a noon meal before starting downcountry. Johnny located Haig's horse, which had been left in brush at the upper end of the valley, and brought it in. The half-breed, he reported, had taken the other and scampered. In mid-afternoon, they started down, and, although a quiet and steady purpose was in Caine now, he knew that the next hours or days would be the supreme test of his life. With Johnny Renshaw, and perhaps with Laura, he was ready to meet it.

IV

Tige Haig continued cursing. "That stinking 'breed! He could have walloped you with his rifle or threatened to plug the button! The dirty, yellow-bellied son-of-a-bitch!"

Johnny snorted. "He heard what you told Caine about beefing Flanders. And he sure cut out. I don't reckon it was because he got scared, either. He was only getting tracker's wages from you. What he knows would be worth plenty, blackmailing Johnson. That is, if he lit out afore he got his own hands too dirty. To my notion, that's what took Jake outta here so fast."

Temper began to give way to worry in Haig's eyes. Caine turned Johnny's supposition over in his mind. He had hoped Jake would pull out if the tide was reversed suddenly. He recalled that, beyond firing a single shot, the half-breed had offered no determined interference. The tracker might hope to blackmail Johnson, at that. But he might also be made useful to Sheriff Engels, since he had witnessed Haig's admission to the murder of Flanders and the earlier plan to kill Laura. . . .

In late afternoon the next day they came out of the foothills above the Bar F.

"Johnny," Caine asked, "think you could take Haig in to the sheriff by yourself?"

The lad nodded. "I'd just like for the cuss to give me a excuse to put a slug in his brisket. But what you figuring to do, Quincy?"

"I'm going to get Injun Jake, if I can. If you're right about his intentions, he'll be hanging around here somewhere."

"Caine," Haig said nervously, "you're fixing to play the fool. If Jake puts the bite on Johnson, he'll just get hisself killed. You won't get no witness there, pilgrim . . . Johnson'll see to that. He won't let me stay in jail, either. When he hears you're back in the country, he'll be after your scalp and the button's. If you're smart, you'll turn me loose and kite outta here."

Caine silenced him with an indifferent stare and watched Johnny head on toward Three Forks, Haig with his wrists strapped to the saddle horn and Johnny trailing with a gun in his hand. Caine had warned him to skirt Johnsonville, to give Haig no chance to escape, and to tell the sheriff of how useful Injun Jake might be. He knew the boy could be relied upon. Johnny was more mature mentally than a lot of men Caine had known.

Caine waited until dusk, then mounted and rode to Bar F. He dropped down off the last rim, left his horse, and went in afoot, keeping low. Lamplight peeped peacefully from the house. He made the compound without disturbance, crossed it, and stepped lightly onto the back porch.

He saw Laura in the kitchen; she appeared to be alone. He crossed to the door and knocked, seeing through the glass that she had heard him and caught up a carbine.

"Who's there?" she called, her voice unsteady.

"Quincy Caine."

He saw relief flow across her face. She came cautiously, however, and had the gun lined as she bade him open the door. Identification, Caine thought, put a kind of gladness in her face.

"You came back!"

"Then you're not sorry?"

"I'm glad, Quincy. I've had time to think. Then Injun Jake was here today. He told me what happened in the mountains and what he'd learned. But I'd changed my mind before that. I couldn't make myself believe that you'd killed Fred. It was just that there seemed to be no good reason why Johnson would, at that point."

"Jake a friend of yours?" Caine asked.

Laura made a wry face. "He offered to serve as a witness against Johnson and Haig for a thousand dollars."

"Ah," Caine said. "But that was only to get a bargaining point to use on Johnson. It was Johnny's idea that he'd try to blackmail Johnson. He propositioned you to have a lever to use on the man. Haig says Johnson will simply kill him. I've got to get hold of Jake first."

There was a worried look on Laura's face. "It may be too late. Jake was pretty eager. Maybe he's gone over there already."

"Then I'll go there," Caine said.

"No, Quincy. Not alone. If he's heard Jake's story, he'll kill you on sight."

"I've got to have him," Caine said. He lifted her hands, and her grasp closed, warm and strong, upon his fingers. "I had to see you first. I had to know I stand right with you."

"You do, Quincy."

"A girl was killed. My bride of six weeks.

She died horribly. But I'm over it now. I wanted you to know."

"I'm glad, Quincy. I know I would have liked her."

"And she'd have liked you."

Caine left, mounting and striking the trail to Johnsonville. He had a gun in his holster, another shoved beneath his waistband, and his nerves, he found, were steady. He felt as he had before the now dimming tragedy and knew that, no matter what the outcome of the next hours, he was his own man again.

The night was serene. He had never been in Johnsonville but knew it to be a mean place, boasting only a roadhouse and several shacks. It was this iniquitous nucleus that Ford Johnson proposed to build into a railroad town, killing Three Forks, giving him power and organization in the country in addition to reaping his revenge.

Caine sighted the lights of Johnsonville where the trail crested a final hill. He left his horse in a copse, checked his firearms, and went on afoot. He dreaded dogs but none lifted a warning racket. Keeping low, he picked his way, coming in upon the roadhouse from behind.

He had no assurance that he'd find Injun Jake here, or, if he did, that the half-breed would be alive. But he dared wait no longer, not even to get the support of Sheriff En-gels. The rear area of Johnsonville was brushy. Caine concealed himself, gun in hand, and studied the situation. A pole cor-ral and a crude barn were to his right. Two darkened shacks stood at a distance to his left. The box-like rear of Johnson's roadside shebang was ugly and unadorned, and one shaded window showed light within.

No one stirred, although Caine could hear the buzz of voices. He felt safe to assume Johnson wouldn't expect anything as bold as this move. He speculated on Jake, if the half-breed had been here and if he were alive or dead.

He rose from his crouch and moved silently out of the brush. He crossed to the rear wall and pressed against it flatly, strain-ing his ears to pick up inside talk that he could understand. That failed, and he slipped toward the rear door. The doorknob turned easily. With slow patience he shoved the door open. He stepped into the hallway and scanned it. Bars of light showed under two doors ahead. There was no racket to indicate that any sort of a crowd was out in front.

Caine placed a hand on the second door, but now he moved boldly, twisting and wheeling the door wide and stepping through. He hadn't expected luck as good as this, for he stared at Ford Johnson and Injun Jake. His gun covering them, Caine stepped into the room, kicked the door shut.

"Don't move. And don't lift your voice."

It was Johnson's bedroom, Caine decided, for it was well-furnished, large, with a desk standing in one corner. The door of a large commode stood open, and he saw dude clothing within. Jake's expression didn't change, but Johnson sucked in a long, slow breath.

"Howdy, Caine," Johnson said.

Caine moved closer. He had the half-breed alive, but getting him away alive was a different matter.

"Struck your bargain?" Caine asked.

Johnson shook his head. "There'll be no bargain. This 'breed'll never get away from here alive. Nor will you, Caine. Did you kill Haig?"

Caine shrugged, knowing it would be dangerous to divulge where Haig was headed until Johnny Renshaw had had plenty of time to reach Three Forks with him. "Don't count on him, any more," Caine said. "I'm taking you and Jake out of here, and, if there's any interference, hold in your guts, Johnson. That's where you'll get it."

69

"You've come a long ways, pilgrim," Johnson grunted.

Caine made them stand apart. Shoving his gun against their sides, he disarmed them successively, taking a knife from the half-breed and an armpit gun from Johnson. Both watched balefully, but Caine felt Injun Jake was relieved by the development, which might furnish a chance for him to escape.

"I'll go out behind you," Caine said. The pair obeyed, stepping through the door just ahead and turning toward the back door. Caine's breath was quick and shallow until they had emerged into the night. He felt certain Johnson would make a break but, once outdoors, the man strode at Caine's gesture toward the distant pole corral.

Horses were there, and Caine's thoughts ranged ahead. If he succeeded in getting away with his prisoners, he would turn both over to the sheriff, trusting to Jake's testimony, however reluctant, to justify holding Johnson. They reached the corral, and Caine saw a gate built on a frame and hinged with a weighted rope to keep it shut. Johnson placed his hands on the gate and suddenly he was jerking it, and the *clang* of a cowbell rang loudly in the night. Johnson dived for the shadowed open door of the barn, and got through as Caine fired. The half-breed bolted behind him, trusting to the obvious fact that Caine wanted him alive. Caine fired at his legs and dropped him in the barn doorway.

Men were pouring out of the main structure. Bent low, Caine sprinted the length of the corral and made the corner. Behind the corral he came in against the barn and followed its wall to the end, where he found a door. Relying upon his feeling that he had picked his ex-prisoners clean of firearms, Caine stepped inside. He understood Johnson's willingness to emerge now. The man had thought of that cowbell, sometimes used to sound warning if gates were opened.

A gun blasted, but Caine knew it came from outside the barn. He prowled into the black interior, feeling his way along stanchions until he came to an open space, which he turned through. He recalled that the barn was high enough to have a hayloft, and it might be that Johnson had crawled up there for safety's sake while awaiting rescue by his men.

Caine heard nothing, no sound even from Injun Jake who he knew to be wounded. He heard running steps in front and on both sides of the barn. At least three men. Caine had no chance now of getting away from there with Injun Jake, and Johnson would kill the half-breed immediately if Caine escaped. Caine knew there was a dim hope Engels would come out at once to Johnsonville after Jake, if not after Johnson himself. Johnny Renshaw was smart and had heard Haig's statement that Johnson would shut Jake's mouth forever. Johnny also had been a friend and something of a ward of the sheriff's. Caine knew his only chance of escape lay in this moment. But he let it slide. He reckoned he'd stick.

The men outside the structure had apparently taken shelter. They feared exposing themselves by entering the barn. They dared not shoot into the interior as long as it held Johnson, as well as their prey. Caine decided to sweat it out.

Caine's eyes made out the shapes of the barn openings, slightly less sable than the rest, and he could watch them all from his position. His immediate worry was the close presence of Johnson and the mystery of his position.

Then something came at him out of the darkness. Caine felt it only a second before it hit him, from the left hindquarter, shoving him forward and down. Caine twisted, coming to his knees, lifting the gun. He fired, the blast loud in his ears, the flash of fire only blinding him a few seconds. There was no more movement close at hand, but a gun fired to his right, its flash showing Caine it had been aimed through a crack between weathered boards. He heard the tearing impact of the slug ahead of him.

He crawled forward, and his hands touched a still shape. Long hair told him it was Injun Jake. His heart sank. By his own hand, he appeared to have destroyed the thing he had come for, the thing that had held him here. And now he was trapped in a spot where he would find no mercy.

He sent a slug ripping through the boards whence the fire had come, and he heard a man grunt. His lips pinched flatly against his teeth as he considered the impossibility of escape. But his regained courage held. He was going to make it costly for them to clear their barn of its menace.

Then a voice ripped out: "Ford, where the hell are you! Declare yourself, man! Give us a chance."

Johnson apparently lacked the courage to answer. Caine was glad. His one advantage was the fact they dared not riddle the structure. He watched the openings closely, to keep anybody from slipping in but mainly to keep Johnson from trying to get out.

Johnson's unknown position was wearing on the nerves. Caine kept imagining the man moving up on him. He wondered if he could imitate the man's voice closely enough to get himself through one of those doors. It seemed unlikely and might even draw attention to such a move. He kept his eared-back gun in his hand and waited, the other shoved into his waistband.

Quiet built eerily in the surroundings as men waited and watched and probed with their minds. They dared not shoot wildly into the structure, or to set it afire, with Johnson inside. They apparently lacked the men to make a rush for the three openings in the walls. Then turmoil arose on the corral side; Caine heard hoarse shouts and a whacking sound. Looming shapes appeared in that doorway, crashing against its sides — two ponies driven in together. Caine jumped aside, reaching a wall and pressing hard against it.

Kicked up dust fouled the air, the black bulks of the horses wheeling and snorting. One smashed into a post and jarred the barn structure. A gun spat, and Caine knew men had followed the horses in, screened by them. He fired at the flame, and a second gun fired from the opposite side of the doorway. He answered this, shifting position, then his gun snapped on an empty chamber. He threw it, jerking out the other,

74

moving silently to his right. Two in here with him, perhaps unhit, and he had no reliable estimate of how many remained outside.

The horses cut, darted, and wheeled, keeping the air filled with dust, and Caine pressed to the wall. He judged Johnson must have climbed to the loft. Caine reached a corner and edged to the doorway there. He'd be highlighted to the pair within the barn if he tried to use it, and if they were still in the fight. He decided on the gamble, bent low, and drove through.

It drew no interior fire; apparently he had not been detected. He was on a clear side of the barn, with no close cover. He kept against the wall. The horses still milled inside. He came to the forward corner of the barn, investigated, then went around it. He still could locate no enemy. He prowled on to the big front door through which Johnson had ducked to start it all. He got to the corral and saw a couple of remaining horses but no human figures. It dawned on him that their play in driving the two into the barn had resulted in the situation reversing itself. He was outside and certain that Johnson at least was able-bodied within.

Four horses. It struck Caine that the saddlers regular to Johnson and his henchmen would be kept in this corral. Injun Jake had ridden in, but his mount would have been left on the roadside, at the hitch rack there. A horse for Johnson and for three men. Johnson and two others were inside. There was another out here somewhere.

Caine remembered the position of his own horse in the copse a few hundred yards south of here. He had a chance now to make it there and get away. This mission had accomplished nothing, for he probably had killed Injun Jake with his own gun. He worked his way along this wall, meaning to make a run for the nearby brush, on the far side of which he might make his mistake. A gun blasted through a crack in the barn and something slammed him flat. Shock rose in his left shoulder. He scrambled around the corner of the barn.

A man came at him. Caine fired, saw the figure pitch down. Caine raced for the shelter of a water trough, the situation wholly out of hand suddenly, shock dragging at his limbs and freezing the thought in his brain. He hunkered beyond the trough and got a bearing on the barn's front. Fire blossomed there, lead *thunk*ed into the heavy planking of the trough. It gave Caine a good shot, and silence followed.

After long moments Caine began to wonder at this silence. They were waiting for him to move, for it seemed impossible that one man could have beaten at least four deadly, determined men. But he had had several good targets, had himself been hit. It was then that he heard the drum of fast-ridden horses far down the trail. It could be friend or foe, but Caine listened to its growing louder, excitement forcing through the cold chill of his shock. Bent over, Caine made it to the corner of the roadhouse structure, then walked the length of the building. A mounted party whirled up, coming along the north trail, and relief broke in him when he recognized Johnny Renshaw. Then sickness and revulsion combined with his shock, the figures reeled, and he fell forward. . . .

It was daylight when Caine opened his eyes, and he knew without being told that he was in bed at Bar F. Flowers on the stand table and dresser, the lingering aroma of some perfume, all spoke of feminine occupancy. He was undressed, his shoulder bound and throbbing, and there were clean sheets over and under him, a pillow beneath his head. It took a moment for his head to clear, then he called out.

Laura came quickly through the doorway,

nearly running as she crossed the room. She bent at the side of the bed, her eyes shining, her soft hair touched with light.

"I knew you'd be all right, Quincy," she breathed. "But it seems years I've waited for you to get the shock and weariness out of you."

"Johnsonville?" Caine asked.

"Wiped out. You'd got a couple of them. The other two, including Johnson, gave the sheriff's posse a fight. To the end, because Tom Engels ordered Johnson to submit to arrest."

"Two's plenty," Caine said, more to himself than to Laura. He didn't like killing, he didn't like violence, and it was not because of the old dread, for that was gone.

"Injun Jake lived a while," Laura resumed. "Long enough to confirm Johnny's story about what happened in the mountains. Tige Haig's the only one left to hang for Fred's murder."

Caine saw an eagerness in her eyes, knew that the answer he wanted to make was the one she wanted to hear. "I'd like to stay here on Bear River. I want to see the first train run into Three Forks, and know it was mainly you who put it there."

"And you, Quincy."

Caine made a motion with his usable

hand. "I want to learn the cattle business, if you'll be patient."

Disbelief rose on Laura's face. "Patient? Quincy, I'd love that. It's you who'll have to be patient with me. I'm headstrong. I'm used to running things."

"You've never tried double-harness," Caine said, and his free hand caught hers.

She could only smile back.

I

■ ■ ■ ■

NIGHT RIDERS

■ ■ ■ ■

I

It was past midnight with Splinter Rock dark except for the dim light in the windows of the Stag and Rialto saloons and a smoky lantern hanging on a hook beside the livery door. Tully Gale halted his string of horses in the barn's center aisle and let out a Rebel yell. The barn was an old structure, trapping the smells of countless years, and it was an old man who shuffled out of the tack room to stare at him sharply.

"So you come back alive!" the stableman gasped. He eyed the red mustang that Tully rode and added: "Besides catchin' that danged stallion!"

Tully grinned. He sat tall in the saddle, the lean face under his brown hair matching the genial good humor of his gray eyes. "I got the stallion," he admitted. "As to being alive, I can't tell without a shot of that horse liniment you call whiskey. I'm some tired."

"Come on."

The oldster was Ed Handel, who was a runty, unshaven man with wild hair and habitually skeptical eyes. He turned back into the harness room, and, as Tully dismounted, a lamp came alight in there.

Tully paused to pat the red mustang on its touchy rump. Although smallish in the way of the wild breed, it was a perfect specimen, wiry, compact, and explosive. The bronco wheeled away from Tully's hand, snorted, and bared his teeth, communicating his nervous energy to the pack horses Tully was returning to Ed. Tully tied the reins to a ring on a pillar and went on into the tack room, where Ed had put a jug on the table.

"So you outfoxed Sugar Lagg," Ed said. "Son, that don't happen very often. Too unhealthy. Even the wild hosses are leery of that *hombre*."

"Lagg's only a crooked horse dealer," Tully stated. He swung the jug to his lips and took a healthy pull. Wiping his mouth with the back of his hand, he added: "It's an old trick he pulled. Selling a stranger a green horse that'll dump his load and come home."

"This 'un sure dumped his load," Ed pointed out. "Cuss who calls himself a rider.

83

Pitched him into the middle of next week."

Tully frowned at the painful memory. "Anyhow," he drawled, "that cowpoke went out to the *malpais* and brung him back. If Lagg's settin' there, waiting for the bronc' to show up, he'll get corns on his bottom. But the steed's yours, Ed, till I catch up on sleep."

Leaving the livery, he walked the length of the town's main street. It was a tired, dried-out settlement on the banks of a creek that was all but gone because of weeks of rainless heat. He was mindful of that dangerous drought condition. He knew why the creek was drier than any man could remember, even though there had been many spells of weather just as arid and hot. Maybe, in pulling that old green-horse trick, Sugar Lagg had made a mistake because he had a secret that, during his week in the badlands, Tully had unearthed.

Passing up the town's best hotel, Tully went on to a less pretentious structure standing athwart the end of the main street. It bore a sign that said: **THE PAINE HOUSE.** Just as he entered its plain lobby, a girl came through the dining room archway. She carried a plate covered by a napkin and gave a start when she recognized him.

"If you're sneaking a snack to your room,"

84

Tully told her, "you got company. I could eat the label off a can of beans."

"You filthy tramp," the girl breathed. "You'll clean up before you can even stay in my hotel. Tully, it's good to see you again. I didn't expect to." The surprise left her face to show a look of real pleasure. It was a plain but fetching face, crowned by fine black hair. Her lips were full, parted now, white teeth wetly gleaming. Her nose was straight, flared at the nostrils, and set off by the brownest eyes he had ever seen. But it was her body that Tully noted, slim and lithe and womanly.

"Then I better clean up," he said. "If you'll loan me your pump."

"I'll do better than that. You can use my bathtub. We'll have to heat water, though. Come on back to the kitchen."

"Thanks, Maggie. You're the girl I been hunting for."

"Liar."

But she was gratified, he saw as he let her lead him out through the hotel dining room and into the big, darkened kitchen. There she said: "You'll have to start a fire, and you'll find a wash boiler on the porch. Soon as the stove's hot, I'll fix you some supper."

" 'Way after hours," he said. "How come I rate it?"

Maggie Paine gave him an intent look, then slipped out of the room in her quick, quiet way. He grinned as the door swung shut behind her. Her scent lingered in the room, which had been lighted only by the lamp out in the main lobby, and scent and darkness had quickened the life in him. She was a puzzle to him as yet, a challenge, and he meant to settle it with her before morning.

The thing that hooked at his imagination was what he had learned of her in the few weeks he had been in Banca Basin. Until two years ago, he had heard, she had been married to the man who had owned this hotel and who ran it between drunks. Then the man had dropped dead, an abused heart quitting him on one of his bouts with Splinter Rock's dubious whiskey. But, although he had stayed here before, Maggie herself had never referred to that part of her life.

Lighting a lamp, Tully kindled a fire in the stove. He found a wash boiler on the porch, filled it at the pump, and carried it into the kitchen. He slopped water lifting it onto the stove and was hunting a mop when Maggie returned.

She got the mop and took care of the floor herself, then started his supper. "I thought you'd drifted on," she said.

"Not yet," he said. "You know Sugar Lagg?"

"I know of him."

"Well, I hit this country on the stage," Tully told her. "Man said I could buy a good, tough bronc' at Lagg's horse camp. I went out there on a livery horse of Ed's, and Lagg sold me a green one he claimed was gentled. But it was only halter-broke. Had no reason to distrust Lagg then, and I brung the critter to town before I tried to fork it. When I did, I nearly went over Ed's barn. The mustang hit for the *malpais*. It still had my saddle on, and that's what Lagg expected. He figured to pick the cayuse up again the next time he flushed wild stuff outta there. And have my money and saddle and horse, all three."

"It didn't work?" Maggie asked, smiling.

"That red stallion's in Ed Handel's barn right now," Tully informed her. "I packed into the *malpais* and caught him myself. Didn't come out till I'd busted him the way a mustang ought to be before he's sold to a trustin' stranger. Now I got a riding horse, and Lagg's got no laugh on anybody."

"From what I hear," Maggie murmured, "he doesn't like people he can't run over."

She was pleased by what he had told her,

87

Tully saw. He rolled a cigarette and smoked it while she brought dishes from the cupboard. He liked the quick, even motions of her body, the neat way her dress matched its lines. He was honest about his direct, fundamental interest in her. He wanted her, but only physically, and this interest sprang from a restlessness and need that he sensed in her. She was a ripe woman who had known marriage and, rightly or wrongly, a man expected more from that kind.

Moreover, there was a veiled, evasive attitude in the town about Maggie Paine. He had sensed it more than once. Since he had already met and liked her, he hadn't pried into that. He formed his own opinions and was inclined to defiance of prevailing judgments if he saw fit. This was a kindly, sincere woman who from the first had seen more in him than a transient to be put up. Her pleasure in his return, which she had not expected, was evident. That was all he needed to know of matters.

Maggie had laid bacon in the spider, which was beginning to smoke. She was starting coffee, when she noticed his close inspection of her. When she looked at him questioningly, he said: "You're a pretty girl, Maggie. You fill a man's eye."

"Why, thank you," she answered. "I don't

know about the eye filling, but you're wrong about the pretty. I'm not. I'm plain, and, if I didn't know how to use what I've got, I'd be ugly."

"Then I'll take mine plain and ugly," Tully said heartily.

She turned, lips parted, a perplexed look in her eyes. "May I say that you know how to fill a woman's ear, Tully Gale? I guess that's a sore point with me. I had a sister who was really beautiful. My mother wasn't tactful in the matter of comparisons. I never got over it."

"How'd your sister turn out?" he asked.

"Married. Happily so. Contented." For a moment something rose on Maggie's face, a lost, in-turned unhappiness standing there. Then she shrugged and was back in the room with him. "Water's hot. But let's eat before you have your bath. Supper's ready, too."

The subject had got a little ticklish, and Tully was glad to let it drop. They ate together, idly talking of his venture into the *malpais* and of the drought that each day became more of a menace to the basin's great herds of cattle. The depression lifted from Maggie; twice he caught her giving him the same secret search he had given her. Her life, as well as her experience in running a cow-town hotel, had given her worldly wisdom. He thought that he attracted her and sensed that, if so, she would be guided by mood rather than convention and he believed that the mood was coming up. His excitement increased when, after they had eaten, she left the kitchen without having bidden him good night.

He lighted a lantern and took it out to the woodshed, then carried out a washtub and filled it with hot water. Desire mounted as he prepared to wash away the grime of the trail. The awareness between them had built to where it had to reach its climax this night. On his first stop at her hotel they had become friendly. On the second she had promoted him, giving him a different and better room reserved for privileged guests. There was something special about that room, and Tully's breath caught as he remembered. A door opened onto a private upper gallery, as did one other. In the night, too hot for sleep, he had gone onto the gallery for air and had discovered the other door. He could see into the room, the bed and its occupant, a reposed face framed by dark hair. Tonight he must have that room again, and he had a feeling it would be assigned to him. . . .

Maggie was still absent when Tully returned to the hotel kitchen. He blew out the lamp, crossed the big dining room, and found the lobby empty, also. He was moving along the upper hallway toward her room when its door came open. She was in a thin white silk nightgown. Tully stared openly at the fullness of her breasts and a smile spread across her face.

"I'm afraid I'll have to give you a poor room," she said. "I had no idea you'd show up. You'll have to take Twenty-One, back by the stairway."

His face stiffened, disappointment kindling a quick, heedless temper. "Somebody in the one I had last time?" he demanded.

"Not yet. He's out having his fun. But his stuff is in there."

"Then I'll toss it out," Tully said promptly. "Any man who's got to go out for his fun doesn't rate that room."

She gave him a quick, sharp stare, her cheeks coloring. For an instant she seemed on the point of matching his temper, then she shrugged, laughing softly. She said: "I'm afraid you've been misled by the gossip, Tully Gale. The only advantage to the gallery room is that it's quieter and sometimes cooler. I'd still let you have it except for the fact that Nick Daimler has been coming here too long to be treated that way."

"Nick Daimler?" Tully repeated sharply. "Know him?"

"I've seen him," Tully answered. "Without liking what I've seen. Friend of yours?"

"An old patron and one-time friend of Mark Paine. That was my husband, in case you haven't heard. Don't be a sorehead, Tully. If you drift, that's your own doing. But if you stay, there'll be another time." The smile was on her mouth again, warm and a little provocative. She knew the ways of a man and the wants of a man while keeping her half promise shrewdly mixed with doubt. Else why had she dressed this way before bringing him up so short and hard at the end of her catch rope?

He turned and went back down the hallway, aroused and unsatisfied, and in the mood for violence. He didn't hear her door close, but when he glanced back before entering the stuffy cubicle he was to use, he found the passage empty.

It was just daylight when he tossed a key and coin on the lobby desk, leaving early to avoid having to see Maggie and check out formally. The street he came out upon was cooler than on the previous evening but still too warm for comfort. A dog lay asleep on the far walk, some stray that found the days too uncomfortable for rest. Its ribs stuck out, reminding him painfully of the thousands upon thousands of steers likewise starving on burned-up range.

All at once this concern was uppermost in Tully's mind, taking his thoughts away from Maggie Paine and the way she had made him feel like a panting adolescent. He had a job to do, a special one with which he had been confronted in the *malpais.* Banca Basin relied upon Splinter Creek for its water, and the creek came out of that *malpais.* He had stumbled upon something in there. When the Land Office opened, he meant to see a map and straighten out a few geographical puzzles in his mind.

He went on to the livery barn where he found Ed Handel up and cleaning out the stalls. "You can take care of that red mustang yourself," Ed said. "Mebbe you won his affection, but he figures I've got horns and a tail."

"Who is there around here," Tully asked, "who knows as much about the *malpais* as Sugar Lagg and his bronc' twisters?"

"Me, for one," Ed said. "Used to mustang myself long before Lagg started his horse camp in there. But age got me to where a livery nag's all I can handle. What's on your mind about it?"

"Show me how Splinter Creek gets outta that wild country and into this basin."

Ed pondered an instant, then hunkered. He ran his finger through the dust at their feet, drawing a shape like a kidney. "That's Banca Basin," he reported. "The *malpais* lays just above it. Splinter Creek starts in there from three forks and does a lot of hellin'. Lagg's got his horse camp on the south fork. Other two fan out above him, eight or ten miles apart. After the forks join up, the main creek runs west a piece. There's places where it's gouged deep in the rock so a man can't ride its whole course."

"Then I'm right," Tully said.

"About what?"

Tully was studying the crude map in the dust. He pointed, saying: "Must've been the middle fork where I found it. A lake, Ed. Big enough to drown all the dried-up steers in the basin. How come Splinter Creek's all but petered out?"

"One reason," Ed retorted, "is that there ain't any lake in there. If you thought you seen one, it was a mirage."

"Took a swim in that mirage, then," Tully rejoined. "And found it as wet and cool as the real thing."

Ed stared at him, shaking his head. "Don't

try to josh me before breakfast, boy. It makes me mean."

"We better get you some breakfast, then," Tully said. "Because I'm sure going to tell you about the lake I found on the middle fork. The reason you never heard of it is that it's brand new. No vegetation around it even. I figured a landslide done it, then I got to wondering. A landslide probably plugged up a cañon somewhere, all right. But I reckon it was man-made and intentional."

Ed shoved to a slow stand. "You telling that straight, Gale?"

"No reason I should do otherwise, is there? Ed, Sugar Lagg's behind that. He's helped the drought along by damming up the main fork of the creek. Why?"

After a long moment, Ed said: "You ain't drunk and you ain't crazy. So you took a swim in a lake that's got no business in that *malpais.* Gale, I got a feeling like I was coming down with ague. This basin's dying for water. If it don't get it quick, it's going to war with a ranch called Two Hump that's got artesian lakes and won't share 'em. Sugar knows that, and the lake's got some connection, and it scares the hell outta me. Let's go eat breakfast."

"Go wash your face first," Tully said, grinning at him.

While waiting for Ed, Tully sat on the bench in front of the livery barn thinking over his short experience in this country and what he had learned of it. Two Hump, the cattle ranch Ed had mentioned, was the big outfit, occupying a valley all to itself and blessed with plentiful artesian water. He knew about Two Hump, all right, for it already had entered his life and cost him plenty. But now he considered the outfit objectively. It was run by a man named Daimler — the Nick Daimler who had got the gallery room in Maggie's hotel the night before. Its lakes held sufficient storage that it could pull the rest of the basin through the drought if it wanted. This it had refused to do, so that the ranchers in the suffering basin were talking of taking water and pasture by force. Now it was evident that the creek had been tampered with. Sugar Lagg had to be the one who did it, for his mustanging would have shown him that lake long since otherwise, and he would have reported it to the drought-harried basiners. Therefore Lagg, and perhaps others, was trying to put something over on Banca Basin.

Tully thought he had an inkling of what it was. He had neither drifted into the country as Maggie supposed, nor had he been hunting work as a man called Ellery Vines had judged. But he had been offered a job by Vines, a gentleman rancher who had organized the basiners into a stockmen's association and been elected its leader. Vines had figured out a scheme for wresting help from the Two Hump outfit and had needed an outsider to put it over. His sympathy aroused by the drought conditions, Tully had agreed to take part. The association wasn't yet ready to act, so lately he had been killing time.

Now he wasn't sure that he trusted the situation he had let himself be drawn into. Right after he had committed himself to the part he was to play, he had caught Vines, Daimler, and Lagg powwowing secretly in a deadfall called Valen's, here in Splinter Rock. It had seemed odd enough, even then, with Vines and Daimler assumed to be bitter enemies because of the water wrangle. Now Lagg had entered the water picture, even more prominently than the other two men — Lagg, who knew that there was a vast reservoir of it in the *malpais*.

Dynamite, Tully thought. *He dynamited a cañon somewhere in the stretch nobody can ride through. He built a dam that could be called a landslide if anybody did find it. But dynamite blew it down and it could be blown out again.* Tully shivered slightly in spite of the morning's heat. Since he had discovered the secret, it looked like that was his responsibility.

Ed emerged, flattening his hair with his hand only to have it rear up again in disarray. They turned down the street, which was coming alive. The doors of business houses stood open. At several points men were at work sweeping off the sidewalks. A horse had appeared at a hitch bar in front of a restaurant. Tully saw a man cross over and enter Maggie's place at the end of the main street. Ed noticed the same thing.

"If you figure on breakfast at the Paine House," he said, "you can eat alone."

"You don't like the cooking?" Tully asked.

"Cookin's fine." That was all Ed had to say about it.

After the two had eaten breakfast in a high-stool place that Ed preferred to the Paine House, they went over a block to the government Land Office. It was a small, deserted-looking place, for the settler movement was only starting in the area. Its door was open, and, when they emerged fifteen minutes later, both men looked disturbed and riled.

The badlands had been mapped only crudely by the government survey, yet Splinter Creek and its tributaries were shown with what Ed said was fair accuracy. Across the middle fork of the creek lay a half-section of land the clerk had shaded on the map. "That piece is filed on," he had said tiredly. "Sugar Lagg took it up last spring. Don't ask me why. Nothing in the law says a man can't homestead a piece of *malpais* if he's crazy enough to want to. . . ."

Out on the sidewalk again Ed said: "If your thoughts are running like mine, you better cut it out. I'm old and useless, but you're too young to die."

"All right, he's homesteaded the land around his secret lake and dam!" Tully exploded. "But that don't give him a right to ruin Splinter Creek by plugging up its main fork. If you've got a lawyer in this town, he'll tell you so."

"Don't need to have no lawyer tell me," Ed answered. "Lagg's got no right. But by the time you could get a court to tell him so, Lagg'd be done with that dam and could afford to blow it out and make apologies."

"I know that, man," Tully snorted. "I'm talking about blowing his dam out ourselves and countin' on the court to justify it afterward."

"Lagg's homesteaded that piece," Ed reminded him. "He'll stand on his right to keep off trespassers. Fool around there with dynamite and you'll be plugged before you've lit the fuse."

"We could organize a right smart army in the basin," Tully retorted. "Men who'd be happy to go in there a-hellin'. Ed, I don't aim to lay eyes on another ribby, bloating steer knowing there's water wasting in the *malpais*."

Ed looked at him worriedly. "I know how you feel, bub. Only don't go off half-cocked. You let it out about that dam, and this country'll blow sky high and good men'll be killed right along with the bad 'uns."

"I'll blow the thing out by myself, damn it."

Ed dropped a hand on his shoulder and smiled at him sadly. "Son, I sure admire your salt and vinegar, but you leave it to a older head a while. You keep your trap shut and your nose outta that *malpais* till I've seen a lawyer and the sheriff. They're both good men. They'll tell us the best way to go about it with the least cost in money and time and blood."

"All right," Tully said tiredly. "But don't ask me to wait too long, Ed. I ain't built that way. I just can't."

II

They parted on the corner of the main street, with Tully striding on at a slow and thoughtful gait. The visit to the Land Office had reminded him of a previous visit he had made to the place in connection with the job he was yet to undertake on behalf of Ellery Vines. *You're a homesteader yourself, you know,* Tully reflected. *And you'd better move onto your land claim the way they want. Maybe that'll keep you from building a fire in this here powder magazine.*

He was passing a restaurant when its door opened, a man emerging. Tully saw the figure out of the corner of his eye and checked the impulse to swing half about. But the other man had less desire to avoid a meeting.

"Just a minute there, bucko!" he bawled.

Tully paused, turning around in forced unconcern. "Talking to me, Lagg?" he asked indifferently.

101

Sugar Lagg was in his early thirties and stood four inches over Tully's own six feet. It was all hard, well-built flesh that now was clad in sweat-streaked, dirty working clothes. Lagg also wore a gun with shiny grips. Two of his bronco-stompers had followed him out of the restaurant, and all three looked hard and mean. Part of it, Tully surmised, was hangover from a night in Valen's deadfall, but a goodly portion came from plain dislike of the man they scrutinized.

"Talkin' to you," Lagg agreed. "Heard that red I sold you got away. Another man told me he seen you ride the critter into town last night. So you been messin' around in the *malpais.*"

"What do you find wrong with that, Lagg?" Tully asked softly. His hackles were up, giving him trouble. It wasn't his recapture of the mustang stallion that disturbed Lagg, who was thinking about that reservoir of water and the secret dam that had impounded it and wondering what all Tully Gale had seen in the badlands. On the other hand, Tully was remembering droughted herds and harried stockmen, with his hatred of a man capable of exploiting such a situation swelling to the bursting point. It would take a miracle to keep him mindful of Ed's counsel of caution.

Lagg stepped forward and used a stiffened finger to tap Tully's chest. "I don't want you pokin' around my horse runs. I got traps all through that country, and I don't stand for anybody bucketin' around in there and scatterin' the wild 'uns. Folks hereabouts know that. If you figure to stay, you better get it through your own head."

"Pull back that finger, Lagg," Tully warned, "before I take and run it up your god-damn' nose."

"Tough 'un, are you?" Lagg said, but he quit jabbing. "Gale, just where did you latch onto that red?"

"Why do you care?"

"That stud had a harem I'd like to locate. Ain't seen hide nor hair of it since we took him. If you tracked him in, he must've led you straight to it."

"That ain't what's worrying you, Sugar," Tully murmured. "You're wondering if I got a chance to wash my feet."

There it was. Tully knew in the same breath that, as so often happened to him, impetuosity had carried him too far. But he had never had the ability to hold in while somebody breathed fire on him, and he watched reaction change the expression on Lagg's face without regret. The mustanger was doing an outrageous, unholy thing, inflicting widespread suffering, so let him worry a little as to his own security in the matter.

"Ah," said Lagg, "maybe that's what I'm wondering, Gale. If you got the chance, you better not even think about it, let alone make talk. Don't forget that . . . not for a minute." Swinging then, the big mustanger went down the sidewalk.

Tully stood there until they had turned the distant corner, his temper pushing hard against restraint. Then something caught his attention, the sudden howling of a dog in the other direction.

Turning, he saw a man in leather cuffs and a stained apron boot a dog out of a doorway. It was the skinny stray whose nap he had observed when he came out of Maggie's hotel. Tully moved forward, frowning. As he had surmised, he came to the front of a butcher shop. The butcher had gone back indoors, but the dog still lingered on the walk, looking back wistfully.

"Tough going on the grubline these days, huh?" Tully asked it. He went on into the shop.

The butcher had a different attitude for a possible cash customer. He tipped a halfway pleasant nod and said: "Howdy. What's it to be, friend?"

"A steak," Tully answered, "and a big one. Cut a round off that quarter there."

"You must be hungry."

"Friend of mine."

He told the butcher not to wrap the meat and tossed a coin on the counter. The butcher had caught on and was looking perplexed but he put the money in the till. Tully carried the meat outside and let it be snatched wolfishly from his hand. He grinned as the dog cut for safety of the notch between the closest buildings, not even trusting him. Then he started on up the street.

It was only to stop at the end of that block to stare. He had come abreast the broad porch of the Commercial Hotel and absently, at first, had detected a small, shapely figure seated in a round-back chair partly concealed by a dog-eared newspaper. He swallowed hard, for the first time having come upon the magnet that had drawn him across mountains and deserts to this place. She was as lovely as he had remembered her.

At that moment she looked up as if aware of being watched. The newspaper fell limply and her mouth opened, and in her lovely eyes was astonishment that slowly turned into delight.

"Tully!" she cried. "The moon rider!" She rose from the chair and ran toward him.

He'd had a bad moment trying to keep his hands off Sugar Lagg, and he had a worse one trying to keep them off this trim girl. He caught her elbows and stopped her at the point of flinging herself into his arms. The action caused her to step back and look at him in surprise and wonder.

"It's all done?" she asked falteringly. "It was only fun you had one time on a stage?"

"You know better than that," he said harshly. "You're why I came here. But you could have saved me the trouble. Louise Bentham of Bentham Valley, owner of Two Hump and rich as sin."

"That makes a difference?"

"You knew it would or you'd've told me all about it, Louise. It wasn't hard to find Splinter Rock. But once I got here, the only Louise anybody knew of was a Bentham. And they had plenty to say about the Benthams and Two Hump. And you . . . pretending to be a schoolma'am coming here to work!"

"Come and sit down, Tully, so that your arms won't look so tempting."

She led the way back to the row of chairs, which were all empty now. She was a small girl, whose amber eyes were flecked with green, whose hair was honey-gold and worn in braids wrapped about her head. On the stagecoach she had worn city clothes but now was dressed in whipcord skirt with boots and a pale-green blouse. She seated herself thoughtfully and waited for him to take the next chair.

"At least," she said thoughtfully, "you tried to hunt me up. Why?"

"I was hunting a pretty schoolma'am who'd only tell me she was called Louise and that she was coming to this country. Didn't know why then. I do now."

"If you'd found her in a schoolhouse . . . ?"

"I'd've tried to talk her into marrying me."

Louise Bentham sighed softly, shaking her head. "I didn't lie about it, Tully, unless withholding information is lying. I was a schoolteacher then, and happier than I've been since. I've thought and thought about the days we had together. Your saddle in the boot beside my trunk. Just us two passengers. It was no time to tell you I'd just inherited a ranch I'd never seen from an uncle I knew nothing about. Anyhow, I knew you were a moon rider . . . just heading for yonder. It wasn't likely that I'd ever see you again. And it did take you quite a while to get here."

"Been here a few weeks," he informed her stiffly, and he fell silent. Scent was a powerful sense. The subtle perfume he caught from her brought back vivid memories of that stage trip, a chance meeting that had grown into something far deeper than a passing flirtation. Yet he had not realized then that it was deep enough to hold them together always, and they had separated at the Julesburg junction.

"And you let what you heard keep you from coming out to see me," Louise accused.

"Well," he said awkwardly, "as a matter of fact, I did start out, anyhow. But I swung my cayuse around when I seen all them Two Hump steers and the fine big place you call headquarters. All yours, they tell me, plus a fat bank account. I never lied to *you*, Louise. We made a little love. . . ."

"A *little* love?" Louise gasped. "What's more you said you'd come here just as soon as you could. You were lying in your teeth and I knew it, even if you did change your mind afterward. Don't you carry on about me deceiving you!"

He had to grin at her vehemence. She had him cornered, because it was true he hadn't been altogether honest with her.

"You win," he said. "And since we're going to be neighbors, we might as well be friends."

"Neighbors?" Louise Bentham looked interested.

"That's right. I've taken a homestead claim right next to you in Bentham Valley."

"In the valley? I don't understand, Tully. Two Hump owns all of it."

He shook his head. "I see you haven't learned too much about your property. Your uncle took what he could get hold of, but some of it's government land. That part's been opened to homesteading by anybody with the nerve to tackle it and the will to stick. Both of which I've got."

"Welcome," Louise said readily. "As long as it's you."

Tully smiled at her innocence. "Your ramrod . . . that fancy Dan, Nick Daimler . . . won't agree with you on that. He'll try to gun me off."

"Why?"

"If he lets me get away with it, other homesteaders will try to follow suit. Soon your valley will be cut up by a pack of greasy-sackers. I know. I took a good look at the land situation on the government map. So Daimler . . . if he's worth his salt as a ramrod . . . won't let it get started."

"Tully," Louise said suddenly, "I wish

109

you'd come to work for me, instead. Now that you've mentioned him, I don't trust Daimler."

"How come?"

"For a lot of reasons," she said. "One is that he doesn't like my questioning him about what's supposed to be my own ranch. He says I'm not to worry, that he'll take care of everything."

"Think he might be taking care of Daimler, to boot?" Tully asked.

"I don't know what. Nobody knows better than I do that I'm a greenhorn. I certainly don't mean to interfere with ranch operations until I know what I'm doing. But it seems to me Daimler doesn't mean for me ever to learn anything about it."

"He ever tell you," Tully asked flatly, "that the basin hates Two Hump worse than poison?"

"I've heard there are hard feelings about water now that there's a drought," Louise admitted. "We've got it, and the basin hasn't. That, I understand, is due to Uncle Cass's being the first stockman to come into this country. He got the choice range. Why the hard feeling?"

"You've got water wasting," Tully said. "And grass till hell wouldn't have it. But Daimler says no smoke when it comes to helping your neighbors. They resent it. Which is as natural as your Uncle Cass latching onto all the best graze and water."

"I asked Daimler why we weren't helping out," Louise told him instantly. "He says there's sickness among the basin stock, and that, if we let it come in on us, our own range is liable to be infected."

"Sickness?" Tully snorted. "The basin steers are starving and dying of thirst. Daimler's filled you with hot air, girl. If you want to throw a surprise into him, ask him why he offered to buy up basin steers at five dollars a head if he thinks they're sick with some disease."

Louise looked surprised. "I didn't know he'd made any such offer."

"Well, he did. Which makes it look like Two Hump's out to profit from the basin's troubles."

"It is not!" Louise blazed. "Not while I own it!"

"I'll bet my right arm Daimler's got a different notion about that. And speaking of the cuss . . . ain't that him in that buckboard coming yonder?"

Louise cast a glance at the rig coming along the street behind a team of fine bay horses. "Yes, drat it, and I haven't talked half long enough with you."

There was no chance to continue the conversation, Tully saw. The buckboard turned in before the hotel and halted. Nick Daimler swung down to the sidewalk, glancing briefly at Louise and touching his hat. He called: "Ready to go home, Miss Bentham? Howdy, Gale. Didn't know you two knew each other."

"We're old friends, Daimler," Tully answered.

"That a fact?" Daimler said mockingly. "Catching up on visiting, I take it. Your bag inside, Miss Bentham? I'll get it and we'll get going." He was tall and wiry. His kinky black hair, under a pushed-back hat, showed gray at the temples. His eyes were jet black, and belligerence lurked in them. Without waiting for Louise to answer him, he went on into the hotel.

"Going to tell him about me homesteading on you?" Tully asked Louise.

"No. He can find out for himself. Suddenly I have a feeling that you're right. He'd go gunning for you. I don't like that man, Tully. Come be my foreman, and I'll fire him."

"No smoke. Pretty soon I'd be marryin' you."

"What's so wrong with that?"

Tully shook his head. "Everything. I own

what I wear and what I ride, and that's all I got in this world. I couldn't work for a girl I'd like to marry. I couldn't marry a girl who put up my spread, bank account, and even the roof over my head."

"When will I see you again?"

"That depends on a lot of things."

Daimler was coming out of the hotel, carrying a valise. Tully touched his hat to Louise and headed for the porch steps.

He waited until Daimler's buckboard had rolled out on the basin road. Then he saddled the red mustang and hit the same trail himself. His discovery in the *malpais* was forgotten for the time being, and his thoughts ran ahead.

Ellery Vines had asked him to file quietly on a piece of open land that lay on the Two Hump side of the ridge that separated Bentham Valley from Banca Basin. Thereafter he was to lay low for a while. During the interval, he had bought the mustang from Lagg and found himself launched upon that adventure. That had been incidental. The basiners were to assemble the equipment and supplies he needed to set up on his claim, and it had ought to be ready by now.

He rode slowly into the monotony of a flat, unbending plain. On the south, sky and earth met in a blaze of heat, but northward lay the low, hazed shapes of the badlands. The road he followed was pocked by hoofs and rutted by the iron tires of many wagons, and it seemed scarcely to change direction as it lost itself in the heat shimmer ahead. It was dry country at best, and the drought had made it look even more forbidding.

In mid-afternoon hills began to show on either hand, nearly lost in the purpled distance. He was nearing the end of the basin, and ahead was the pass to Bentham Valley. He had crossed it that one time and knew that on the far side lay a staggering contrast to this side. The valley was large, mountain-hemmed, with a concave bottom that was its prime asset, for under it was an artesian table that the ridge broke off from the basin.

Tully left the main road short of the pass, taking a trail that seemed to meander aimlessly to the left. The land made a slow, scarcely discernible rise. At long last it crested, and he looked down upon the spread he sought. It was the little King Pin, owned and operated by old Sam McNulty, who had become as good a friend of Tully's as had Ed, in town.

Below him a single scrawny poplar broke the monotony. Beneath it stood a small structure that was half soddy and half stone. Behind it was a stone barn, a couple of pole corrals, and a water trough. On the encircling range, Tully knew, ran some fifty beat-up steers, Sam's entire herd. Sam had nearly killed himself trying to dig wells to keep the herd alive. That was the main reason Tully had bought chips in a game that was growing more and more sinister. He rode onward to the house.

A woman came to the soddy door and stared out at him. To Tully's mind she looked as out of place there as a hair ribbon on the tail of a steer, for she wore a city dress and slippers. But she had compromised with her situation to the extent of wearing a scarf about her head to protect her hair from the dust.

She said: "So it's you again."

"I couldn't keep away from you, Missus Meade," Tully said. "Even if you are a married woman."

Aurora Meade tossed her head. She was a slender, attractive woman for all her outlandish clothes and ways. Another redeeming feature to Tully was the fact that she was old Sam's daughter come to visit him.

"Confidentially," said Aurora, "I could stand keeping away from you."

"Where's Sam?"

"Too busy eating his supper to be bothered by even you."

"That a subtle way of inviting me to light down and eat?" Tully inquired. "Thanks, Missus Meade. I'll be there in a minute."

He rode on to Sam's corral, grinning. Aurora was range-bred and trained but had married a railroad engineer and gone East to live. She had come back on a visit to find Sam fighting a losing battle against the drought. That had been much to her liking because she had divulged plans for taking Sam back with her to live in comfortable retirement. That had scared the very life out of old Sam, and Tully knew why. Aurora Meade had revealed herself to be a resourceful and determined woman. Everything Tully had done to help Sam hang on had heightened the conflict between him and Aurora.

Tully washed at the horse trough, sparingly because like all the others on the range the headquarters well was nearly dry. Then he went on to the house and stepped in uninvited because he knew that, as far as Sam was concerned, he had the run of the place. Sam was at the table, a knife in one hand, a fork in the other, but eating with the knife. The old man nodded gruffly. He was a bantam with bowed legs and a nose

116

like a tomahawk.

"Where in tunket you been? We thought you'd skipped the country."

For all her truculence, Aurora had made an extra place at the table, and Tully took it. "See you've got your wagon hid in the barn," he told Sam. "Also seen that it's loaded with my homesteading stuff. Am I ready to set up in business?"

"And get yourself killed," Aurora said cheerfully. She took the remaining place. "Anybody fool enough to trust Ellery Vines deserves to be. I smelled a rat the minute I laid eyes on him."

"Vines is an Eastern gentleman," Tully retorted. "Or does it take one Easterner to smell another?"

"Vines is a crook," Aurora insisted. "You think he's trying to help the basin through the drought, but I don't. Yet why should I worry? The sooner Dad admits he's ruined, the sooner he'll come home with me and get some pleasure out of life."

"Pleasure?" Sam snorted. "Tully, I was back there once. So crowded a man's got to take a trolley to the country if he wants to spit. I seen Vines while you were gone, boy. He says the minute you're dug in on your claim, he'll see Daimler and lay down the law. Two Hump can take its pick. It can help

117

us basiners or face a plague of nesters."

"It won't work," Aurora reflected. "And I don't care, Tully Gale, as long as you don't mess around and get Dad's head shot off. That worries me, and I'm warning you. If anything happens to him, I'll hold you responsible."

"By damn," Sam breathed, "I ain't forgot how to dust your tail feathers. This boy's risking his neck to help us basiners, and you set there lecturing him. If you think it's him keeping me from going home with you, you got another think coming. If I go busted, I'll take to the *malpais* and start rustling."

"Take it easy," Tully told him. "Me and Aurora are really in love and trying to hide it. She's already trying to figure out how to get rid of her husband."

"Oh, flapdoodle!" Aurora said, laughing.

When evening came on, Aurora lighted a lamp against the gathering melancholy of the empty space about King Pin. Once, Tully knew, she had been a range girl, used to solitude and self-dependence. But the years of congested living had turned her into a herd creature, needing noise and bustle and numbers of people about her. To Tully that was deterioration for, out here, there was God and countryside to keep a person company, and that was sufficient.

Gale rose from the table and went to the barn to bed down. But sleep failed to come in its usual quick way. He lay in the hay wondering why he lacked the stability that kept Sam on this hard-scrabble little spread, bucking every kind of adversity yet more frightened by the prospect of being dragged off by Aurora than by any possible local trouble. Not that he found it hard to appreciate Sam's attitude toward city life. The puzzle was in Sam's sticking to this one bare, baked spot of ground when the whole world was open and calling. At least it called to Tully Gale, who could not remember spending more than six months in one place since he was on his own.

He received no answer to his question about Sam's tenacity and presently found himself thinking of Maggie Paine. She acted on him in a different way from Louise Bentham. Louise had beauty and Maggie was not beautiful but she left little doubt in a man's mind that her nature was just as warm. Yet the pull of Maggie was persistent, more obsessing to the male mind. A fellow wanted to marry Louise, as well as possess her, to share with her all kinds of things. Maggie — he meant to master her, and, as far as he knew now, that was all.

■ ■ ■ ■

At breakfast Sam said: "Aurora, we'll move Tully onto his claim this morning. You can ride Bess over and bring the wagon home."

"Me?" Aurora asked, astonished.

"You," said Sam. "And get into some sensible duds. Them affairs you wear are plumb ridiculous."

"I haven't been on a horse for years . . . ," Aurora began.

"That's the p'int," Sam cut in. "And your brain's softened, the same as your bottom. Pound leather a while and sweat a little, and see if you're still so willin' to lay down and roll over for this drought and Two Hump's ambitions."

Aurora saw the grin spreading on Tully's face and tossed her head. Sam was getting his teeth in the problem with which she had confronted him; he was wresting the initiative from her, and she knew it. But she went into the bedroom.

They loaded the wagon and struck out, Sam driving the team and Aurora astride his old saddle mare. Tully rode beside the wagon, which headed directly across the open range. They crawled forward slowly. When finally Sam pulled down the horses, he stared at Two Hump's barbed-wire fence, then shifted an uneasy glance to Tully.

"This is the big jump," he remarked. "But cutting their bob wire won't rile Two Hump a mite more than squatting on its range."

He started to climb down from the wagon, but Tully said: "You let me do the cutting, Sam. They'll try to beef me, anyhow. Besides, Missus Meade warned me not to let you get hurt in this ruckus."

"Hell with her," Sam answered.

But Tully took the cutters away from him and quickly snapped the strands of wire. Tully laid back the wire then, and a grave-faced Sam drove the wagon through. All three of them knew the ethics involved. Cutting another's fence without his knowledge and permission was less injury than insult. Sam drove on for 100 yards, halting at a point Tully had picked as the best place for his camp.

By then, however, Sam's eyes had begun to gleam. They unloaded the wagon, which held a tent and cot, a stove and cooking supplies, together with groceries and an assortment of tools. But the thing that drew Sam's interest the most was an earth auger some basiner had provided. There was no spring on Tully's claim, but Bentham Valley's artesian table lay beneath it, with the water under considerable pressure. A six-inch hole drilled into that water would provide for Tully's needs and then some. This fact had been a primary consideration in the plan Ellery Vines and the basiners had worked out for Tully.

Sam started Aurora home with the wagon as soon as it was unloaded. He stayed to help make camp, and it was late in the day when they finished and cooked a meal. Sam had neglected his own chores, so he took Bess off picket and saddled up.

Before riding out, he scratched an ear and said: "We'd better not fool ourselves, Tully. It ain't going to be easy to pull off this caper. Aurora, dang her hide, has got me uneasy about it."

"Her suspicions of Vines?" Tully asked.

"Well . . . mebbe. That cuss has always been a puzzle to me. He's a basiner and not a big operator, just like the rest of us. Needs water just as bad. This caper to scare Two Hump into helping us out is the only thing I know of that can save us. But . . . well, I just don't trust it, somehow."

"You don't think Two Hump'll scare."

"Not easy. But that ain't it. I got a feeling there's things going on most of us don't know about."

Tully made no comment to that. He had

seen Vines, Daimler, and Lagg talking together in Valen's saloon, and he had seen Lagg's impounded water in the badlands. Sam was certainly correct about there being ulterior motives in the situation. Even Tully Gale knew things he dared not tell, at least not yet. So he let Sam ride home without disclosing his own doubts.

But Sam was back bright and early the next morning, eager to help sink the well. He and Tully picked a site, a point where the flow of artesian water would be caught in a declivity to form a pool. They took the earth auger and extension rods to the place and set doggedly to work.

It was slow going down through the hardpan, which they were still in at noon. They had laid off for dinner when Sam straightened to stare down the slope toward Two Hump's line fence.

"There comes Daimler's outrider," he communicated. "We'd best buckle on our irons, Tully. No telling what he'll do."

They walked up to the tent and were armed when the Two Hump rider swung away from the fence line and headed for the camp at a gallop. As he approached, Tully saw that he was young and the kind of cowpuncher to be found on countless cattle spreads. But the Two Humper's face was dark with anger, which was mixed with shock. This reaction informed Tully that the man had had no inkling of what he was going to find here.

"McNulty!" the cowpuncher bawled at Sam. "What the hell's going on here? What're you doing on our side of the fence? What's that tent doing? Who's this jigger here? What do you think you're digging?"

Sam's eyes were cold, yet he grinned. "Clyde, you're too full of questions. But I've got the answers. I'm on this side of the fence to help my new neighbor get set up in business. That's Gale, here. This ain't your side of the fence but his. He filed on this piece of land. What we're digging is a hole. Tryin' to set Gale's homestead to squirtin'. That satisfy you?"

Clyde looked anything but satisfied, and his stunned expression told Tully two things. Louise had not informed Daimler about it, keeping her word, and Ellery Vines had not yet laid down the law to Daimler as he had promised to do as soon as Tully was on the claim. It was that, or Daimler had not passed the word of it down to his crew, which did not seem probable if Daimler knew.

"So Gale figures he's got hisself a homestead!" Clyde yelled.

"You can check up at the Land Office, Clyde," Sam said.

"Check, hell! This is Two Hump graze, and you know it, Sam! I know you been hard put, and a lot of other little fellows. Don't blame you for going after water any way you can get it. But, damn me, I won't stand for you tryin' to nest on any outfit I ride for!"

"Easy, Clyde," Sam warned. "Keep your hand away from that gun. I always had a fair opinion of you, bub, and I'd hate to blow out your brains."

The wildness went out of Clyde as he sat under the cool impact of Sam's eyes. His shoulders relaxed and his right hand fell limply. Tully felt a certain admiration for him. Any rider worth his pay gave a fierce loyalty to his outfit. It had to be that way in a country where the six-gun often superseded the courts. Then Clyde swung his horse and rode off, heading for Two Hump headquarters.

"That's the end of our peace and quiet," Sam commented. "Clyde's all right, and there's others like him on the Two Hump payroll. But they won't take a thing like this layin' down, not a man's son of 'em. Vines, he better get over there quick and tell Daimler what he's up against. That the whole basin's backin' you, not just me. That if he runs you off, there'll be two more squatters on him, and, if he guns them off, he'll get four more. And so on until he sees the light and gives us pasture and water."

"What's Vines waiting on?" Tully demanded. "The night this caper was worked out, he was breathin' fire to take action. But we ain't seen hide nor hair of him. Apparently Nick Daimler ain't, either."

Sam shook his head. "There's a lot of things I'd like to know, bub," he said.

III

Sam stayed until dusk but the earth auger still turned up dry dirt. There was danger that they would hit shale and be stopped. They put on more extension rods and kept going, stubbornly driving the head of the drill toward the hoped-for artesian water. Tully began to fear that they would have to use dynamite or in some other way get themselves tied up for weeks of labor. He didn't mind work, but Sam needed water soon if he was to escape killing off steers or selling the herd to Two Hump. Sam was only one of a number of ranchers in the same fix.

Then, just at dusk, it came. They had the tool out when Tully heard a grumbling, hollow and distant, far down in the hole. He bent above it, not daring to hope yet certain that a water jet was at work far below. The rumble pitched up, then suddenly dirty water boiled out on the surface. It pulsed, and, each time it surged, it rose higher above the ground, still muddy, scouring its way through some kind of raveled opening deep in the earth. Then, with a gush, the stream shot a good six feet in the air.

"We hit it!" Sam yelled. "Tully, we hit it big!" His voice was jubilant with relief.

"Looks like it!" Tully felt nearly as good as Sam did, but was too tired to dance a jig.

They retreated and hunkered to watch the mushrooming water grow clear. It began to pool in the declivity below. They would have a perpetual flow running day and night, and the year around, artificially created but now a natural spring.

"And now I can tell you something," Sam said. "My last range well dried up day before yesterday. I like to've died when it looked like we might not hit water here. How's to bring my steers over, boy?"

"Wouldn't try it tonight," Tully said, although he understood Sam's driving eagerness. "We'll have to close-herd 'em whenever they're over here, till we can fence in the claim. You know what would happen if there was any straying on Two Hump. Have Aurora help you fetch your bunch over the first thing tomorrow."

Sam got his horse and rode off, eager to tell Aurora that her last hope of whisking him East was gone. Tully fixed and ate his supper with a deep sense of satisfaction filling him. For all the war clouds on the horizon, it was a peaceful, triumphant twilight.

He was down looking at the red, which he kept hobbled, when the mustang's sudden attention to something out in the night warned him. Tully turned around, staring in the direction the horse searched intuitively. Presently Tully could hear the beat of hoofs coming in from the west, through the hills separating this and Sam's little King Pin. The openness of the approach reassured Tully, and presently somebody called a salute.

It was the voice of Ellery Vines. Tully walked back to the camp and was waiting there when Vines rode in.

Vines spoke another greeting and swung down. He was a blocky figure in the darkness, and it was a body that never seemed to relax. "So you're here," he said. "Have you had any trouble?"

"Two Hump's line rider stumbled onto me today and was some shocked," Tully told him. "Either you haven't laid down the law to Daimler, or he's keeping it under his hat. How come, mister? I've got no hankering to set here like a duck for them to shoot at."

Tully's voice was harsh.

Holding the reins of his horse, Vines seated himself on the grass. "I had to be sure the stage was set, Gale. Something kept me from getting over here sooner."

"This whole caper," Tully said, "is intended to scare Daimler into opening Two Hump's spare water and grass to us. When are you going to make that plain to him?"

"The first thing in the morning," Vines assured him. "I understand your worry, Gale, but I promise to spike the man's guns. It'll be a chore I'll like. For twenty years Cass Bentham lorded it over me. I only wish it was Cass I'll deal with tomorrow." He was overly stimulated, although Tully could see no signs of drinking. It struck Tully that he had been the same way the night he organized the basiners for this move, all but drunk on the sense of power it gave him.

"So it's your hatred of Cass Bentham more than your worry about drought cattle," Tully reflected. "That's a poor motive for anything, Vines."

"I'm worried about the drought cattle," Vines said irritably. "But you're right about me hating Bentham, too. I did. He prided himself over something that was sheer luck. He found Bentham Valley, and it gave him everything he had. Yet he took credit for it.

He set himself a notch above the rest of us."

"The way I heard it," Tully drawled, "Bentham rode into an unclaimed valley and had the sense to latch onto it. Wouldn't you have, Vines? If you ask me, I don't see you divvying up with anybody, either, if it had been you."

Vines made a sound that was pure anger, then turned it quickly into a laugh.

"You see Daimler," Tully went on, "and find out if it's going to get us water and pasture. That's what I'm here for. That's what I want done. I want no piece of your getting revenge against a man who's dead and gone."

"Sure," Vines said, and his manner was easy again. "I'll see Nick in the morning." He rose to his feet.

"Wait a minute," Tully said. "There's something I want explained. One night I saw you drinking with Lagg and Daimler in that stinkpot they call Valen's in town. How come?"

Vines straightened, then laughed. "I remember that night. It happened that I bought some horses from Lagg. That's the kind of place he hangs out. If you want to do business with him, you see him there. Daimler happened in. He's a friend of Lagg's. I didn't think it was necessary to walk out on him." Vines swung up to his saddle and rode away.

Tully had barely risen, the next morning, when the bawling of steers caught his attention. He looked west to see Sam's little bunch spill out of the draw, with Sam and his daughter behind. But the thirst-drawn steers needed no herding. Having scented water, nothing could have held them back. Sam waved his hat, and Tully grinned as he watched the bunch break and run for what was now a considerable pond of sweet water that had already drowned out its boiling intake.

Aurora turned toward the camp, but Sam stayed with his bunch to watch it ease the thirst that had so long tormented it. His gaunt frame was erect in the saddle, so that he looked like a runty old warrior astride the equally aging Bess.

Tully touched his hat to Aurora. " 'Morning. How does it feel to fork a horse again?"

"Inelegant," said Aurora, "but otherwise not bad. Tully Gale, I could skin you. Dad's got so much water, dynamite couldn't move him off of King Pin now."

"Never could've," Tully retorted. "And you never had a leg to stand on. Look at him down there. If we weren't watching, he'd be down on his knees drinking with his steers. He's that close to them."

"You may think you're joking," Aurora said, "but if he had a choice between shooting me and a cow, the cow wouldn't need to worry."

"Light down, ma'am," Tully said, "and make yourself comfortable. I bet you haven't had your breakfast. I was just fixing to cook. You can rest and eat beans or you can cook and eat better."

Aurora swung out of the saddle. Tully had noticed that she knew how to handle herself on a horse. Dust kicked up by the moving bunch had darkened her skin. Perspiration had risen to form a vague coat of unladylike mud, and for all her bluster she looked like the morning's work had enlivened her. In shirt and work pants she was more attractive than before, he observed, the shirt showing an appealing fullness, the Levi's rounding fetchingly over long, slender thighs. She noticed his quick, surprised inspection and was not displeased. Since she didn't offer her services, Tully started breakfast.

With their thirst quenched, the steers fell to grazing on the better grass over here and showed no inclination to breach off. Sam came in to the camp for breakfast, and Tully told him about Ellery Vines's visit.

"Yeah, I seen him," Sam said. "You're right about him having a personal grudge against Two Hump. Vines is getting a lot of relish out of being able to talk tough to it, even if Cass ain't there any more. Mighty queer critter, Vines. Never understood him. Never liked him much, either. You wipe that smile off your face, Aurora. Mebbe he's going to skin us. I dunno. But I'd sure like to know how he's going to make out over there this morning."

"The frog could jump the wrong way," Tully admitted.

Aurora kept right on smiling. "And Gale with his neck stuck out too far to pull back. Do you know what I hope happens to it?"

"A carbuncle," Tully answered, "with a rope pulled tight around that."

"You took the words out of my mouth," Aurora told him. "And I wouldn't be surprised to see something like that. I warned you two not to trust Vines. You went right ahead. All you have is his word as to what he means to do. His intentions could be considerably otherwise."

Tully had to admit that. "But if he don't do what he's agreed, what else can he make of it?" he asked. "You got a woman's insight into that, Missus Meade?"

"Unfortunately not," Aurora acknowledged. "Except I've got the feeling Dad had better bottle as much of that water as he can. He might not be able to get to it very long."

"Aurora," Sam said, his face darkening, "you can take them steers home by yourself. I aim to stay with Tully today, just in case Daimler don't take the bit the way we hoped."

Although he didn't want Sam exposed to any more danger than necessary, Tully consented, partly because of the look of consternation that rose on Aurora's face. She started to protest, then changed her mind. But Tully had to admire the expert way she rounded in the little bunch, disdaining help, getting it out through the fence opening, and on its way up the draw.

"Her heart's in the right place, Sam," Tully said, and meant it.

"I reckon," Sam said grudgingly. "Only I don't like to be took into it lock, stock, and barrel."

"Maybe she'll throw in her hand, now that it's hopeless."

"Hah," Sam said, and let it go at that.

They ditched along the ravine that day, so that the cattle could drink without crowding. The job was finished by noon without much left to do, and there had been no sign of trouble from Two Hump. Sam's interest had been caught by the idea of making this King Pin's headquarters, the two of them becoming partners. They fell to talking of cutting juniper logs and sledding in rock for a house. Sam offered to buy barbed wire so the half-section could be used as a part of King Pin, with no special effort required. It got so interesting, Tully wondered if he was going to mind the time it would take to prove up on the land. For a man whose sojourns were inclined to abrupt endings, this was a surprising and not unwelcome change.

"You know, Sam," he said wonderingly, "if I was to settle down, I wouldn't mind running a horse ranch."

Sam nodded, pleased. "Horses is fine for them that likes 'em better. But with me its cows. Dog-gone, there's something about a cow critter. . . ." Sam's voice trailed off, incapable of expressing his feelings.

Tully grinned. "If I could catch a good mate for the red stallion, I'd be set up in business, wouldn't I?"

"Plenty mares in the *malpais*," Sam said. "Wouldn't be hard to find one willing to marry that good-looking red."

Tully fell to thinking about that. It would

be fun to invade the *malpais* again and catch a mate for the red stallion, snatching it out from under Sugar Lagg's nose. A half-section of land and two wild horses, he thought, and a man would be setting pretty. His feet were itching him suddenly, but not to travel to far places. He had again thought of the water Lagg had pooled in the bad-lands. He had kept quiet about that, as Ed requested, but suddenly it became a gnaw-ing temptation. The droughted basiners would certainly swear off drinking if they got a sudden flash flood in Splinter Creek.

Sam stayed for supper and lingered on. When Tully suggested, finally, that he go home, Sam shook his head. "If they aim to wreck your camp, and you to boot, they'll come at night. If Vines seen Daimler today, and Daimler kicks over the traces, this is apt to be the night. Reckon I'll hang around just in case you should get visitors."

The moon was hazed. Stars sprinkled the sweep of sky linking the surrounding hills. To be on the safe side, Tully agreed when Sam suggested that they take turns and stand guard. The day's excitement and activity had tired the old man, and Tully insisted that he sleep until midnight. After Sam had turned in on the cot in the tent, Tully stretched his legs lazily by the cold ashes of the cook fire.

The night's serenity seeped into Tully, and it was hard to credit that human passions had so divided this country against itself. Although not given to self-searching, he had found that, of late, these rare intervals of repose caused it to take place in him. More and more he was questioning the kind of life he had lived. He was twenty-six, with the first flush of manhood worn away. Adventure and excitement had lost a little of their pull. It struck him suddenly, in the night's tranquility, that, given the right woman and place, he would like to settle down. Maybe both were here. He hoped so. He wanted to get his teeth into something worthwhile.

He had known that this hunger had brought him to Banca Basin in search of Louise, only to be buried temporarily when he found out the truth about her and her wealth. Now he caught himself comparing her with Maggie, wondering if he could not find the same anchorage there. Reason told him that, all else being equal, Maggie would be the better mate for a man cut out like himself. She understood him, she liked him, and he doubted that she would try to make him over to suit her taste. She stirred him and gave him physical pleasure if nothing else. Yet, for some reason, this quality did not register in the deep quick within himself. Without consideration of qualities, Louise still made an impact there. She was going to be hard to erase from his mind.

Tully would have let Sam sleep on through the night had not the old man roused voluntarily. Sam came out of the tent saying: "Thunderation, boy, it must be past midnight."

"Wasn't sleepy," Tully said.

"You ain't tried it to see. Now you get in there. Won't have you falling asleep on me in the middle of a gun ruckus."

Tully went into the tent, started to unbuckle his shell belt, then thought better of it. Stretching out on the cot, which was yet warm from Sam's body, he found himself still in a mental unrest that would not relax. He thought: *Five years you've chased your own tail.* The fancy pleased him because he was close to admitting that a man's pursuit of his self was also a flight away from it.

His reflections were destroyed by a sharp, loud shot in the night. He heard Sam's low curse as he rolled off the cot. The tent walls were no protection, and two more shots came in quick succession. He crawled through the tent flaps and saw Sam stretched by the cold fire. The old man chopped down with his pistol and fired up the slope.

Tully crawled to him, whispering: "They took you for me and figure there's only one man here. You keep 'em interested, while I wiggle up to that thicket and hand them a surprise."

Sam didn't answer and Tully slipped away. The shooting came from the top of land east of the camp. His pistol in hand, Tully crawled around behind the tent and began to work his slow way up the open slope, moving toward the thicket that fringed the top. The night had turned quiet again, and he could detect no movement of horses. He was certain that the attackers had mistaken Sam for himself. The assault had been swift and heavy, and the quiet suggested that they figured it had been successful. He reached the edge of the thicket after what seemed long, dragging minutes.

He had drawn no fire. Emboldened by this, he climbed to his feet in the grove's entanglement. He crossed hurriedly to its far side, hoping he could locate their horses. He saw two and was instantly energized.

The riders were there, also, but too far away to be identified. One man was in the saddle, the other swinging up. They considered it a finished business and were getting away as quietly as possible. Wildness ran through Tully. He wanted to know who it was. He fired once, and then sent a quick second shot at the same target.

The horse stumbled forward, going down. Half risen to the saddle, the man spilled across it while the other rider wheeled off. Tully fired at the man still mounted, saw him bend widely in the saddle. Excitement swirled in Tully. The mounted man threw down and fired, and Tully dropped flat as he heard the lead cut leaves and twigs close to him. The spilled man scrambled to his feet, trying desperately to clutch the other's saddle and swing up behind.

Tully fired at this one, and the horse bolted. But the man on the ground hung on and was dragged, now on the blind side of the horse. The other bent low in the saddle, urging the mount on. Tully emptied his gun as the animal thundered down the slope, but the range had grown too great for effect. Far below, the horse stopped while the dragged man swung up double. Then it pounded on. They swept south, which meant nothing since they would make their escape in as evasive a manner as possible.

They're sure wondering who popped out of the ground, Tully reflected bitterly.

The horse was dead, and he discovered

that he had put both bullets through its head. He struck a match for a brief moment but scarcely needed it to make out the small Two Hump brand, a **B** on its face, burned on the animal's front shoulder. This gave Tully no surprise, and the only thing unexpected was the furious nature of the attack. But a couple of Two Hump riders were wishing they hadn't left a dead, ranch-branded horse at the squatter claim. A horse carcass wasn't a thing a man tucked in his pocket to tote off and hide somewhere.

Tully crossed the rise and began to hurry down the slope, calling: "You all right, Sam?"

There was no answer. A pulse began to beat in Tully's throat and he hurried. He entered the camp on the run. Sam was still stretched by the ashes of the cook fire, unmoving. Tully spoke again and dropped to his knees. He saw the stain on Sam's shirt even as his fingers touched its wetness. Alarm crawled through him. He caught Sam's wrist and made out the stringy rhythm of a pulse. Afraid to move the man, he ripped away the shirt and was eased a little. Sam had got it through the left shoulder, probably in that first flurry of shots. He had held onto himself long enough to fling a shot in retaliation, and this cemented him to Tully forever. Then shock and blood loss had got Sam.

Tully was weak with apprehension. Sam had taken that bullet for him, and this had created an obligation. He thought: *The devil with the rest.* He couldn't leave Sam here while he went to get help. He had to get him home, then ride for the doctor. He got Sam onto the cot in the tent and bound the flowing wound as best he could. Afterward he sucked on a cigarette, his fingers trembling. He had scarcely finished it when the old man opened his eyes.

"They sure come up quiet," Sam gasped. "Never heard a thing till they began to wham lead."

"They knew right where to shoot," Tully said. "Clyde got a good look at this camp."

"They sure showed powerful openers," Sam muttered. "I expected rough-housing, but not that rough. It'll rile the basin, boy, if it gets out. We'd better keep it under our hats."

"The devil with that!" Tully exploded. "I'm already keeping too much under my hat to suit me, so as to keep peace in the country. Well, to hell with peace. They've asked for it, Sam. We'll see they get prompt delivery."

"Boy," Sam said, and his voice was very

tired, "peace is a thing you young 'uns don't appreciate. Now, I'm going to get up."

"You'll lay there if I have to hog-tie you," Tully said. "Sam, there's a dead Two Hump horse across the rise. I killed it, and I bet it's got them smarting in their britches. Daimler will have some fast talking to do when the sheriff or the basiners ask how come it got there . . . you winged, and it with two slugs in its head."

"We'll keep the sheriff out of it, too," Sam said solidly. "Should this get out right now, it'd start a bloody range war. I've seen 'em, boy. Nothin's worse."

"Man's better off dead than tucking his tail when somebody shoots at him!" Tully blazed.

Sam grinned weakly. "Mostly you've got what it takes, Tully. But there's a shortage. That's seasoning."

Tully made Sam rest for an hour, then brought in old Bess and the red. Sam was shaky, sore, and fevered, and had trouble getting into the saddle even with help. Tully was too experienced to make light of a gunshot wound. Sam was drawing on reserve strength now, but the real reaction would come soon and at his age might be serious.

They rode out for King Pin, Tully taking

time only to close the barbed-wire fence behind them to prevent straying from Sam's cattle. Dawn was breaking when they poked down into Sam's little saucer, riding carefully. There was no sign of activity below at the soddy, and Tully would rather have faced the guns again than Aurora, who had said: *If anything happens to Dad, I'll hold you responsible.*

They came down to the soddy where Tully dismounted and rapped on the door. Even Sam looked more sheepish than injured at that moment. Then the door swung in. Aurora stood there in her nightgown, an exciting figure even though she held Sam's shotgun in her hands. Her mouth swung open when she saw her father's blood-soaked shirt and the way he grasped the saddle horn.

"Two Hump paid us a call, ma'am," Tully said. "We squabbled a little. You better help me get him down from that horse and into bed."

"Dad!" cried Aurora. She put down the gun and ran out to Sam in her bare feet.

Sam grinned down at her. "Now, don't get excited, honey. I've cut myself bad as this shaving. When I used to shave."

With Aurora's aid, Tully got Sam into the house. He helped the old man undress and

145

slide into bed, forcing him actually, for Sam protested proudly.

To Aurora, Tully said: "Reckon you can keep him there till I fetch the doctor. Or should I knock him cold with a gun barrel?"

"I can handle him," Aurora answered. "And any Two Humper that ever lived!" There was anger in her face at the men who had done it, and for a moment she looked just like her father.

"I'd put my wages on you any day, ma'am," Tully told her. "They can take a range woman East, but they can't get the range out of her. Don't fear that anybody will come here from Two Hump. They had a flimsy excuse over there. Wouldn't have here, and they won't bother you."

"I wish they'd try," breathed Aurora.

IV

All through the long ride down the basin Tully was grateful for the tough little mustang stallion under him. He was in Splinter Rock in less than three hours, still chafing against Sam's request that the shooting be kept as quiet as possible. He rode the length of the street, looking for the doctor's shingle. He found it between the barbershop and the Commercial Hotel. But the door was locked.

Not knowing where to look for the man, Tully rode on and pulled up before the Paine House, feeling that Maggie could be trusted with some inkling of the secret heating so explosively in his own mind. He saw that the stage was just leaving at the depot across the street, and, when he entered the hotel, Maggie was in the lobby checking out what, from the luggage, appeared to be a drummer. She gave Tully a quick look of surprise and the faintest smile.

When the man had struggled out with his luggage, yelling for the stage driver to wait for him, Maggie repeated the smile, making it broad and warming. "Here we are again," she murmured. "Fairly clean this trip, but apparently on the warpath."

"Where would the doctor be if he wasn't in his office?" Tully asked her.

"Anywhere in a fifty-mile circle. Tully, what's wrong?" Maggie looked worried.

"Man come down with lead poisoning," Tully told her, worry running through him, too. "And the sawbones must be out of town."

"Better check at the livery," Maggie advised him. "Doc Burne keeps his horse there. Ed'd likely have the best idea where he is. Tully, have you been getting into trouble?"

He gave her a searching look, then said: "Where could we talk with a fair amount of privacy?"

"Like to come up to my room?" Without waiting for an answer, Maggie started across the lobby and he followed.

His heart was speeding up, causing him to frown for this was no time for private interests. At the top of the stairs she walked swiftly down the hallway to her door, opened it, and let him step in ahead of her.

She closed the door carefully behind her, facing him with a look of wonder.

"You're perfectly safe," Tully assured her. "I've got worries."

"If I can ease them, I'll be glad to."

He held her gaze. "How well do you know Nick Daimler?"

She straightened and lifted a hand only to let it fall. Something jerked very slightly at the corner of her mouth, which she made into a smile. "Why, Tully?" Her voice was low, cautious.

"Daimler," Tully said, "is close-mouthed and unfriendly with other men. But sometimes a man like that opens up to a woman. You called him an old friend, and I got to wondering. There are things I'd like to know."

"Such as what, Tully?"

He thought about her uneasiness for an instant, then said: "I'd like to know something about the man himself. I think he's out to trim the Eastern girl who inherited Two Hump. He'd like to scare her into going back where she came from and letting him have the run of the spread. Maybe selling to him at his price, with terms that would let the ranch pay for itself."

Maggie's relief was visible. "What makes you think I'd be aware of it, if he did?"

"I told you one reason. A woman notices things and senses more. Then there's the fact that I stampeded you for an instant, just now, when I brought him up."

Maggie turned from him and walked to the window. She stared outward for a moment, then moved back. "All right, you stampeded me. I knew you were angry about him the last time you were here. I thought you meant to pick a quarrel. If you're worried as to Two Hump, I'd be inclined to say you're guessing shrewdly. You've pegged Daimler pretty close. He clams up with other men. But a man has to talk to somebody, sometimes, and he does to me. He drops things, now and then, that make me wonder about him. I'd have told you that at the start but I didn't know you were interested in Two Hump. What got you interested? Louise Bentham? I've seen her, and she's very pretty."

Tully waved an impatient hand. "The insolence Daimler's been showing the basin is meant to cause trouble. He's refused to pasture or to share water. Instead of offering help, he's tried to buy up drought steers at five dollars a head. He knew that would put the basin on the prod and maybe stir up enough trouble to sicken Louise into dealing with him."

"I wouldn't know, Tully," Maggie said. "Honestly I wouldn't."

"What do you know about Ellery Vines, then?"

Maggie smiled. "Nobody knows much about him. Maybe not even Vines himself. He's a proud man with ambitions too big for his talents. He never drops a grudge. That's all I can tell you."

"Thanks," Tully said. "Now, would you keep an eye on the doc's office and send him packing for Sam McNulty's if you see him before I do?"

"Of course." Maggie crossed to him and placed a hand on his arm. "Tully, don't breathe a word of what I said. It's not good policy for a woman in business to talk about people who are often her patrons. Promise?"

He grinned. "Why, sure. Me, and the only ones I'd be inclined to mention it to, we don't happen to be thick. Vines and Daimler themselves." She stayed in her room when he left, changed by his visit, quiet and a little withdrawn.

Tully swung onto the red and rode back down the street to the livery barn. Ed Handel was canted in a chair at the door and lifted a hand in greeting.

"Seen you fog into town like a dog running a rabbit. Seen you go down to the

Paine House. You in that big a itch to see the widder?"

"Have you seen Doc Burne?" Tully demanded, scowling at the implication.

"Doc got me out of bed before daylight," Ed reported. "He was called out to Half Diamond."

"Half Diamond?" Tully swung around and found his voice weak. That was Ellery Vines's spread. "Somebody sick out there?"

"Doc didn't say. Keeps his lip buttoned about his cases. Smart, too, when some of 'em are lead poisoning. But I'm nosier. What do you want of Doc Burne?"

"Sam McNulty's not so spry," Tully said evasively. "Ed, I'll try to catch the doc at Half Diamond or somewhere between. If I don't connect, you send him to Sam's. Another thing. The red's had all the pounding he can use for one day. You better let me take another horse."

"Dog-gone," Ed said, but he got to his feet, "that pesky mustang might as well move in and live with me." Then, as they walked down the darkened aisle of the barn, he said in a lower tone: "Sheriff went out to see Sugar Lagg and ask how come he plugged up the middle fork. Lagg was fit to be tied when he heard it had got out. You better watch him. But we guessed it right.

Sugar told the sheriff to come back with a court order saying that dam had to come out. Then maybe it would. But not before. Sheriff and me seen Chet Canby, the lawyer here, and Chet hunted through his law books. There's ways of fixing it, but they all take time."

"Dynamite's mighty sudden," Tully said.

Ed nodded sourly. "Too sudden in the hands of a sudden man. Not yet, Tully. Not till you have to. Lagg claims that pretty soon his pool will spill over the dam and there'll be as much water in the south fork as ever. That's right, too. Trouble is, that ain't apt to happen soon enough to help the business. There's so many whereifs and whereases about it, Tully, a man gets dizzy. One thing Canby says is certain. Lagg could sue the pants off of anybody who destroys that dam without legal backing."

Tully grinned. "All I got to lose is Red and a land claim I ain't proved up on."

"And your life," Ed retorted.

"Oh, that," Tully said. They had a fresh horse about ready, and his mind had gone back to his present needs. "Would Doc Burne ride the basin road or take some short cut to Vines's?" he asked.

"If there's a short cut in this country, Doc knows and rides it. In fact, he blazed most

153

of 'em."

"If he comes in without having seen me, Ed, you send him to Sam McNulty's."

"What's wrong out there?" Ed asked sharply.

"Sam's off his feed."

Ed snorted. "That old goat could eat tin cans and get fat on 'em. You're lying, but it's your business."

Tully led out the horse, mounted, and hit the basin trail. An enormous curiosity was in him as to why the doctor had been called out to Half Diamond. Someone had come for him around daylight that morning. A man riding hard would make it about then if he left Vines's ranch an hour or so after midnight, not long after Sam had been shot. Tully had had the feeling of having winged one of the attackers. But Half Diamond — Vines's own spread? A shiver ran along his spine.

Two hours out of town he came to a place where a side trail angled off in the direction of Half Diamond. He hadn't yet met the doctor, nor did he meet him on the long cut-off he followed thereafter. He dropped down the slope to Half Diamond headquarters with the sun burning hard on his right. No horse stood at the yard hitch rack, and, if the doctor was there, he had been tied up long enough to have had his mount turned into the day corral.

Tully swung down in the yard, looking around, then strode to the house and crossed the porch. The kitchen door stood open, and a sour-faced oldster stared out at him.

"Howdy," Tully said. "I'm hunting Doc Burne."

"In with Vines," the man answered.

"Might I ask where Vines is?"

"In bed."

"Shot?" Tully asked.

The man pulled straight. "Kid, how did you know that?"

"Take it easy, Pop," Tully retorted. "That was a shot in the dark on my part."

"It was a shot in the dark that got Vines, too," the man intoned. "A bushwhack bullet. Somebody plugged Vines, up on our east boundary, last night. Vines got home and spilled out of the saddle and got that much out. Been unconscious since. Jake went for the doc. I don't like the way you talked just now. We figured us and the 'busher to be the only ones who know about it. Vines was alone. Likes to ride around by himself at night. Don't sleep good."

"Send for the sheriff?" Tully asked.

The man shook his head. "Vines said not

155

to. We don't want to start trouble, considering the way things stand. Figured it was Two Hump that done it, but now you've got me wondering. You know a lot about it."

"Tell Doc Burne I'd like to see him," Tully said. He needed all his self-control to keep from showing the disturbance working in him. It didn't make sense that a bushwhacker would know where to wait for a man riding around alone at night because of insomnia, or that an attack would be made on Vines at the same hour as the one on the camp at the claim. He thought: *I'd bet my teeth Vines was with that Two Humper and that the Two Humper was Nick Daimler. I've been taken by a double-crosser who aimed all along to kill me and start trouble.*

A tired-looking man, younger than Tully had expected, appeared in the kitchen doorway. He gave Tully a civil nod. "I'm Doc Burne. Did you want to see me?"

"You're needed over at Sam McNulty's," Tully said.

"What's wrong with Sam?"

"Got in the way of a slug himself."

The doctor stared at him a moment, sighing. "How bad is he hit?"

"Through the shoulder, but it needs tending."

Doc Burne shrugged. "Vines is in bad

156

shape, and I'd ought to stay with him. But it isn't far over to Sam's. Tell that old kraut-face in the kitchen to saddle my horse." He turned back into the house.

". . . You got off easier than Vines, Sam," Burne was saying two hours later. "The bushwhacker shot him through the chest. I don't think he'll pull through. But you . . . thunderation, a cannon couldn't blow a big enough hole in you to kill you."

"Cannon couldn't," Sam agreed. "But your probing come mighty close to it. What size lead did I catch, Doc, in case Vines lives and takes to bragging?"

"He was shot by a Forty-Five, of which there probably aren't more than a couple of hundred in this country. Now, you stay in bed a couple of days, Sam, and take it easy till you heal up."

Sam's voice was thunderous. "Hell, I've got cattle to tend to."

"I'll take care of them, Sam," Tully said.

"You've got enough on your hands," Sam growled. His mouth pulled up in a wicked grin. "I reckon Aurora will have to take over King Pin. The work would be good for her. Hone her down a little and bring back her lost girlhood, mebbe."

Aurora pulled up her shoulders. "I can

take over, Sam McNulty. City life doesn't waste a person away like you prefer to think. I can likewise tend to you. You'll stay in bed a month if I have to tie you there."

The doctor went out with Aurora. Sam's face was ash-gray, and now he let worry seep back into it. "Who shot Vines?" he asked presently.

"I did, likely. Where does that put us, Sam?"

Sam shook his head. "Anyhow, Ellery Vines is out of it for the time being. The stockmen's association has got to elect a new leader. This time, one we can trust. I'd say you, Tully. Why don't you ride around and call a meeting? Hold it here where I can take a hand."

"Not me," Tully said instantly. "Not till we know what we're up against, anyhow. The only thing that makes sense is that Vines and Daimler figured out the caper together. Start a war. Kick Two Hump so far to pieces its new owner would be relieved to sell. Then split the profits. My squatting on Bentham Valley grass was no surprise to Daimler, and there was no need for Vines to go and see him with that so-called ultimatum. Their try at killing me was cold-blooded, a way to get the basin into a fighting mood real fast. I reckon you were smart about wanting it kept quiet, Sam. Then there's Lagg."

"What about him?" Sam asked with interest.

Tully caught himself up short, then grinned. "Sam, I've promised too many people to keep my mouth shut. It sure hampers a man. But I've got reason to figure I'm right about what's going on. For one thing, I seen Vines and Daimler drinking together in Valen's place, one night."

"We ought to re-organize," Sam muttered, "and start something they never figured on."

"I'm against calling another association meeting just yet," Tully told him. "It'd only turn into a fight. And there's something I might try first."

He saddled the livery horse and rode back to the claim, rounding in Sam's close-hovering little bunch and taking it on with him for water. When he had thrown the steers back out, he returned to the camp. There was no sign of anything having been disturbed. He went up the rise and saw that the stiffened Two Hump horse still lay where it had dropped, which wasn't surprising since moving it would be no small task.

He wanted to see Louise. The girl was already discouraged and turned against Two Hump. She felt herself to be friendless, surrounded by men she couldn't trust and knew she was the target of widespread animosity in the basin. No woman would like to be in that position. Tully didn't know how much pressure would be needed to make her willing to bargain with Daimler. But a deep compassion for her rode him, and he wanted her to know that she had a real friend. That might steel her against any overtures that could already have been made by her ramrod when he reported Vines's supposed ultimatum.

The only way Tully knew to see Louise was to go to Two Hump himself. Since he didn't want anyone else over there to know that he had done so, he would have to do it by stealth. That would require darkness, so he stretched out on the cot and was instantly asleep.

It was night when he awakened. He ate a cold meal, saddled the livery horse, and rode out, striking straight into Bentham Valley. He knew that ranch headquarters lay due east of the pass, which he had crossed on his first visit to the valley. Now he swung widely to the north, clinging to Two Hump's high range.

Although night covered the land, the earth still gave off its warm waves and here, where

160

vegetation was ranker, the rich, raw smells rendered by the heat. A quarter moon lay well down the sky, turned coppery by the haze in the air, and all about it stars hung in veiled brilliance. His nostrils caught the scent of dust kicked up by his horse, and he kept a careful study on the rolling plain. Far off a coyote called, and these familiar impressions brought back many memories of trail herding and plain itchy-footed travel. It struck Tully oddly that these things seemed behind him now, things that would always warm him, but in retrospect and no longer bearing upon his life. He thought: *This is it, I guess. This is where I want to dig in.*

When he figured he had ridden better than an hour, he swung his horse south. He passed one of Two Hump's water tanks, came into a draw, and followed it down. At last he halted his horse on a low rise and, far off, could see the lake where Cass Bentham had set up headquarters. He could see no glint of light and knew that, on these isolated ranches, darkness and bedtime coincided closely. He started the horse again, keeping it to a patient walk. On his previous visit he had seen no sign of dogs, which most cowmen regarded as a menace to young calves. He also had in mind the fact that the big white house, where Louise lived, had been set apart from the rest of the buildings.

His problem was to gain the house undetected and get hold of Louise without warning anyone else. There was a chance that she had her own cook or a companion of some sort, but he would have to risk that. He came onto the lake margin without trouble and followed it on to the poplar grove surrounding the big house. There he left his horse and went on afoot, his shoulders pulled high, his breath caught. He paused at the edge of the private yard to stroke his chin and study the place. It was dark, silent, and somehow forbidding. Then he stepped out boldly, crossed the porch, and laid his knuckles on the door.

It seemed a long while before there was any response, and his mouth was dry. At last he heard a creakng board beyond the door. If it was Louise, she would assume it to be one of her ranch hands.

When the door inched open, he said softly — "It's Tully Gale." — and waited to see what response that would bring.

The door swung wide. "Tully!" Louise cried. "What are you doing here?"

"Peddling horseradish, ma'am," he said. "But you'd better ask me in. If one of your boys catches me here, I'm a gone gosling."

"Come in, Tully."

He stepped through and closed the door carefully behind him. In the dim indoors light he could see only that Louise wore a nightgown and that her honey-gold hair was now in braids that hung down her back.

"I was in bed," she said. "For once it's lucky that I don't sleep much in this creepy house. I'm glad to see you and more than curious about what brought you here."

"We need a powwow," Tully said, "and maybe to make some medicine."

"Interesting," Louise said. "Should I start a fire?" The perfume he remembered came at him, and she was a slim, small shape in the obscurity. The emptiness of the house spoke plainly of her loneliness, while across the darkness her scantily clad body cried to him.

"Don't even light a lamp," Tully warned. "We'll gnaw our bone in the dark. It's no time to pay a call, but some things have happened. Do you know that the basin has organized against Two Hump? That it's issued an ultimatum . . . pasturage and water or a plague of nesters cutting up Bentham Valley?"

"Daimler told me today."

"What's his attitude?"

"Daimler said he laughed in Vines's face," Louise reported. "He said that, if we give in to a thing like that, we might as well go out of business. He says we'll stop any nester invasion real fast."

"He tell you the first squatter's moved in?" Tully asked.

"Yes. You. And I didn't tell him I knew you were going to."

Tully gave a sour laugh. "Don't reckon he told you he knew, too. But never mind. Did he tell you Two Hump hit my camp last night, trying to kill me? And, as far as it knows, did?"

"Oh, no, Tully!" Louise cried. "Are you all right?"

"All here," he assured her.

"Tully, if they'd hurt you . . . !"

The urgency in her voice sent something boiling through Tully. She had turned toward him, her hands half lifted. He stepped to her and, when she didn't turn and run, placed his hands on her shoulders. Her face tilted up, then his arms swept about her, and his lips found hers. She sighed and was slack against him, and he thought: *This is more than I figured on.* But for a long while it made no difference. They had parted this way, and it was as if they were just now coming back together.

Then she whispered against his mouth: "So you do care. Then why didn't you do this in town? Tully, they can have it all if I can have you. It's been this way with me since the day we parted. After I saw you in town, I tried to forget it. I can't. I'm not rich. I don't want Two Hump. Just let me ride the moon with you."

He stepped back, shaken. He had known it was deep with her, all along, but this was coming out of her very soul. He said: "Are you sick enough of it to quit?"

"I have been from the start."

"That's the caper, Louise," he warned her. "Daimler's done all he can to get you to feel that way. There's worse planned than you've seen. He'll offer you a cheap price for Two Hump when he figures you're sick enough to take it. If you refuse, he'll sicken you some more."

"He can have it!" Louise cried, her arms still fiercely holding him.

"No!" Tully thundered. "Even if I have to force you to stay rich. You can't let a thing like Daimler beat you, Louise. We got to lick him."

"I'll fire him in the morning," Louise warned. "Tully, won't you come and work for me?"

"I can't," he groaned. "I've thrown in with

165

Banca Basin and I can't change sides. But you've got to hold on, no matter what comes along. Promise me that."

"I'll send Daimler packing anyhow," Louise threatened. "Most of the crew would go with him, I think, which has kept me from doing it already. But a few of the older men might stick. I . . . I guess I could run things all right."

"Don't fire him yet," Tully advised. "They've tried murder, so we know they won't stop at anything. You scare me, girl. Don't let the man know you're even suspicious. You play along like you're ready to give in. When we've shoved his scheme down his own throat, you can give Two Hump away for all of me. Till you've whipped this thing, you're its owner and responsible for it. Remember that."

"Me," moaned Louise. "When sometimes I used to think a roomful of kids was too much to handle. But I'm afraid for you, too, Tully. Daimler said we'll bust up the squatter play forevermore. The next time you might not be so lucky." She clung to him again, then looked up abruptly to blaze: "And another thing! Daimler tells me you've been intimate with that widow I hear about."

"Daimler tells you that?" Tully said. "I

wonder why."

"That's beside the point. Have you been?"

"Depends on what you mean by intimate," Tully said. "She let me use her bathtub, but. . . ."

"Who *can* I trust?" Louise wailed. Then, bewildering him completely, she was kissing him fiercely. "When will I see you again?" she whispered.

"I don't know."

"What if it's never?" she cried, clutching him tightly. "I won't let you go and be killed. Stay with me. At least until morning."

For a long minute he could only stand there with desire pounding through him. Louise thought she might never see him alive again. By the same token, he knew that any of the gun hands working for Daimler wouldn't hesitate to cause trouble for her. He knew he could stay on any terms he called for, because Louise, out of love for him and fear of never seeing him again, would draw no line as to what might take place that night. She might have to make a few hours last a lifetime.

"All out?" Tully's voice was tense.

"Yes," she cried, "Yes, I want you, Tully."

She crushed herself against him, her breasts hot against his chest. He sighed and

167

longingly kissed the moist, parted lips she offered. Then Tully moaned, as if in agony, and broke away.

"It's no good this way, Louise. You don't really want it to happen like this and neither do I. It ain't our way a-doin' things. When the trouble's over, then maybe it'll be different. . . ."

He groped his way to the door and stumbled into the moonlit yard, cursing to himself. He knew how hollow his words must have sounded because Tully Gale knew how badly he had wanted her.

Back in the house, Louise ran to the window, her body racked with sobs. She was conscious of how tightly her hands were clenching her breasts and she murmured: "Come back, Tully, come back. I need you."

V

The moon held its sway upon the range, and starlight filled the sky. Once he had lost sight of Two Hump headquarters, Tully cut boldly toward his claim. The ride gave him time to think.

Louise was frightened and turned against her vast property at present. But it was only because of the bewildering responsibilities upon her inexperienced shoulders that she felt that way right now. Two Hump had inspired avarice and cunning in men she feared, but once that had passed, if it did so favorably, she would feel the pull, a sense of power and place in her neighborhood, the affluence that few people could resist. She might still want Tully Gale but would come to want him on her own terms. That would never do, being what he was. His staying put anywhere would depend on remaining his own man.

I've played the fool again, he thought. It

had been bad enough remembering how she had looked on the stage, how wistful she had been in that parting. Now he knew her full abandon in his arms, the hunger that she had had for him. Yet, although knowing it would only serve to widen the gulf between them, he wanted to help her hold the spread. It was hers by right of inheritance. Tonight it didn't seem vital to her, although later she might feel differently about it.

Coming in against the hills that separated his claim and King Pin, Tully found himself confused because of his unfamiliarity with the area. He stumbled upon Two Hump's fence somewhat below his claim and rode along its length at an easy jog. Then he sighted the white blob of his tent, across from him, and pulled down his horse.

There was another horse dimly outlined against the tent's reflected moonlight. Tully dropped his hand to his gun, urging his mount forward at a careful walk. He saw a man rise from the ground and come out from the camp, a squat figure that he couldn't yet identify.

Somebody yelled: "That you, Gale? I'm a friend of your'n. Matt Beer, from the basin."

Remembering the name, Tully relaxed and rode in. As he neared the camp, he saw a second horse. There was only one man in sight, and Tully's uneasiness stirred again.

Beer said: "You been gone a long time. There's another meeting at Sam's, and they sent me to fetch you."

"Who's your friend?" Tully answered. "I don't like jiggers who stay out of sight." He jerked his head toward the third horse.

Beer laughed. "Oh, him. He's there on the ground, Gale. One of Two Hump's cowpokes. Take a close look, and you can see their brand on the cayuse."

"How come?"

"I caught the cuss prowling around here a while ago," Beer explained. "They told me to be sure and bring you to the meeting, and I was waiting. Clyde Colby figured you were asleep or that the camp was deserted. I sure gave him a turn. He was looking at a dead horse over the rise there. I throwed down on the viper and tied him up."

"Clyde Colby?" Tully walked over to the man stretched out on the far side of the fire. "Howdy, Clyde," he said, staring down at the Two Hump rider who had raised hell the day he found the camp here. Tully had sort of liked his looks that day. Beer had used pigging strings to tie Clyde, who lay on his side with his wrists and ankles lashed behind him. "What were you after, man? Trying to do what Daimler couldn't cut?"

"You go to hell, squatter!" Clyde growled.

Tully shrugged, motioned to Beer, and walked away from Clyde. He said: "How come a meeting tonight? Sam wanted one, but I told him I figured it better not to call one with things so touchy."

"It called itself," Beer said. "Johnny Babbage was at Sam's today. Learned Sam had been bushwhacked. It happened he'd just come from Half Diamond, where he heard Vines also had stopped lead. Everybody bleeding and keeping it quiet to stop trouble. Me, I call that foolish. So there's a meeting, and they want you there. You'll be a big cog in what we're fixing to do."

"What's that?"

Beer laughed. "If I told you, you might not come, and the boys would peel me good. I don't reckon Colby'll be unwelcome, either. After what's happened, the boys'll swing him to that one tree Sam's got on his spread."

"You go on," Tully said. "If they haven't got tired of waiting, tell 'em I'll be along pretty soon. Without Clyde. We won't start the next dance with a hanging. But I mean to have a little talk with the huckleberry."

"You're a fool if you turn him loose," Beer said. "He'd only try it again." But he walked to his horse, rose to the saddle, and rode out at a hard pound, the energy in the man proving that something big was in the making.

Tully pulled out his jackknife and cut Clyde's bonds, which Beer had knotted with determination. The Two Hump cowpuncher rolled onto his back and began to work his legs and arms to restore circulation. Knowing how painful that could be, Tully hunkered near, rolling a cigarette and saying nothing. But he watched Clyde carefully. The man was boiling mad and he was no coward.

When Clyde sat up, Tully said: "What were you after, Clyde? You're no killer. It wasn't you who shot Sam McNulty by mistake for me. Nick Daimler was the man who left that dead horse across the rise. So what are you after?"

Clyde was silent a moment, then said: "I ain't done any shooting, Gale. And I don't figure to go to jail for it, if you aim to turn me over to the law. I had orders from Daimler to get the saddle off that horse. My cayuse nickered, and I should have been warned. But I figured it was your horse, and, when I couldn't see anybody, I thought you'd turned in. I was trying to work the saddle off when Beer sneaked up on me. Never heard him."

"The saddle?" Tully asked. "Seems to me it's the branded horse that's dangerous to Two Hump."

Clyde's laugh was sour. "The cayuse might be dangerous to Two Hump. But it's the saddle that's dangerous to Daimler. It's his, tailor-made, and the saddle maker in town could identify it in a minute. That being the case, I don't see why I should go to jail for him."

"Ah," Tully breathed, "it sounds like you're not so sweet on Daimler."

"I don't like Daimler, but I like Two Hump. I worked for Cass Bentham before Daimler ever set foot on the spread. So Two Hump's squabbles are mine, Gale. I'd like to see you blasted off this claim. But I come over tonight on Daimler's orders. He had to go some place, and, since I work this piece, I know it better than the other boys do."

"When it comes to Two Hump's troubles," Tully said, "are you sure what they are? I'll let you go, but without that saddle, if you'll answer a question. Are you for or against Cass Bentham's niece?"

The cowpuncher's answer was prompt: "I like Miss Louise, woman or no woman."

"Which is where we differ again," Tully reflected. "It's the fact that she is a woman that's got me mighty interested. Do you boys realize Daimler's out to take Two Hump away from her?"

"That's talk around the bunkhouses," Clyde admitted. "But Daimler claims the basin's out to carve up the spread. So we've got to fight for our jobs. Your moving in here bears Daimler out. It's got the boys riled."

"That's what Daimler wants," Tully said. "He's got the basin mad at Two Hump, and Two Hump's crew is sore at the basin. It doesn't matter much who was shot the other night. The basin's about to spew over about it. If there's a reprisal, your outfit will hit back."

"It sure will."

"But," Tully said, "if there was a break between Daimler and Miss Bentham, which one would the boys throw in with?"

Clyde thought for a moment, then said: "About two to one with Daimler. Maybe more. Some are scared of him. Some figure they'd like the place better without a woman running it. It seems to all of us that Miss Louise come into something mighty easy. That don't set good with a man who puts his life in hock for forty and found and has nothing better to look forward to. Right or wrong, the edge is against her, I reckon."

"But which way would you turn, Clyde?"

Clyde's answer was evasive. "I can't figure

you out, Gale. Save for your having the gall to squat here, I'd say you're all right. What're you really after?"

"Not money," Tully said. "But I've got reason to be concerned for Miss Louise. Daimler means to make the going so tough she'll be anxious to get away from it. He wants the spread or a chance to run it to his own profit. He's got help. Dirty, under-handed help, outside. You boys and the basiners are all being used by him. Do you want to see him get away with it?"

Clyde swore. "All right. But what could I do for Miss Louise?"

"She needs a friend over there and doesn't know who she can trust. Wish you'd tell her you and me had a talk and that she can depend on you if she needs help. I'm not turning you loose on the strength of that, but because you look like a white man."

When he had considered that a moment, Clyde said: "Gale, I'll do it. Beer took my gun off me. It's in your tent. Do I get it back?"

"Why not?" Tully found Clyde's six-gun and handed it to him casually. He was smiling, making a heavy play for the man's respect. The gesture seemed to remove what little doubt Clyde still entertained.

Clyde said: "I'll tell Daimler you run me

off before I could get his saddle. I'll see Miss Louise. But how'll she know I really talked to you?"

"Tell her you saw the horseradish peddler and he was walking around in circles. That will persuade her. Keep her courage up, Clyde, and get hold of me if you need help yourself." Tully was pleased as he watched Clyde ride out.

Afterward he went across the rise and worked Daimler's saddle from the bloated carcass of the horse. He carried the saddle back to camp, hoping he had something tangible with which to bring about a show-down. Reflecting a moment, he tied a rock to the saddle, carried it to his ever-growing pond, and tossed it in. When it had sunk from sight, he went to his horse.

He didn't like the idea of that meeting at Sam's. He knew that blood would be boiling there, that it would be hard to stop headlong action after what had taken place. But a reprisal strike at Two Hump would only be playing into Daimler's hands, for Clyde had declared the crew over there to be equally unstable. Tully rode out for King Pin.

He saw from the last rise that there were more saddle horses in Sam's ranch yard than there had been at Half Diamond the night the stockmen's association was organized. Tully learned, also, that they were watching for him, for somebody bawled: "There comes the varmint now!" Tully rode on in.

Sam's shack was too small for the aggregation, and the ranchers were scattered about outside. They came together quickly at Tully's arrival, and he saw that Sam had got out of bed and was seated in a chair in the doorway. He had a blanket across his shoulders, which would be Aurora's compromise. Tully swung down, exchanging greetings and recognizing men he had met that night at Vines's. The late hour and the fact that they had waited for him accented the urgency he could sense in them. Tensions and tempers were high. Daimler's medicine was about to boil over.

Matt Beer was there and said: "It's all cut and dried, Gale. We've elected Johnny Babbage to take Vines's place. But it needs your consent."

"Now, look," Tully said. "Nobody made me the guardian of this basin, and I sure don't want the job. Why mine?"

"On account of it can't be cut without you," Beer said cheerfully. "Johnny, you met up with Gale the night we got organized. You do the talking."

Tully recognized Johnny Babbage, a tall man who stirred and stepped forward as Beer spoke. He was young, a cheerful-looking individual, but there was a look of responsibility in his face.

Babbage said: "It sure appears we've been sliggered, Gale, if anybody can figure out how. Me, I never liked Vines's plan in the first place. I got a notion that took me over to see him today. They weren't anxious to talk over there, but I got it out of a man that Vines is hurt. Then I come by Sam's and found he'd stopped lead, too. Funny how bullets have took to paralyzing a man's tongue."

Tully saw that Sam had not revealed how they figured Vines had come to get shot, and it wasn't surprising that Vines's man had not disclosed it.

"Anyhow," Babbage continued, "Vines's squatter idea never struck me as worth much. It was what I figured to be a better one that took me over there. Wanted a look at a map Vines made at the Land Office, one that shows where the open land is in Bentham Valley. I made them let me take it. It proves I'm right in what I figured. We've got something that will take care of things without any fancy capers like his'n. Something Vines ought to have seen right off himself, and either didn't or didn't want to."

"Let's hear it," Tully said.

Babbage spat, wiped his mouth on his sleeve, and said: "There's some open land in Bentham Valley that checkers out from your claim. I figured we might make up a herd of stuff we can't care for ourselves. We could run it on that joining graze if we have men enough to hold it there. But there's no water, and that's where you come in. You'll have to supply it. Your one tank won't be enough, but with your permission we'll dig a dozen if we need to. Also, we'll have to cross your claim, coming and going. That's why we wanted to see you tonight."

Looking at these aroused ranchers gathered in Sam's yard, Tully had an awesome sense of the explosion he could create by revealing the secret of Sugar Lagg's stored water in the badlands. But Ed and Sam were right. The plan Babbage had worked out was less dangerous than an attack on the dam. It would have to do until something permanent could be done about the water problem.

Tully said: "You've got my permission and a warning to boot. Two Hump's crew is about to blow up already. Open land or not, they'll take to a herd invading it with even poorer grace than they took to my squatting on it."

"We'll risk it, if you're willing."

A shout of agreement went up, and Beer yelled: "Ride home, boys, and get at it!"

Tully's blood was heating as he thought it over. He saw a gleam of approval in Sam's lamplit eyes. When the others had moved away from the soddy, Tully grinned at Sam.

In a low voice, Sam said: "If them jiggers knew the whole story, they'd be on the warpath right now. As it is, they're working at something that stands a show of doing some good. It's risky, but it's best."

"I reckon I could send Daimler to jail right now," Tully told Sam. "His tailor-made saddle was on that Two Hump horse I shot. I've got the saddle cached."

"Then what're you waiting on?" Sam demanded.

"When we send Daimler over the road," Tully retorted, "we've got to send his sidekicks with him. That two-faced Vines might not be any more guilty, but he's the more despicable the way he's sold out his neighbors. We've got nothing on him, nor Lagg, who came into the game with that dam. . . ."

"What dam?" Sam asked puzzledly.

"Slip of the tongue, Sam. I wasn't supposed to tell anybody. But Ed Handel wouldn't mind your knowing, seeing how careful you've been to keep from starting trouble. When I was in the *malpais,* I found where Lagg had dammed the middle fork of the creek. Lagg's filed on the land, and the lawyer in town told Ed the only way to get rid of the dam is to law it out."

"I'll be blamed," Sam breathed. "It was cut and dried from the start."

"From the minute they heard a greenhorn girl was coming to take over Two Hump," Tully agreed. "Turning Daimler over to the law now would deal him out of it. But there's still Lagg. And Vines, if he lives. We've got to bag all three of them."

"If they don't bag you first," Sam said.

"That's the chance I've got to take," Tully said, and for once he sounded serious.

Sam's chuckle was dry. "In other words, you hanker to help that little gal over there even if it costs your life."

"What makes you think that?"

"Knowed you were sweet on her the day you showed up here from the questions you asked about her." The old man's voice was sympathetic. "You figure she's too rich for you. Son, it ain't steers nor graze nor a bank account that makes anybody rich. Maybe someday you'll know it."

Tully rode home, worn out from the hard pace of recent days. The more he thought it over, the more hopeful he became of Babbage's plan. But it depended on how Daimler reacted. This, a justified defiance of range tradition, would take Daimler by surprise and wrest the initiative from him. But, at best, Johnny's plan could bring only temporary relief to the harassed basin. There was only one sure way of solving the problem for good and all. Again Tully's mind had gone to Lagg's dam. He was well convinced that a group effort to destroy it could end only in tragedy. He was equally impatient with the drawn-out process of the law. One man with a few sticks of dynamite might make his way in to the dam undetected. The proper charge, at the right place, might well restore Splinter Creek to its proper, seasonal level and put an enduring end to the dissension. With the strife put down, dealing with the schemers against Louise would be a simpler matter. *Sooner or later,* he told himself, *I'm going to try it.*

He was tempted to do so at once for he had no concern for Lagg's legal rights, real or assumed, in something that was patently a dishonest undertaking. The only thing restraining him was the fact that it looked like suicide for the man reckless enough to

183

attempt it. He would have to outfit in Splinter Rock for the venture, as he had done the first time. He had the livery horse to return to Ed in exchange for his red mustang, anyway. He decided that, once Johnny Babbage and his men were launched on the new plan, he would take another trip to town as the grazing invasion of Bentham Valley would be Babbage's to handle.

By the time he reached camp, Tully had admitted that his desire to revisit Splinter Rock revolved around Maggie as much as anything else. He thought: *You keep mooning over Louise, a girl you can't ever have. While there's one better suited you could at least court with some hope. That's Maggie.*

He placed the horse on picket, wondering at the perversities in men that drove them toward the impossible and kept driving even after the impossibility had become apparent. He undressed and went to bed, eager to see Maggie again, sure that her mouth would be as warm as Louise's, her generosity as full. She was within his reach, and he would not have to deny himself.

The peace of the night closed about him. It was hard to realize that this site would soon become hotly contested ground, having already prompted a try at murder. Restlessness began to grow in him out of the false tranquility. Probably, if he had any sense, he wouldn't toy with the idea of settling down at all. Some men were meant to ride the moon, as Louise had claimed of him. That breed was built so that peace was a thing to be enjoyed at intervals, coming and going without a man's having much to say in the matter. He thought — *And she'd pack up and travel whenever I wanted to ride.* — and was trying to keep his desires centered on Maggie.

The man was standing in the tent opening before Tully came fully awake.

"Howdy, Gale," Nick Daimler said. "You sleep late. Maybe you don't get to bed bright and early, like you should."

Tension crawled up Tully's spine. The man was armed, but his hands were empty and he looked slack as he stood there. Yet there was a noticeable ugliness to his eyes, which never wavered as they stared at Tully. Tully swung off the cot and groped for his boots. His own gun was under his pillow, and he considered it unwise to reach for it. He pulled on his boots and began to dress.

"I lead a come-and-go life," he said. "You look proddy, Nick. Haven't you had your breakfast?"

Daimler frowned. "Maybe I'm just proddy

185

by nature. Gale, with you I see no need to beat around the bush. It stands to reason you've added up things with some accuracy. Now, it happens that I'm short a saddle I'm right fond of. I want it."

Tully shook his head. "I used to have your saddle, Nick. But no more. You should have told me how attached you are before I got shed of it. How bad do you want it?"

"Bad enough a girl you know might help me get it."

Tully swallowed. "How?"

"By getting so messed up you'll wish you'd turned that saddle over to me right now."

"You could mean Louise Bentham," Tully reflected. "Or it could be Maggie Paine. With Louise you've got to play the gent, Nick, if you hope to do business. With Maggie, I dunno."

"I don't mean Maggie."

Tully made himself laugh. "You're bluffing, Nick. If anything happens to Louise, there's nobody to sign any papers. And another thing. I'd drop you in your tracks." He had a stomach full of buckshot, but he finished dressing as carefully as if he were going to his own wedding.

"You could hedge that bet, Gale," Daimler drawled, "by forking over the saddle."

186

"You make strong talk."

"For strong reasons. Answer me a question. You figure to turn that saddle over to the law?"

Tully shook his head. "Not right off, if that will calm you down any." He was sick with concern. He had figured that the saddle was his hole card. He knew that, at this point, Daimler was bluffing. But there was no telling what all was in his mind, what he might do in the working out of the things that were yet to come.

"Has the law been let in on this ruckus?" Daimler asked softly.

"It hasn't."

"Why not?"

Tully turned and looked straight at him. "In the first place, there are men in this country less anxious for gun trouble than you are. Besides, we've got three skunks to trap. When you go to jail, Nick, I want you to have company, such as it is. Lagg and Vines . . . if he survives the little caper you and him pulled here the other night."

Daimler rubbed his chin. "You're a smart boy, Gale. I pegged you that way at the start. So be smart enough to fork over that saddle and save your little Eastern filly a bad time. You're wrong about me caring what happens to her. There's more than one

187

way to skin a cat, when a man sets his mind to skinning it." He made an impatient motion with his hand. "Now answer me another question. How did you know that saddle's important? Did Clyde Colby double-cross me?"

"That was a fancy hull and a little too steep for a plain 'puncher to pay for," Tully said readily. "Besides, I figured I recognized you that night. When I found out it was Vines I shot, I was sure it was you with him."

"You had a powwow with Colby, blast him."

"Nick," Tully said, and he grinned, "you should have seen that huckleberry you sent, whoever it was, light a shuck when I popped a shot at him. I swear he passed that slug on his way out of here."

He hoped that he kept it off his face, but fear ran in him that the fat was in the fire. If Daimler grew suspicious of Clyde, Louise would be wholly at Daimler's mercy. For a moment Tully was tempted to fish the saddle out of the pond and hand it over. But at that moment Daimler swung and stared to the west. The scowl on his face darkened. In the quiet Tully heard the distant bawling of steers and realized that Aurora was bringing Sam's little bunch in to water. Daimler didn't object when Tully came out of the tent to take a look. For a moment the tall ramrod stood quietly, watching the oncoming cattle.

"That's a woman," he said. "Who is it?"

"Sam's daughter," Tully said. "From back East. In case you decide to leave, Nick, let me tell you something I didn't seem to get across. I don't like to be pressured through people I like. Let something happen to Louise Bentham, and I'll kill you on sight."

Daimler turned his head. "You mean you'd try," he answered.

Out in the distance Aurora rode around the halted bunch, swung down, and threw back the strands of wire. The cattle spilled through the opening, cutting for the pond. Aurora rode on, halting an instant when she noticed Daimler, then coming on.

The ramrod met her stare, stonily touching his hat.

" 'Morning, Missus Meade," Tully said. "You know Daimler?"

"Fortunately not," Aurora said. "Because I know of him." That was all she had on tap for Nick Daimler.

"Nick dropped over for breakfast," Tully said. "We'll make it a party, and I hope you can stay all day. You could show me that crocheting stitch you told me about."

Aurora straightened, then seemed to catch

the urgency in Tully's voice and realized that he wanted her help. "Why, I meant to," she said. "I've been going to write down those recipes of yours. Mister Daimler, have you eaten codfish custard?"

"Reckon I've stepped in it, ma'am," said Daimler. He gave Aurora a searching look, then swung toward his horse. He cast a glance at Tully. "About that business we were talking, Gale. You can come over to Two Hump when you're ready to deliver. Don't take too long about it. Things have a way of going wrong." He mounted and rode off.

"Now," Aurora said severely, "what kind of jackpot did I get you out of?"

"If I was a bolder man, I'd kiss you," Tully informed her. "He was giving me a bad time." Since she knew most of it anyway, Tully explained, concluding: "That saddle's sunk in the pond. You'd better tell Sam. It might be useful to him if something should happen to close my big mouth."

"Which could be any time now," Aurora said optimistically. "Yet, Tully Gale, I don't want you hurt at anybody else's hands. I'd love to humble you, and I will yet. On the other hand, I've taken a piece of this ruckus, as Dad would say. I've been remembering some things I'd forgotten. For instance, how good it feels to spit in the eye of a man like Nick Daimler."

"I reckon we got him in both eyes, ma'am."

"Now," Aurora said, "I suppose you're worried about his threat to that Eastern girl. He's probably bluffing, but there's the off chance that he isn't. And a man in love doesn't want to take even an off chance with his girl."

"Now, look here, who said she's my girl?"

"If you're not in love," said Aurora Meade, "I've got four legs and a tail. So, you'll probably let her know about Daimler's threat?"

Tully shifted his weight. "I'd sure like to tell Clyde he's suspected. And warn Louise again not to turn her back on Daimler for too long."

"I'll go over and talk to her," Aurora announced. "They wouldn't dare trifle with me. And what would be more natural than for two Eastern women to get together? To discuss styles, say, and wonder how much they've changed since we saw anything that could be called that."

"You mean you'd do it?" Tully asked, surprised.

Aurora smiled. "And after what you've done to me, I consider that mighty decent."

"It sure is," Tully agreed. "Tell Louise to

warn Clyde. If she's too worried, tell her to take Clyde and light out for town. Leave Daimler a note saying they've eloped."

"I'll take her a dried apple pie," Aurora said thoughtfully. "I'll bet she hasn't eaten more than a thousand since she's been out here."

Tully was smiling to himself when he watched Aurora ride out with the steers. The West was reclaiming her, and she had sense enough to know it. He hoped to see the day when, instead of whisking Sam home with her, she would send for her husband and settle down for good on King Pin.

VI

The first drought cattle came in from the basin in the deep of that night, a cut of nearly 100 head from Frying Pan, which lay on Sam McNulty's west boundary. There were two cowpunchers handling the cattle. The thirst-maddened animals came rollicking out of the draw and nearly piled on Two Hump's barbed wire in their frenzy to reach the water. It was only with difficulty that they could be driven from the pond before they became water-logged. Afterward, the bunch was moved east to clear the way for the great numbers that would be coming in as fast as the hasty roundups could be made and the short trail drives accomplished.

By noon the next day Tully figured there were 800-odd head of steers close-herded on his claim and fast denuding it of grass. Babbage got in with his own drought cut, and, as the basiners had elected him to run the operation, Tully kept in the background.

Johnny was competent, cool-headed, and smart enough to have thought up this expedient.

The one pond was too small to accommodate so large a herd, and Babbage set men to work probing for other artesian flows at scattered points on the claim. There was no way of knowing if Two Hump was onto the move, and Tully had a tight-nerved wonder as to what would happen when the big herd, finally assembled, struck out into the open range yet existing in Bentham Valley. It wasn't a thing that Daimler had plotted and planned on. The man would hit back hard.

The cow camp was established on the east end of the claim, where open terrain permitted approaches to be watched carefully. The tough, determined outfit was made up of fifteen men finally, many of them owners who had left their spreads to their families, while others were cowpunchers from bigger outfits. Vines's Half Diamond was not represented.

Babbage's plan was to graze the steers in close herd through the day and return them to the water tanks for bedding down. That way they could be maintained for a long period, provided Two Hump could be held in check. By the following morning there were nearly 1,500 steers in the waiting herd. Feeling as if he were in the midst of a roundup camp, Tully rose and had his breakfast. Interested as he was in seeing the cattle move out onto what would be contested grass, there were other matters pressing him.

He saddled the livery horse that he wanted to exchange for the red mustang and rode over to Sam McNulty's. Old Sam was chafing at the luck that had made him an invalid at so exciting a time. Although he had let the *malpais* secret slip to Sam, Tully said nothing of his half-formed purpose of going in there again by himself.

Aurora was looking pleased and, when she got Tully alone for a moment, said: "Louise is lovely. And in love with you. She made no bones about it, which I expect is a rocking surprise to you."

Tully grinned. "How did she like the pie?"

"It thrilled her to death. She gave me one in exchange. It was even up, because hers was an apple, too. Tully, I hope you won't be proud and stubborn and let that sweet girl get away from you."

Tully frowned. "How did she take the news?"

"About Daimler's threat? She promised to be careful. She was thrilled to learn that

195

you've worried about her. She says you're wonderful, Tully. I wonder why."

Tully touched his hat.

Leaving word that he was going to town and might not be back for a few days, Tully rode out along the trail leading to the basin road. It was a hot, bright day, so monotonously like all the others in Banca Basin that he wondered if there had ever been any cold weather. But he knew there had been, that in season this same land would feel the bite of sub-zero temperatures and the blast of killing winds. It was plain, ordinary cow country.

He was short of the basin road when he saw a rider coming toward him. He thought little of it until, in the near distance, he recognized the sour-faced oldster he had talked with at Vines's Half Diamond. The man returned his stare with equal interest.

"You saved me some riding, Gale," he said when he came up. "Vines sent me to fetch you. He said to tell you it's important and for you to hurry."

"Why'd he want to see me?" Tully asked.

"He didn't say. But he's in bad shape. Doc went back to town, but he said it's a toss up with Vines."

Vines doesn't want to remember me in his will, Tully thought. *But if the man had some-*

196

thing to say, at this time, it might be worth hearing. Tully didn't like the extra ride required but decided to gamble on picking up something of value. At his nodded assent, the old man turned his horse and they rode on.

The oldster wasn't talkative, which suited Tully. They left the basin trail at the Half Diamond turn off and made the long ride toward the foothills.

When they swung down in the ranch yard, Tully's escort said: "I'll rack your cayuse. Reckon you can find Vines's room by the medicine smell. It's powerful."

Tully stepped through the kitchen doorway and crossed that room. Another door stood ajar that seemed to open into a bedroom. He went across and saw Vines. The man had heard him come in and was watching the door. The sight of him gave Tully a start. He had thought of Vines as a man still in his prime. What he saw now was an aging wreck, almost lifeless. The man was far gone.

Vines motioned for him to come on in. His odd Eastern speech was thick and raveled. "Glad you came, Gale. Close the door and take a chair. I hoped you'd want to talk to me."

"What about?" Tully asked. "I know I'm

the man who shot you. It might turn out that I killed you. What could we talk about?" He took a seat at the head of the bed, the strong medicinal smell of the room mingling there with the fevered scent of the dying man's body.

Vines's eyes narrowed. "I'm in no position to argue with you. And when you're where I am now, a lot of things don't seem to matter. We were there to kill you, so why should I hate you for killing me? You have, Gale. I'm done for."

Tully didn't like it. It was bad enough to take a man's life without having to talk it over with him afterward. Impatiently he rasped: "What's on your mind, Vines?"

"I said some things don't matter," Vines reflected, speaking slowly and with extreme effort. "Others do, and they matter like hell. I'm out of it. Daimler and Lagg will live to reap the fruits of my planning, while neither could have figured it out for himself. The hell of it is, Gale, they'll be glad to get rid of me, now that they don't need me. Daimler told me as much the night I was shot. I don't take to that kindly, and that's where you come in."

"Let's get to the point." Tully had no pity for the man, whose fever-lambent eyes still showed arrogance and rancor and bitter pride. "What can you do about it?"

"Hire a good man to help me. You, Gale."

"The devil with that," Tully said, and he stood up.

"Wait," Vines protested. "I know what you're thinking. You hired out to me once and nearly got killed. But I'm helpless now, because you were capable enough to turn the tables. I admire proficiency. I never had much myself. I only had cunning. It's a poor substitute."

Tully sat down again, leaning his weight forward. "Start off, Vines, by telling me the whole deal. Then I'll decide whether to trust you."

Vines rested a moment, then said: "Why not? You're my only hope. Even if you take it to the law, it will stop Daimler and Lagg, and I'll die happier. I expect you know what's up. Lagg dammed Splinter Creek to run the basin short of water. I formed the stockmen's association to create a fighting force to throw against Two Hump. Daimler struck an antagonistic pose to add fuel to the fire. We meant to make Two Hump too hot a proposition for Louise Bentham to handle. Then you arrived, blast you, and I was fool enough to think I could use you. Does that satisfy you that I mean business?"

"You've told me nothing new," Tully said.

"And I know of nothing I can do to help you."

"I hope you'll want to earn a handsome sum of money," Vines offered. "By acting as my agent. Knowing Miss Bentham and enjoying her confidence, you might persuade her to sell Two Hump to you, if for no other reason than to keep it away from Daimler."

Tully's eyes widened. "You think I'd betray her confidence. Vines, it's a good thing you're a sick man right now . . . !"

"Wait," Vines cut in. "It would be to her benefit. If things go as planned, she won't have much left when it's over. Lagg plans to rustle so heavily on Two Hump that it will be brought close to bankruptcy. He knows where he can conceal cattle in the badlands for a long period. When they've forced her to sell Two Hump, they'll bring back the steers. That was my planning, Gale. Two Hump was to buy itself for us. You can't do Louise Bentham any good by getting your back up at my new plan, too. Gale, think it over."

"I've thought it over all I need," Tully rapped. "I'll have no truck with you."

"You have your basin friends to consider," Vines reminded him. "I've heard what the basiners are trying to do. That's right up

200

Daimler's alley. He'll destroy that cow camp ruthlessly. Step in and buy Two Hump on the quiet for me, Gale, for everybody's good. And hurry . . . before I die."

"We're wasting time," Tully said, and again he rose. But he was getting excited. Whether or not Vines realized it, he had let his frenzy carry him into a disclosure of things yet to come from Daimler and Lagg. That would be useful in the effort to come.

Vines's laugh had a rattle in it. "Think it over, Gale," he said again. "Go to the law, if you want. If I can't have what I wanted, then I'll keep Daimler and Lagg from having it, too. But I'm not through bargaining. I want to own Two Hump before I die. Get it for me, and I'll make a will leaving it to you. Think, Gale. Two Hump would be your spread, not hers. Marry her, and she'll be taken care of for life. That's the perfect solution for both of you, isn't it?"

Tully only turned to walk out.

Vines's voice kept coming, although now hopeless. "All right. You can't be bought. And I'm going to die. So just break it up. That would still keep Daimler and Lagg from profiting from my ideas. You know what they mean to do. Stop them."

"There we see eye to eye, Vines," Tully said, and he left the room.

Gale's excitement climbed as he mounted his horse and struck out for town. He had gained information that completed the puzzle and gave him concrete knowledge of what to expect. But he knew that he couldn't take the case to the law as yet. Vines was dying and without fear for himself. What he had said simply reported as hearsay would have little weight against Daimler and Lagg. Tully could send out the sheriff, but, reconsidering, Vines might refuse to repeat. Even if he told all to the law, he would not live to appear in court against Lagg and Daimler. So it was just as it had been before this talk. The problem was still to get water for the basin cattle and, after that, to bring Vines's confederates to account.

In that respect, Tully's interest was held by what Vines had said of Lagg's plan to rustle Two Hump poor before the ranch changed hands. The *malpais* abounded in places where stolen stock could be hidden for long periods. The rustling could already be going on, Tully realized, and it seemed the best way to get evidence against the two men still active in the undertaking. A visit to the *malpais* seemed all the more necessary to Tully, not only to destroy the dam but to find out if Lagg was already whittling on Louise's cattle. He hurried his horse, eager to reach Splinter Rock and make the preparations. . . .

Ed came sleepily from the harness room of the livery, late in the night, to frown at Tully tiredly through the yellow light of the lantern he held.

"Aren't you ever out of your clothes?" Tully asked.

"Sure am," Ed snapped. "They don't wear forever. You're getting to be my cross, boy, but, if you've come to take away that red, you're forgiven."

"He acting up?" Tully asked.

"Pining away in that stall," Ed reported. "No spirit left at all. Doubt it he'd even pull a plow for you in his present frame of mind."

"Ed," Tully said, "go tell that little horse I'm in town. Mebbe we'll see his kin in a day or so."

"You mean to go into that *malpais* again?" Ed demanded. "If so, you'd better go tonight. Sugar Lagg's in town, and so's Daimler. Probably over to Valen's right now."

"No fooling?" Tully asked with interest. "Ed, they're likely plotting their next move. Vines got himself shot up. He's out of the caper. So they're figuring out what to do about Johnny Babbage. Scratch the hayseed out of your ear and listen." He gave the stableman a summary of what had developed and what he had learned of the probable future. "The question is," he concluded, "can we believe Vines as to what Daimler and Lagg are trying to put through?"

"He's sure right about them dealing him out of it now," Ed said. "They'd jump at the chance. And I'd say he was talking straight about Lagg meaning to rustle Two Hump poor. That's Sugar's stripe. Besides, Daimler ain't got the kind of money it would take to buy Two Hump, even at a sheriff's sale, unless they rustle it broke first."

"Then what we've got to do," Tully said, "is catch 'em rustling. I'm going into the *malpais* for a look."

"When?"

"Starting tomorrow morning."

"Got any ideas on that dam?" Ed asked.

"Just thought I'd take a look around," Tully said evasively.

"Now, look here," Ed snapped. "Leave aside the fact that we got to leave that dam alone. Don't even think you could blow it out easy. Sugar might be away a lot, but he's got it guarded night and day, now that the secret's leaked out. Besides, I heard a rumor the other day. He's hiring some of the saddle bums that drift through the back country all the time. Gun hands, that's what. He's expecting some damn' fool like you to come in there."

"Ed," Tully retorted, "would the hardware man sell you a few sticks of dynamite and a box of caps and keep it quiet?"

"If I asked him. Which I won't, damn your hide, and quit tempting me!"

"Which you will," Tully contradicted. "Have it here in the morning, bright and early, or I'll make you take the red over for feed charges." He grinned at the spluttering hostler, left the horse he had ridden in, and walked away.

Cow ponies were strung along the town's hitch bars, and the public corral was the wide gravel bed and the dribble of water that meandered through it, water that had disappeared down at Sam McNulty's end of the basin.

Valen's was a low, rambling structure nearly lost among old locusts. It was double-doored, a sure sign that its activities were not meant for public inspection. In the smelly, narrow passage between doors a drunk brushed into Tully and lurched on. Tobacco smoke rolled out as he went on inside, and the racket, detectable since the bridge, swelled to a steady grind.

The barn-like room was divided into halves. Beyond a wide arch, Tully saw gaming tables with a considerable attendance. Private card playing and drinking were conducted on the near side of the arch, where stretched a crowded bar as well. Tully's first sweeping glance showed him Sugar Lagg. The man at the corner table with the mustanger had his back turned, but he was Nick Daimler. Tully could see a couple of Lagg's bronco-stompers in the crowd.

He moved idly across the room, heading for the arch and passing a little closer to Lagg's table than necessary. A little beyond it he swung, as if in idle recognition, and his glance touched Daimler's.

"Why, howdy, Nick," Tully said. "Glad I run into you. When you going to come and bury that stinking dead horse?"

The ramrod straightened, making a slow, startled study of Tully. "What are you doing in town?" he demanded.

"Having a fancy saddle made, maybe," Tully retorted. The man's discomfort pleased him. He had a notion Daimler was wondering like hell if that menacing saddle had come to town finally to be turned over to the law.

"Gale," Daimler intoned, "thought I made it clear about that saddle. I want it. You ain't delivered it. What's holding you up?"

Sugar Lagg was staring at Tully with steady, angry eyes. Tully had a feeling Daimler had told him about the saddle, that it, too, had been discussed tonight. Lagg's lips muttered soundlessly, but he said nothing.

In a voice almost silken, Daimler resumed: "Gale, you must not have understood what I told you. You were to turn that saddle over to me or be sorry, remember? I said pretty soon. It's past that time already, and I've got tired of waiting. But if you've brought the hull to town, I'll take delivery here."

Tully shook his head. "Relax, Nick. I didn't bring it. Let's call that a stalemate. You're scared of what I'll do with the saddle. I'm scared of what you'll do if I do something. Let's keep on scaring each other, and not go hurting people who had nothing to do with it."

"Mebbe," Daimler said. "As long as you show sense."

Tully didn't betray his relief. Daimler was worried enough to be willing to make this strange, silent deal. Tully was sufficiently concerned for Louise to let it ride. He started to turn.

Lagg's chair scraped noisily as he came to

his feet. "Just a minute, Gale," he said. "I hear you talked out of turn about *my* business. I don't like that."

Tully had nearly forgotten Lagg's reported rancor when the sheriff had come to ask questions about the dam. So the mustanger's driving vehemence now caused him a little surprise. They were hemmed in by other chairs and tables. Lagg's hand had seemed loose but suddenly it closed and swung up, driving for Tully's chin.

Tully knocked the fist aside, temper backing up in him. He drove headlong at Lagg, trying to force him into an open space behind the men. But Lagg stood solidly, chopping again with a short hard blow that missed. It threw him off balance, and Tully closed with him. Hooking an arm around the mustanger's waist, he bent and violently swung the man across his hip. Lagg's boots arced in the air when Tully made a quick, full turn and threw him. The mustanger hit the sawdust on the floor, out in the room's cleared center.

"If you want a fight," Tully breathed, "let's go at it proper."

The violence drew the room's attention. Men shoved to their feet and spewed in from the game room to form a gallery. Lagg got up slowly, shaking his head in astonishment. He stared at Tully, who waited cautiously. The mustanger's face was twisted by the churning in him. The wild, murderous look of him sobered Tully. The man was big and mean and had killer instinct all through him. Tully balanced himself, still watching Lagg, who came slowly toward him.

Suddenly Lagg surged forward, an arm held on guard, a heavy fist bolting in. The blow landed, staggering Tully back. For an instant something like heat waves seemed to dance in the room. He blinked and shook his head. Lagg cut in again, hammering without pauses, forcing Tully into a clinging retreat. Lagg kneed him; he slashed at Tully's eyes with stiffened thumbs; he poured it on with both fists. Tully took a dozen smashing blows, turned sick and despairing, but still Lagg assaulted him.

The room grew hushed, the press widening to give them more room. Aware of his superiority, Lagg drove Tully against the bar and tried to nail him. The smoky yellow lamplight swirled in Tully's vision. When Lagg pulled back to drive in a killing punch, Tully lifted a boot. He caught Lagg in the belly and sent him back to crash against a table. Lagg rolled onto his back in the sawdust.

"Stomp him while you've got the chance!"

somebody called. "That's what he'll do to you!"

But Tully waited, knowing he would receive no such consideration from Lagg. The mustanger climbed up, puzzled, worried. Suddenly Tully sensed the man's weakness. Lagg was confident, when on the mauling initiative, following familiar habit patterns. Change confused and threw him off stride, upsetting his timing. That insight did more for Tully than a half dozen cracking fists to Lagg's jaw could have done.

Standing off from the mustanger, Tully wove back and forth and made an elaborate business of measuring him. Each twist he took caused Lagg to take one, like a worried animal turned wary by a strange enemy. Once Tully moved forward slightly, and Lagg pulled back. Sure he was right, Tully bored in.

This much Lagg understood and he stood his ground, snapping out with his fists. Tully made an elastic shift and hit the man by surprise on the side of the head. He did it again and yet again, trying to cuff him often and unexpectedly instead of hard. The steam, the smashing onslaught was for Lagg, and a smart adversary would offer him no chance to employ it. So Tully tried to give Lagg no opportunity to shift to the attack again.

His anger had given way to something closer to hatred, checked by a feeling that, if he went down, he would die. This was a primitive, merciless man, at one with the mustangs he pitted himself against as a way of life, as tough and wiry. He was big, with enormous stamina. Tully hooked in a punch that made a solid connection with Lagg's jaw, yet seemed to have no effect. He slammed the heel of the other palm against Lagg's upturning chin. With the first hand he ripped in another punch, this time to Lagg's belly. Lagg's arms hung suddenly. He stumbled backward but couldn't get away for the bar stopped him.

Lagg braced and used the bar to catapult himself forward. Tully caught him on the chin before he slid out of the drive's ramming path. Lagg stumbled on, hunting Tully. He tangled with the overturned table and went down again, his fingers digging into the sawdust.

"Blast it, kid, stomp him!" the same man bawled again.

Tully doubted now that there was enough left in himself to stop the man. He ached in every bone, hurt in every fiber of his flesh. His breath was a torture; his brain reeled. He saw Lagg take a sharp look at him and start to come up. He stared back into the puffed, wicked eyes of the man and felt the last caution go out of him.

He made a running jump and came down, heels first, on Lagg's chest, flattening him back. A backward skip brought his heels down again, this time on a muscle-slabbed belly. Wind broke from Lagg's gasping mouth, a retch and a sob of anguish. Tully sprang to come down on the mustanger's face, but heaved hips turned Lagg in a backward somersault that threw Tully hard on hip and elbow.

Lagg came back on all fours, with Tully still down and able only to jab out a kicking leg at him. The boot narrowly missed the man's sweaty face, Lagg jerking his head up and back even while snaking out to clutch Tully's ankle. He caught hold and dragged Tully in to him, twisting to take the other boot's pounding on a heavy shoulder. Then, absorbing brutal punishment, he pinned the one leg with his weight, caught hold of the other, and Tully found himself nailed in a crotch split that threatened to rip open his trunk.

Spreading out with his powerful arms, Lagg gasped: "I'll make you a filly! I'll split you to your belly button!" Suddenly he tried to do it.

Tully's only escape was in a hard twist to the side to break Lagg's purchase. He seemed to feel the flesh tearing but used patience to gather himself and give a quick, twisting wrench. It failed to bring him free but took the terrible strain from his groin. Holding onto his ankles, Lagg shoved to a full stand and began to turn, swinging Tully off the sawdust.

Thereafter Tully was helpless while the spinning Lagg gathered speed. He felt his ankles come free of the man's clutch and tried to fold himself as he sailed through thin air. He had the sense of something slamming into him, rather than the reverse, and all at once was a limp, helpless heap in the sawdust. He felt Lagg land on him, feet first, and eager to end it.

Somehow he got his arms wrapped about these heavy legs, tangling and halting their killing, crow-hop strikes at his exposed flesh. He bored forward with all his might, carrying Lagg along and at last toppling him. Shaking his head violently, he managed to clear his blurred vision. Lagg's heel caught him on the neck and broke them apart. They came up together, and thereafter stood staring and gagging for breath. For a moment it had been his kind of fight but once more Lagg was uncertain.

The mustanger gave a bent, shoving lunge forward, one fist feinting, the other thundering out. Tully drove through it and split his knuckles on Lagg's teeth. He could still move faster than Lagg and was at the man's flank instantly. He hit him with his last strength, the blow driving straight and hard to a point on Lagg's heavy jaw. It was his Sunday punch, his best and last. He heard Lagg's torn breath. Lagg shoved himself and impetus carried him a full step forward into empty unseen space. He shook his head dizzily as he hauled around. His glaring eyes stared. He was out on his feet but wouldn't go down. Despair ran in Tully as he watched. He had shot his bolt, and it had not been enough to end it. Dropping his head, Tully rammed him fully in the face, driving him back against the bar. Lagg groaned and had to brace himself.

The mustanger stood there, shaking his head, showing a mounting bafflement. His mouth hung open and he sucked air noisily. He made an angry, frustrated sound and his unblinking eyes stared stupidly at Tully, who was as tough as he was and a shade or so smarter.

Beat, Tully thought suddenly, *I've beat that stinking little mind of his but not the body.* For the stubborn, brutal, powerful frame was still there, upright. The feet slid from the suddenness with which the body started to move once more. Tully stayed away, just beyond reach of the blindly driving fists, letting them thunder out and jerk the giant shoulders as they spent their fury on thin air. An empty punch turned Lagg half around and he tangled his own feet, yet once again he managed to stay up.

Neither Tully nor the watchers were prepared for what happened next. Lagg emitted a long, gusty sigh, let his arms drop to his sides, and he didn't look at anybody as he started for the outer door. Hatless, bleeding, Sugar Lagg was destroyed psychologically but still going physically. Somebody opened the door, watched him stumble through, then dusted his hands, grinning.

"Splinter Rock waited a long time to see that 'un tuck his tail!" he yelled at Tully.

The rest of the room was silent, caught by it. Some, like Tully, were repelled by the humiliation. Tully walked back to the table where it had started, looking for his hat. He was spent, deflated, anything but the man who had come in here in high spirits ready for anything.

Daimler stood against the wall there and had watched it through. He looked at Tully in a kind of reluctant admiration. "First time I ever seen Sugar quit, Gale," Daimler murmured. "Sugar's had 'em tough and he's had 'em smart, but not both together. But he'll figure you out, Gale. The next time he'll know how to handle you. I wouldn't feel too cocky about it."

VII

Tully walked toward the Paine House, irritable and uncertain. There had been no satisfaction in his fight with Lagg and as little sense. The whole visit to Valen's had been impulsive and foolish. That awareness struck up a strange curiosity in him. Why did he feel that way, when impetuosity had been a main characteristic of his adult life? Now the thing he had done only worried him. He had tweaked Daimler's nose needlessly, and the next time he met Lagg things might go differently. For Lagg had not really quit, he realized, but had only pulled off to gather his wits.

Entering the Paine House, Tully crossed the lobby and was glad to find it deserted. He disdained the bell that would have summoned Maggie and headed for the stairs. A sheepish feeling bothered him as he gained the upper hall. *Daimler's in town,* he remembered, *and he's probably already latched onto*

217

that gallery room. But he strode on determinedly.

He was still at a distance from Maggie's door when it came open. She stepped through, looking preoccupied, then she recognized him. He saw that the pale light of the hallway lamp had failed to conceal his battered appearance. Her mouth opened in mixed surprise and amusement. Her dark hair was in braids, he saw, and she wore the revealing silk nightgown.

"You're a man of many guises, Tully," she breathed. "And you never show up in the same one twice. Who have you been fighting?"

"A man," Tully said. "Can you spare me a room?"

"Certainly," Maggie said, "and a good one this time."

"The gallery room?" He couldn't help showing surprise.

"Why not?" she retorted. "But come on into mine first, and let me have a look at you."

Following her into the room she used, Tully found his heart speeding up. She closed the door quietly. This was only a sitting room, but a bedroom opened off to the right. And Maggie had given him the gallery room, even with Nick Daimler in town!

He was finally making headway with her.

He said: "Don't mind me. I'm like a tomcat. Chewed up and healed overnight and brainless enough to go back for more trouble."

She looked him over. "That's a bad cut over your eye. It ought to be tended to. Sit down while I get some hot water."

It made him feel foolish, but he took a seat. She slipped out through the doorway, her body slim and smoothly moving beneath the silk. Her ankles were bare, her feet in small slippers. He looked about the room, when she was gone, even more interested in it now than on his other visits. It was pleasant and, like her, not cluttered or smothered in frills and fripperies. He leaned back in the chair, pulled in a slow, relaxed breath, and closed his eyes.

This was where she had lived with her husband, the man who had hit the bottle and come to a premature end. She couldn't have had anything to do with that. She had a genius for making a man feel good.

He let her fix the deep cut over his eye, when she returned, and cluck over the other cuts and bruises and show him her sympathy. He liked it fine. But her manner was casual, he noted, and he sensed that she had no special mood for him tonight. His weariness came back full force, and he thanked her, said good night, and went to the gallery room he had coveted.

He couldn't sleep. For a long while he lay puzzling about himself, why he had come to Banca Basin, why he had been so outraged at learning the truth about Louise, why he had wanted that fight with Lagg and failed to find satisfaction in it, why he couldn't make up his mind to court Maggie properly instead of coming at her in the way he did. He couldn't answer one of those questions.

Smoking occasionally, twisting and turning, he lay for a long while in the darkness. The scent of the locusts beyond the gallery came in to him through the open door. At last he rose, pulled on his pants and crossed the room, stepping out to the upper porch. Again he made note of the other door that opened onto this private retreat, the still shut screen that kept out the night insects. Originally the whole must have been a private apartment of the Paines, or of some previous owner.

From where he stood he could see through the screen door of the other room. His breath caught, and he moved quietly as he stepped nearer. He saw the figure in the bed within, her braided hair, her face in the

220

repose of sleep. He put his hand on the screen door and pulled gently. The door wouldn't budge. He tried again, harder, and realized that it was latched on the inside. Then, as violently as he had been thrown into the fight, aggression seized him. Pressing his back to the wall beside the door, he began to mew softly like a hungry kitten.

For a long moment he thought it was having no effect, then he heard the bedspring rattle. A board made its sound under weight, and shuffling feet came toward the door. He heard the low scrape of metal as the screen door hook was unfastened. The door swung outward a cautious distance, then they were looking at each other. "You," she whispered. "I thought it was a kitten."

"Alley cat," he told her. "Didn't I warn you?" He slid a foot into the crack of the door as she tried to close it again.

She simply let go of the handle, turning back into the room. He followed. Moonlight seeped through doorway and window in sufficient quantity to show her to him, clad in the white, thin gown and retreated only a few steps into the room. Her face seemed without expression, her body rigid.

"Aren't you abusing a privilege, Tully?" she murmured finally.

He realized that he had been right in his

feeling that her mood was not with him tonight. The awareness knocked the edge off his own acute need. Yet, oddly, he felt none of the restraints that had caused him to walk away from Louise that night at Two Hump.

Deflated, he said: "You don't really think so. Tonight you've got something else on your mind. What? The fact that Nick Daimler's in town?"

"Why did you say that?" she gasped.

"Idle curiosity."

"You think when he puts up here he makes this little visit?"

"If he's cut out like me, he'd try."

She laughed suddenly. "I suppose I ought to say thanks for trying. But don't again. And don't keep showing me that ugly suspicion, Tully. Want a saucer of milk before you go back to bed?"

He said — "Yes . . . this." — and stepped toward her.

She let him take his kiss but did not rise to it, slack and guarded for the moment she was in his arms. He heard her latch the screen again after he stepped out to the gallery, going back where he belonged.

He rose in a warm dawn, sore-muscled and again truculent. But, early as it was, he found that he was not up ahead of Maggie.

She was sweeping the lobby when he came down the stairs and moved in behind the desk when he threw down the key. She had a cloth wrapped about her head and looked like a teenage girl. Yet she seemed different in other ways this morning. He was glad when she made it plain that she harbored no resentment.

"More rambling to do today?" she asked.

"I reckon," he admitted.

"Better eat first. I haven't had my own breakfast."

Her forgiveness was fully conveyed when she had her morning meal with him in the hotel dining room. But both were silent, self-conscious. He kept noticing her skin with its deep, glowing sheen of copper, her oval face, the strong jaw and chin. There was warmth in this woman, but he knew now that there was no weakness. She was wholly unlike his first impression of her, but still unlike most of the other women he had known. She had no prudish attitudes, no delicate distress at the roughness in men. She seemed to have few of the defenses and pretenses so many of her sisters hid behind. She was honest, he guessed, courageous, and he was halfway glad she had shown him her door.

His mind at ease about her, he began to

wonder about the *malpais,* whether he would be wise to brave it again as had been his purpose when he came to town. Ed was against it in principle, he knew, but a more earthy, human side of the man was tempted to let him try it. Lagg's reliance upon the law's slow process to further his purpose was galling to a stockman and man of action, and Ed was both, exactly as was Tully Gale. Tully decided to see how Ed felt about it this morning.

He reached the livery stable before Ed had opened the big front doors. A little pounding brought the liveryman forth, sleepy-eyed and scowling.

"Wish you'd make a point of having your breakfast before I show up, Ed," Tully told him. "You scare a man with that glower."

Ed looked him over. "So you went to Valen's last night," he commented.

"Got the dynamite?" Tully asked.

"Looks like you should have had it last night," Ed retorted. "Who'd you tie into?"

"Lagg."

"Lick him?"

Tully shook his head. "Yes and no, if you know what that means."

Ed let out a slow breath. "And you still want to go into the *malpais?*"

"Did you get the dynamite and caps?"

224

Tully demanded.

"Got 'em," Ed admitted. "I wrestled with my conscience right up till the hardware was about to close last night. Then I had to give in or it would have been too late. I can't stand Lagg's telling the sheriff to bring him a court order to remove that dam. But I'll furnish you with explosives only on one condition. That's your promise not to tie into something too big for you the way you're inclined to do, and not to do it in a way that'll give Lagg a case against the basiners."

"You've got it," Tully said. "So let's saddle the red."

"That'll be a pleasure," Ed said, "if you'll take him outta here. That horse has got me scared and knows it. I jump if it stomps a foot, which it does all day long."

"I'll let you fork him sometime, Ed," Tully said, "and learn what a real jump's like."

They brought the stallion into the center aisle, where Tully saddled him. Except for his quivering, his barrel swelling, and wall-eyed search for a chance to bite, Red seemed tractable. Ed threw a pack saddle onto a smaller horse. He showed Tully the half dozen sticks of dynamite, in a gunny sack, that he had got from the hardware the night before. There was a short coil of fuse and a box of detonating caps. Ed handed the caps to Tully. "Better stick 'em in your saddlebag. It ain't healthy to pack 'em with dynamite."

Tully did so. Ed would lend him camping equipment, as he had before, but he would have to go down to the mercantile to buy the necessary grub, and he needed extra shells for his .45.

He led the red onto the street, which was still deserted and quiet. Ed brought out the pack pony. The red shied a little when the tame horse came close to it.

"Might give you trouble trying to lead it," Ed commented, nodding at the pack horse.

"Red?" Tully scoffed. "Why, he's got so he eats out of my hand. If you'll throw together some cooking utensils, Ed, I'll go down to Prine's and pick up some victuals."

He swung into the saddle on the red and in the next second had shamelessly grabbed leather. The stallion's hind hoofs shot into the air. It seemed to accomplish the impossible by shaking itself violently while in that position. Tully found himself sailing over the lowered head, and he hit the dust with a *whack,* flat on his back. He groaned, stunned and disbelieving. Then he scrambled to a groggy sit, alarmed.

Hoofs hit the ground hard and fast. "Red!" he yelled. "Whoa, you dag-gummed little devil! Whoa up there, I tell you!" He climbed to a reeling stand. The red was streaking it up the street, reins and stirrups flying. It whipped around a corner, instinct guiding it. It was going home to the *malpais* and it didn't want company.

"Cooped up too long," Ed said at Tully's elbow. "You all right?"

"All right?" Tully bawled. "When I'm out the best damned horse . . . why, blast his dirty, black heart! He had that in his wicked head ever since I caught him the first time! He won't get away with it, Ed! By damn, I'll catch and ride that devil till there's nothing left but his shadow!"

"Yep," Ed agreed. "Sounds like you're out a fine horse."

"Saddle me another!" Tully yelled at him. "And I'll show that crowbait who's got horse sense!"

Ed rubbed his whiskers. "How about them dynamite caps in the saddlebag?" he wondered. "Red had better be careful what he runs into."

Tully fumed for five minutes, while Ed saddled another horse, the best he had left in the barn.

"Red's got your caps," Ed pointed out, "and be damned if I'll get you any more. Catch him, first. That might take the ginger

227

outta you and keep you from pulling Lagg's whiskers." But he was talking to a man with a single-track mind. Tully was going to get Red back before he did another thing.

Riding the rented horse and leading the pack pony, Tully went up the street to Prine's mercantile. It didn't take long to make up a pack of provisions sufficient for the period he expected to be gone, and he remembered to buy shells for his six-gun. It was still early in the morning when he struck out on the basin road. Nothing would give him rest now until he had glued his pants to the saddle on Red and showed that horse who was master.

It was the same old monotonous road, a straight line running out in a flat, hot plain that became irritating to a man's eyes. The heat and lack of vegetation spoke of the life dependent on this land and its suffering when the balancing rains failed to come in sufficiency. But he knew he was heading into worse country for he had visited the badlands before. Yet the thought of its harshness did nothing to discourage him now.

He had followed the basin trail for nearly two hours before he came to the place where the red stallion had left it, bending due north toward the badlands. It was easy to pick up the trail, for the driving hoofs had bitten plainly into the earth. The mustang had headed on a beeline for a high scarp break far in the distance. Tully jogged along, leading the pack horse, pretty sure of where Red was going but prudently keeping an eye on the sign. The stallion had already fooled him badly and wasn't going to be given the chance to do it again.

In late afternoon Tully came to the escarpment. The mustang had dug plenty of earth in its climb up the long talus. Tully ascended patiently to the bench, urging the reluctant pack pony. He was placing himself in trust to the wild horse's instinct, letting it lead him, reasoning that it would head for water and grass the first thing, and then try to rejoin its kind. The trouble was that there was no telling where its kind would be by now. Tully had penned a whole band in a box cañon in retrieving Red the first time. The experience probably had caused Red's harem to penetrate much deeper into the badlands.

Tully figured to make camp at the first good place he came to and work on cautiously from there. He wasn't underestimating the country he was invading. Even experienced men were cautious as to what backland areas they visited. For a short trip, he would have kept dropping something the wind could not disturb to help him retrace his course. This venture, he realized, would take him unnumbered miles. When he had caught Red, he would strike west until he came to one of the headwaters of Splinter Creek.

He had trouble finding where the stallion had got down from the bench on the far side, for the animal had been forced to swing down its length a considerable distance. Once it had turned across the mesa, only to double back and retrace its own steps. That had not been cunning probably, but simply a search for a way down. Then the stallion had gone on for a couple of miles, crossing a rocky moraine that nearly threw Tully off the trail and dropped into a long and narrow cañon thereafter.

Even though he managed to cling to the trail, Tully began to feel uneasy as to his own safety. The shadowed depths of the cañon floor had an unholy quiet. Its blind twists and turns tightened the anxiety that already crowded him. He had two canteens of water, but sharing it with the horses would soon exhaust it. He kept riding, having to trust that the red would lead him to an artesian spring, of which the badlands had many.

It was nearly dark when he came into a small, locked-in valley. The sigh of relief that escaped him seemed loud in his ears. The horses threw their own ears forward and hurried themselves. The grass meant underground moisture, but the animals' reaction confirmed the nearness of surface water. Tully came to it presently, a roaring artesian spring wasting its water here in the empty vastnesses. A creek ran out from it, down the short length of the valley.

He halted at the spring to make camp. It brought his mind back to Sugar Lagg and the probability of his rustling Two Hump cattle. These wasteland oases were ideal for an operation of that nature. The trouble was that there were many of them, too detached to be of use to a legitimate cattle operator, sometimes too hidden ever to be discovered by man.

When he had watered the thirsty horses, he loosened his pack, off saddled, and staked the animals in the grass. There was nothing with which to build a fire but that wasn't important. He ate a cold supper and, thereafter, stretched out on the saddle blankets, hearing the continual chirm of the springs, and smoking as he stared at the star-flung sky. A delight came to him such as he could capture only at rare intervals. It was an animal well-being and an animal's sense of competence. Presently he fell asleep.

He awakened refreshed in full daylight, ready to take up the patient stalking of the escaped stallion. Eating a quick breakfast, he brought in the saddler and cinched on the hull. He left the camp as it was, with the pack pony still on picket. Mounting, he rode down the length of the little creek to find that it disappeared into a sink at the valley's end. Just short of there he discovered where the red mustang had paused to water and graze. Scuffed places showed plainly how it had rolled time and again trying to get rid of the saddle. Thinking of the dynamite caps in the saddlebag, Tully's nape puckered.

The horse wasn't in this area, and the destination in his wicked brain probably wasn't too clear to him. But somewhere within the tangled reaches ahead ran his own kind. Red would keep going until he had joined up with them, and Tully Gale would keep going until he was again in the saddle that still clung to the red's back.

For one more full day Tully followed the red mustang, moving his camp to a new discovery of water and grass to which instinct had drawn his quarry. The wild horse had turned west now, seeking the country that had been his habitat before Sugar Lagg had taken him into captivity, drawing Tully back into the country he had visited the first time. Aware that it was taking him ever closer to Lagg's hunting grounds, Tully followed doggedly. The country grew rougher, but through it the red picked his way with unerring judgment. He expected no pursuit and made no more deceptive movements.

Tully had little idea of where he was when he was recamped finally, except for an estimate that he was somewhere in back of Lagg's horse camp. But this worried him less than the thought that went often through his mind now: *Can I find my way out of this when I'm ready?*

He rode out the next morning for a scout before breaking camp and came upon a wild bunch wholly by surprise. He halted on a high rim to gaze out across a vast, broken open. A pristine excitement stirred in him. A band of forty or fifty wild horses, seen against a distant rise, grazed upwind from him, wholly untroubled. It was a magnificent sight. None of the broomtails were big, weighing between six and eight hundred, but they were strong and tough. This bunch was brilliantly colored, pintos, strawberry roans, *canellas,* blues. They were rough-looking creatures, their wildness accented by their matted manes and heavy, sometimes dragging tails.

Tully dismounted and gently drew back his livery horse to ground-tie it. He slipped again to the rim and this time dropped flat there, knowing that if the faintest suggestion of his presence reached the mustangs they would be gone with the speed of the wind. He let his study play carefully on the band but he couldn't see the red, which would be distinguished by the saddle and bridle. But he knew that the urge to join this or a like group would have drawn the escaped stallion to this point. Tully knew, also, that making the capture would be a delicate operation. But he had done it once and he could do it again.

He remained on the rim for nearly an hour while the wildlings grazed unsuspectingly. The band swirled into motion well before a stallion's sharp whistle of warning came to him on the wind. The mustangs wheeled west and within five minutes were lost from sight. He was on the point of rising to mount and follow when his gaze riveted on the country to his right.

The red stallion came along at a forlorn trot, pursuing the fleeing band, unaware that the saddle he wore had frightened the others. A wild joy leaped in Tully. He walked down to his horse, mounted, and put it at a good clip along the bench land. The dust kicked up by the fleeing wild bunch kept him informed. Then he straightened in the saddle at one more of this country's quick surprises.

Sunlight struck at him from below. The cañon floor had turned a pure silver. It took a moment to realize that it was water, a lost lake of considerable size tucked away where nothing but wildlings could use it. He rode on, bending with the rim and coming above the water. The wild bunch had halted at its edge, and he saw that the lake originated in a traverse cañon. He shoved back his hat, staring at the sight below him in dawning recognition. There was no foliage to be seen around the lake, nothing but the lifeless brown soil and sheer rock cliffs. He had seen it from a different point before, but suddenly he knew that he had once more come upon Lagg's reservoir of impounded water.

VIII

Swinging his attention back to the wild horses, Tully saw that they were stirring again, working up the far rise. Well on the slope the leader turned back in the direction from which they had come. *All you need is to find your trap,* Tully told himself. *They won't let the red join up with them. But he'll keep trying. All you've got to do is take advantage of that. . . .*

He studied this run as he rode back to camp. A high excitement filled him. But he would need patience, letting the band get used to the strange red horse that dogged it, and letting the red grow resigned to his banishment. Tully spent a pleasant evening in camp, making plans. There was stunted greasewood in the locality and he wanted a hot supper. He fried bacon and skillet bread and afterward mingled cigarettes and coffee, scheming against his red quarry.

Up before dawn, he skipped breakfast in

his eagerness to check on the band. This time he kept off the rim and picked his way down into the run itself. He had barely gained the floor when he pulled down his mount in sudden wonder. *I'll be dog-goned,* he thought. *Has that red devil grown himself a set of horseshoes to go with his other trappings?* The prints of a horse's shoes were certainly there on the ground, a horse shod all around, and the prints were fresh.

Worry rolled over Tully. Somebody else was in here with designs on this bunch, and it had to be Sugar Lagg or someone from his outfit. The ridden horse had been moving east. Tully followed the sign a distance, coming upon a place where the horse had been joined by another that, also, wore shoes. Convinced that it was another mustanging party, Tully turned back.

He climbed again to the rim and stayed well over on the bench until he had traveled for some distance. Becoming familiar with the area, he halted presently and swung down. He crossed cautiously to the edge of the rim and once more looked directly upon the wild horses, still at a distance from the lake and well across from him. His eyes narrowed in quick interest.

The red mustang was just below him, staring at the others in a kind of hung-head melancholy. He began to move cautiously toward the group in the distance, trying to sneak in and join it. *No use, Red,* Tully reflected. *You might as well be a camel.* He settled himself to watch. Attention rose in the band, which this time failed to flee when the saddled red horse came into plain sight. Then a beautifully marked stallion wheeled away from the band, neck arched, his screaming whistle reaching Tully as he traveled toward the red.

The red halted. *Better get, Red,* Tully commented privately. *Even if you lick him, you couldn't get a mare in the harem to look at you with that rig on. By the time that latigo rots and the saddle falls off, you'll be too old and feeble to care.* Just the same, it disturbed him a little. Red was only trying to be himself, and mysterious, unreasonable frustrations had been forced upon him.

Suddenly Tully found himself an ally of the red instead of his foe. Red didn't run. He answered the other stallion's challenge, and then the two were driving together at a gallop. Tully thought of the dynamite caps and winced. The two stallions came together in a tremendous crash. The lead stallion went down and Red went head over heels across him. But no explosion rent the air. Both horses scrambled up and now Red's saddle hung at a jaunty angle. He swung in, rearing and striking as the other came up. They pawed, driving sharp teeth at each other's arched throats. The mares in the harem watched intently while the two stallions fought, perhaps wondering if they were destined to bear strangely humped colts.

The fight held Tully fascinated, also, but suddenly he was on his feet, struck cold. Out in the band a younger stallion sent out his warning. The band swung in a bunch to stare eastward, then whirled away together. The drumming hoofs rocked up to Tully. The fighting stallions broke off and whipped away. The band drove straight toward the lake.

Ridden horses were coming in from the east at a gallop. Tully saw three and suspected more, the riders as yet too far away to be identified. His heart sank and he didn't have to be told who they were. The mustangers were bent on driving the wild band toward the lake. He ran for his own mount, not knowing what he meant to do. He pounded ahead toward the bend in the rim that gave a view of the lake. Dismounting there, he slipped to the rim but could see nothing of the wild horses for the moment.

Yet he could hear their drumming and

knew that they hadn't drowned themselves to escape capture. They were running in under him, with the cliff bulge cutting them from sight. He realized that the mustangers would hold the catch in some box cañon on ahead. There was nothing he could do to stop it, and he would have to wait for his chance. Several days would elapse before an attempt would be made to move this explosive aggregation, mixed with broken wild horses to tame it somewhat, to Lagg's permanent camp for topping out and breaking.

Tully paced the lip of the rim for a distance, growing interested in the lake itself. From this new angle he saw more of it than he had before, a body of water like an immense cigar trapped within the walls of a deep cañon by an earth dam. Presently Tully reached a place where he could see the lower end where the cañon continued on and the lake ended. Detritus lay across the cañon, and this he had seen before, the dam Lagg had built by blowing down the bulging cañon walls.

Tully was excited now. Apparently Lagg was also using the lake for a horse trap, the abundant water and good grass drawing in the wild bunches and saving the mustangers a lot of scouring. It struck him that this also would have been an ideal place to hold stolen cattle. He had ruined it for that purpose, as far as Lagg was concerned, by reporting the situation to Ed Handel and thus the sheriff. It was no wonder Lagg had been so annoyed about that. The whole Two Hump herd could have been held here indefinitely.

Again Tully was thinking of the dam and his long hunger to blow it out. Apparently it was not being guarded, as Ed had feared. He had the dynamite back in camp, but Red had the detonating caps without which the dynamite was useless, and it looked like Sugar Lagg had Red.

Returning to his horse, Tully rode back to his camp. Although he felt certain that the mustangers were well away from there by then, he decided against a fire and ate a cold meal. His provisions were showing signs of depletion, and he knew that he dared not dally too long. He loitered about camp, too keyed up to rest, waiting for the day to pass. In late afternoon he ate again. Then, in the gathering twilight, he saddled and rode out. Night would be safer, but he needed a little light for what he meant to do.

He dropped boldly onto the floor of the coulée, the tops of the high, tawny cliffs now softening in the fading day. When he came to the lake margin, he paused, getting his first close look at the situation. There was a flat margin on this side, running on into the cañon. Along this the mustangs had picked their way to escape the horsemen. But it hadn't been escape, Tully knew. Somewhere ahead the mustangers had laid a trap that would have caught them.

Swinging his mount, Tully followed the broadly scuffed path, riding cautiously and not knowing when he might stumble upon his enemies. Ahead now he could see the end of the lake. He was calm, determined. Holding his horse to a patient pace, he went on. The cañon walls ran ahead in unbroken monotony. He found that the mustangs had plunged over the slide that choked the cañon and had gone on. But there were no guards there.

Tully dismounted and walked carefully to the top of the dam for a look, then got his horse and rode over it. His theory about Lagg's creation of the lake was verified by the dry wash that continued down the cañon beyond the choked area. It interested Tully deeply, but right now he was intent upon his red stallion. He aimed to have it and his dynamite caps before the night was much older.

It seemed to him that he had followed the

dry wash for two miles when his alerting horse warned him. He dismounted quickly. Beyond the next blind shoulder he saw a traverse cañon. The one threaded by the vanished creek had been blocked off by ropes and canvas spooks to turn the horses into a side cañon. This was it, the final, closing trap. Tully caught his breath. He kept going. Then he halted, for the camp was just ahead.

He pulled up in relief when he saw only one man at the fire, well ahead of him and in the center of the bottleneck passage. Beyond the fire, ropes criss-crossed the cañon, forming a barrier, disclosing that the day's catch of wild horses — including the red stallion — were imprisoned in the box cañon beyond. The camp tender's companions might be up there in the cañon. On the other hand, they might have returned to Lagg's permanent camp to bring in the gentled mustangs used to take the ginger out of a new catch. Tully pulled his gun and walked on into view of the man.

"Up with the hands!" he called.

The man shoved his arms up hastily, his mouth twitching as he stared at the intruder. He was getting on in years, the nondescript kind of codger who drew camp chores and other menial tasks throughout the range country.

"You're that Gale buckaroo, ain't you?" the oldster gasped. "Sugar said you was the kind of smart aleck as might bust in here to raise hell. He's your huckleberry, man . . . not me."

"Lagg's not my huckleberry," Tully retorted. "That saddled red stud you took today is my horse, though. It's going to be ticklish catching him, because Red's loaded for bear. But I bought and paid for him, dad, and I aim to take him home with me. Where's Sugar?"

"Went to camp to fetch out the gentled mustangs. Be back in a minute, Gale, and you better hightail it. That's friendly advice, because I'm too danged old to do any of Sugar's fightin' for him."

"Take it easy, dad. I'm going to have to rope you. But if you're nice and polite, it won't hurt you a bit."

"You'll get caught, and then, by damn, you'll get plugged," the old man warned. "Sugar, he hates your guts. He's just lookin' for a chance to get at you and the whole damn' basin."

"Hear he's hired himself some gunfighters."

"A mess of 'em. Bub, take a old man's advice and light your shuck."

Tully grinned at him. "Thanks, pop. But you're only trying to scare me off and avoid getting skinned by Lagg yourself. If I've got any idea of what part of the country we're in, Lagg and his hyenas won't make it to the main camp and back for hours yet."

He found a rope and, afterward, made certain that his work on the camp tender was to be trusted. Returning to his horse, he brought it on into the camp. He let himself and horse through the ropes, re-mounted, and rode on up the box cañon. He had his catch rope in his hand. It was getting dark, but he would recognize the red by its saddle in any kind of light.

He heard a sudden, thunderous racket, close ahead, and knew he had stirred up the wild bunch. He rode on carefully, not want-ing to stampede them past him and out over the rope barrier. He hoped that the red was still an outcast so he would not have to cut it out from the rest of the bunch. Even then he wasn't sure he could rope and handle it in the poor light while mounted on an untried livery horse. Moreover, he shud-dered to think what throwing Red might do to the dynamite caps.

He picked his way on into the cañon. It had grown quiet ahead, indicating that he had shoved the wild bunch up against the blind end. He shook out his rope, the loop formed, ready to dab at anything that caught his interest. Then he saw the mustang through the twilight and made out the canted saddle on his back. Lagg's men had no doubt noticed the saddle, but they hadn't taken the time to rope the horse to get it off.

The red was apart from the other mustangs, still in disgrace as Tully had hoped. He had tried to conceal himself in a nest of boulders while he passed on in. Tully halted his mount. For a moment he and Red stared at each other. The mustang swung his head nervously, uncertain of which way to turn or whether he should make a break at all. Tully managed his mount toward the mustang, gently lifting up his rope. The red was away like a shot, instinct driving it toward the cañon mouth and escape.

Tully whipped in at a sharp angle, coming behind him as he streaked out. Tully shot the loop, the rope's end dallied to his saddle horn. The loop fell on the red's back and bounced off. Tully dug spurs, driving after the scuttling stallion, re-gathering his rope. The barrier ahead would turn the horse back, or spill and explode him, or the red devil would break out. Tully pulled down, waiting, and heard no crash or boom up there. Again he moved his horse forward at a slow walk.

Then he could make out the red again, halted now at the ropes, looking warily back at him. He edged up on him. Then the stallion wheeled and shot toward him, but it switched again and cut to the left. Tully threw for the legs, the way he would have roped a calf, hating to spill a good horse and dreading what might come from the caps. The red tangled in the loop and crashed hard but he failed to disintegrate. Tully let out a whoop and swung his mount. Pulling off to draw up the slack, he had his red horse back.

When he had snubbed the red reliably, he went back to the camp tender. He said: "No need for you to be so scared, dad . . . of me, anyhow, though I can't blame you for worrying about what Lagg'll say when he learns of this. He's got no kick, though. The red's my horse."

The oldster licked his lips, then looked uncertain. Finally, hauling in a deep breath, he blurted: "Lagg, he's lookin' for you to come in here and blow up his dam! He wants you to, Gale, and don't you do it!"

"Wants me to?" Tully gasped. "How come?"

"He . . . he wants a excuse to take his gunnies a-hellin' through the basin."

"I'm just one lone-handed, bow-legged cowpoke, pop. I'm not the whole basin."

"Work for that stockmen's association, don't you?" the camp tender demanded. "Anything you do Sugar'll claim to be on its behalf. Gale, take your damned stud and get out of the *malpais.* Me, I got friends out there in the basin. I don't want to see that kind of trouble."

Tully grinned and turned around. The red was simmering down where he had been snubbed to one of the posts holding up the rope barrier. He walked over and took a look at the horse, then whistled and shook his head. The loose, long-worn cinch, with its shifting saddle, had rubbed the red's back too raw for it to be ridden. He removed the saddle and blanket and looked around the camp until he found a can of bacon grease that he smeared on the sores. He replaced the saddle, tightening the cinch only enough to keep it in place.

He returned to the camp, found the man's gun, and unloaded it. He dropped the shells in his pocket and tossed the gun out into the rocks. The oldster probably had more shells somewhere and would find the gun, but it was no country for an unarmed man and Tully was remembering that. He figured to be well on his way before the man could arm himself again.

He mounted the livery horse and, leading the now docile red, rode back down the cañon. It was no time at all until he came to Lagg's dam, where he halted for a more leisurely look at the situation. Excitement boiled in him, a heedless, onrushing drive. Three times he had been warned against tampering with the earth obstruction choking the cañon and imprisoning millions of gallons of badly needed water. He had never wanted anything as badly in his life as he wanted to make a thorough job out of this visit to Lagg's innermost retreats. The job would not be difficult, he judged, as he examined the vicinity. The scarred walls of the cañon showed where Lagg had blown down the earth to fill the bottom. The obstruction was high but not wide, a mixture of rock and dirt. The rocks, where they piled together, offered cracks where he could plant a charge of dynamite.

Yet a warning sounded in some remote part of his mind, the realization that he was flirting with forces he actually knew little about. He knew next to nothing about dynamite and its proper employment. If he took too big a bite out of this dam, releasing all that pent up water, he would have loosened a flash flood that might wipe out the town of Splinter Rock as well as create havoc on the range. In addition, the camp tender had warned him that the stockmen's association would be held to account for his actions. Lagg hoped for something to justify — according to his dim lights — a swift, punitive expedition into Banca Basin. Maybe that rose out of a natural viciousness, or it could be part of some scheme as yet unrevealed. On the other hand, the oldster could have been bluffing, fearful that Tully meant to destroy the dam and trying to scare him out of it. Tully preferred to look at it that way because he ached to put water back in Splinter Creek, saving Johnny Babbage the need of going through with his own risky plan and knocking the props out from under Nick Daimler's scheme for acquiring Two Hump.

A close inspection of the earth fill showed Tully how he could load it in a way that would only blow off the top. There was a fissure near the surface where he could place the charge, lifting the earth above it and lowering the top a foot or two below the level of the impounded water. That would not create a dangerous flood while restoring enough water to the creek to end the drought emergency. The hell with Lagg!

The old man back at the horse camp was only bluffing. Tully knew he was going to do it.

He found a stick and began to poke in between the loose rock to rake out the earth and make a place for the charge of dynamite. He knew he would have to rush it, having no knowledge of when Lagg and his mustangers would return from the main camp with the gentled mustangs. The caps he needed were in Red's saddlebags, but the dynamite and fuse were in his own camp. By the time he could get the latter and do the job, he was apt to have gunmen beating the bushes for him.

The danger only whetted his appetite for the undertaking, obscuring his realization that he was taking precipitate action against the counsel of older and wiser heads. He finished preparing the hole so that he could return, load it, and light the fuse and be off again in a matter of minutes. Then he remounted his horse and rode on.

Presently he reached the place where the rising lake had spilled into the side cañon, forming the area Lagg had used as a decoy for wild horses. It might also have been the place where he had meant to hide the cattle he intended to rustle from Two Hump, a thing he would not dare to do now that he knew Tully Gale was aware of the region. More and more Lagg was acquiring reasons for wanting to strip one Gale of his hide.

Tully was lost in his own thoughts when suddenly his horse stumbled. A split second passed before the sound of a rifle shot carried to him. By then the red had reared back on its lines, while the livery horse was slowly folding, going down. Tully cleared the saddle, holding onto the red, struck numb. Another shot rang out. He placed it as coming from the rim on his right, from which he had spied down upon this reach of the cañon. In the darkness, whoever was up there had been able to make out no more than the shape of the horse. In better light, Tully himself would have been the target. So the oldster had been bluffing to save the dam when he claimed Lagg wanted it blown out, which was all the more reason for destroying it.

The downed horse threshed, badly hurt, but Tully still held onto the red, sawing it in under the cliff to temporary safety. He rubbed his hands across his eyes, his heart racing from the narrowness of his escape. The man at the mustang camp couldn't have gotten up there in the time that had elapsed. It was somebody else. Lagg had had more men left in these parts than had been apparent. The old camp tender had been smart enough to keep quiet about them.

The stricken horse threshed a couple of times, then quieted, although its chest showed it was still alive. The bulge of the cliff kept the ambusher from trying more shooting. It would take the man a while to find a way to get down here — if he had the nerve to try. Tully waited for long moments but nothing more happened. He knew that he could walk on for a great distance in the protection of the cliff overhang. The red couldn't be ridden with that sore back, and the livery horse was down. Tully had no mind to leave the doomed animal to die a lingering death. Drawing his .45, he used it, then went on, leading the red and not wanting to handicap himself by taking in Ed's saddle as he ordinarily would have done.

He picked his way slowly but safely for a long distance, keeping under the cliff. This changed things, he reflected. All he had left to ride was the pack pony he had left at camp. It was small, old, and anything but saddle stock. But it would have to do because he didn't aim to spoil the red by showing indifference to his sore back. He could still blow out the dam, although he knew he would have a fight in doing it, and he was all the more determined to try.

He trudged on toward his camp and had no more trouble from the ambusher. He knew when he had reached camp only by the location and the char of his fire. The pack pony and his pack were gone. Since the pony was not likely to throw on its own pack, somebody had been here. Lagg's man, the fellow who had shot the horse out from under him.

He stood there a moment before he realized the extent of his loss. The first thing he though of was his water canteens. They were gone. He had no more food, no extra shells. And he was afoot. Then it all hit home. "I've got dynamite caps again," he breathed aloud. "And now no dynamite!" All he would have to show for his efforts was a sore-backed, ornery wild horse.

There was only one thing to do. He knew he had to head out at once if he was to live, using the coolness of the night to get as far as he could for he would have to walk it without water. It struck him, also, that, while Red had led him in here, the horse would be less anxious to lead him out again. He would have to risk going by Lagg's main camp, he decided. After Lagg and his mustangers had returned to the horse trap, the base camp would be the easier to plunder for food and a canteen. The way out to the basin would be easier to follow from there.

He looked at the benighted lake behind him, untold quantities of water. He and Red would have to fill their bellies tick-tight before they left, because that was all they had to carry water in. . . .

His thirst was hardest to bear. He halted, holding onto the reins of the stallion that had plodded so long behind him, and stared out of bloodshot eyes at a wild coulée below. Far across, the rusty-yellow badlands lifted again, giving off a shimmering, midday heat and erecting a barrier of space that would finish him if he didn't find water. He thought: *I set out to blow up a dam and I'm going to die of thirst!*

But there had to be water somewhere in here, one of the artesian springs that bobbed up so unexpectedly in this crazy country. The red would smell it. He would have given him his head long since, letting him lead, except for a suspicion that the mustang would only take them back into the deeper reaches of the badlands.

As it was, he thought that he was somewhere in the general region of Lagg's main horse camp. He hadn't met up with them, although he had started hoping he would.

Daylight had found him on the long floor of a cañon that nothing ever seemed to have traveled ahead of him. Thereafter he had admitted that he was lost.

The sun had blunted the sharpness of his mind, and now his sweating body crawled with weariness. He stood on the rim, trying doggedly to figure out where he was. Dimensions had taken to changing under his tired stare so that the same object could seem right at hand and then miles away, without him so much as blinking his eyes. He let his gaze drift the length of the coulée and begin a slow crawl back. There was nothing to catch his interest and pull his bone-tired body on. There was heat and silence, the forbidding mien of vast emptiness, and little else.

He wasn't kicking. He had tried to make a smart play against sound advice. He remembered Ed's original objection to his sally, the old camp tender's warning, and said to himself: "Mostly you've got what it takes, but there's a shortage. Seasoning. . . ." Well, a man could season fast in this.

He pulled tiredly on the reins of the stallion that was himself showing punishment. The docility with which he followed had comforted Tully sometimes. The red seemed to figure that the route they traveled was as

256

good as any. If that wasn't a suicidal urge in the beast, maybe safety lay just ahead if they could keep going.

He had decided on the most promising descent to the coulée floor and now started doggedly along the high bench toward it. His foreshortened shadow crawled drearily ahead of him on the hot and sandy earth. When he reached the point he had picked, he saw that the rim was cut too deeply for him to climb down. He cursed in frustration, forced to stay on the bench in the unobstructed sun and to turn at right angles to the course he had set himself. Panic began to rise again, the urge to hurry senselessly, and that was a bad sign.

He made himself rest once more, and, when he rose, he walked with more restraint. He had reached the end of the coulée when he grew glad of the change in direction inflicted upon him. Ahead, the fault canted down into a traverse cañon. It was mustang country, like much of the rest of it, but the horse tracks he found on the cañon floor showed iron-shod hoofs and were fresh. *One of Lagg's trails!* he thought in wild relief. *It'll take us somewhere!*

But he held himself to his thrifty pace, not knowing how far he still had to go. Around the headland, a little later, he halted and let out a yell. He was at an elevation, yet so stationed that a rim-locked valley opened before him. He saw vegetation — trees, chaparral, and a wide expanse of green bottom meadow. Far in the distance he could see smoke. Lagg's base camp was at hand. Now Tully let himself hurry.

He had little concern as to whether he found Lagg there. He crossed first to the creek that ran down the middle of the valley. It was cold artesian water, gushing from some fault in the rock-grit land and the reason Lagg had picked the site for the base of his horse operations. Tully drank sparingly, allowed the red to do likewise, and they both paused before drinking again. Then he picked up the reins and grew interested in the horse camp itself.

He had been here before, when he bought the red. He remembered that it was an extensive layout of some permanence. The several large corrals were made from poles and woven brush. They hugged a high rock rim and overlapped the creek. Scattered about were various sorting pens and breaking traps that Lagg used in topping out the fierce little horses of the *malpais* and gentling them to what he called a broken condition. Again Tully saw smoke, which rose from beyond the obstructions, and went on, strengthened by the water and caring more now who he encountered there.

As he rounded the outer structures, he saw a woven-brush lean-to forming the backing of an open camp. With a gunny sack tied about his middle, a gaunt man stood at the fire staring in sour interest. Tully remembered him as Lagg's cook and walked up, pulling back his tired shoulders. He couldn't see anybody else.

He said: "Howdy, friend. Helped myself to your water, but I'd appreciate an invite before I pitch into that stew on the fire."

IX

The cook spat into the fire and wiped his mouth with his sleeve. Although he didn't speak at the moment, he seemed to remember Tully and his eyes showed speculation. Finally he said — "Howdy." — and offered no more.

A blackened coffee pot and a steaming kettle hung on a rod over the fire. Tully gave them a longing look, then swung a grin at his sullen host.

"I reckon I'm not hungry," he said.

"You're hungry," the man answered. "Help yourself. Sugar Lagg don't like you, bub. You'd best swallow something and git."

"He go back to the horse trap?" Tully asked.

"Went somewheres," the cook said evasively. "Sugar comes and goes. Wouldn't risk having him jump me here, was I you. Boys told me about that rumpus in Valen's stink hole in town. Sugar took that hard."

"How far to Banca Basin?" Tully asked lightly. He found a cup and a greasy-looking plate. The coffee pot held a wicked black brew, and he poured that first, wanting to take the tired flatness out of his body.

"Ten, twelve miles to where the basin starts," the cook said. "Maybe thirty on to Splinter Rock. Ride 'em, bucko. Me . . . I sort of admire a peppery jigger. But I don't cotton to fools."

Tully drank the scalding coffee, then ladled stew out of the kettle. It was good, and he ate hungrily. The man seemed to have relieved himself of what conversation he had to spare and poked off into the lean-to. Tully was drinking more coffee and trying to fashion a cigarette from his sweat-soaked tobacco when, from a distance, came the sound of massed hoofs.

The cook looked out at Tully, scowling. "Warned you, didn't I?" He disappeared back inside.

Tully had got a limp smoke going when four riders came whipping into the camp. Leading them was Sugar Lagg. Tully could tell from their faces that they had been out to the trap and had fogged back fast when they learned what had happened there. But Lagg's interest didn't seem to be in the red stallion that Tully had tethered to a brush

261

clump nearby.

The mustanger had a satisfied grin on his face when he bawled: "Figured you'd try to make it here, once I heard you'd been set down without grub and water. Howdy, Gale. Didn't figure on this pleasure the last time we met up." A greasy hat was shoved back on Lagg's large, low-domed head with its bristling cover of rust-colored hair. The coarse, bony face still showed the beating the man had taken at Valen's and, with that, a wicked unfriendliness.

Tully returned the grin. "Just dropped in for coffee, Sugar, if you've got no objection."

"No objection," Lagg said readily. "But have you given thought to how you're going to drop out again?"

"I hope to buy another horse from you."

"What's the matter with the red there?"

"Sore back," Tully said. "He was saddled too long. And now I've got the same kind of trouble with my feet."

Lagg stared at him hard. "You hoofed it all that way?"

"That's right."

"You're a damned fool," Lagg grunted, surprised. He reflected a moment and added: "So you want another horse."

"That's right, Sugar. And if I were you, I

wouldn't figure on anything rough. I'm not the only one who knows about your dam, and one of the others is the sheriff. It's also known that I packed in here again after my red."

"You packed in after the red," Lagg said, "and you brought dynamite. Figure he'd crawl in a hole and you'd have to mine him out, Gale?"

"That's not the point, Lagg," Tully retorted. "I aim to show up in Splinter Rock sound and healthy. It wouldn't be smart of you to interfere with that intention again. I already had a horse shot out from under me. That's plenty."

"Mebbe," Lagg reflected. "And mebbe I had no such present intentions, Gale. I'm in the horse business and you say you want a horse. Tell you what. I been gentling a blue that don't take to it any better than the red did. But she's a dandy little mare. Ride her out of here and she's your'n."

Tully felt a touch of cold at the pit of his stomach but made an easy answer. "You mean for free?"

"If you can stay aboard."

"That's right generous of you, Sugar," Tully reflected. "It happens I been looking for a lady to walk down the road of life with Red. Where's this blue?"

"Over in the trap."

Lagg's battered face was heating with some inner satisfaction. Flicking a glance to his twisters, he said: "You boys go throw a saddle on the blue."

The stompers rode on down to a breaking corral. Lagg poured himself coffee and studied Tully as he drank it. From the corral presently there came the shrill scream of an angry horse. Tully flung a nervous glance to see a blue mustang lift head and pawing forelegs into view. It had a rope on its neck, and the mustangers were fighting it down, getting set to saddle it. The horse disappeared from view but not from Tully's consciousness. He felt a cold sweat dripping down his sides. He started himself another cigarette, but his fingers shook. He was in poor shape to go aboard a badlands thunderbolt right then. He frowned and managed to spill only a little of the tobacco.

He doubted that the blue mare had even been topped out. This was just Lagg's way of getting even for the fight in Valen's without resorting again to open and risky violence. If Tully Gale got busted up by a mustang he tried to ride, the basin would put it down as sour luck attending an occupational hazard.

Presently Lagg laughed and said: "Sounds

like the boys have got her ready for you, Gale. If you've got your prayers said."

Tully walked toward the corral on rubbery knees, Lagg striding beside him. The mare was held in a big pole and brush breaking trap. She was roped down, her legs stretched out, and now she had a saddle on her back. Tully took a look at her mean, rolling eyes and saw a temper worse than the red had ever displayed. He forced himself to enter the trap without showing too much of his worry.

"Let her up, boys," he said.

"You better crawl aboard that way, Gale," a bronco-stomper drawled. "This gal's got six parts of Satan to one of tornado."

"Let her up," Tully repeated. "I'll have a look at the cinch."

He saw them exchange glances, but at Lagg's nod they let the mare rise. Stepping in warily, Tully lifted a stirrup and checked the center-fire cinch. Maybe it was because the mustang had swelled its barrel and now relaxed it. But the cinch was so loose the saddle would have been hanging under her belly after a couple of pitches, with the rider beneath her murderous hoofs. Tully tightened the latigo, making no comment to the men but talking to the animal easily.

A new wariness had come into Lagg, an

understanding that the truth was fully re-alized. He watched Tully closely.

Lagg drawled: "You better leave off your hardware. Might rupture yourself."

"I'll worry about that," Tully said, "and I'll take the loan of a quirt."

"Quirt?" Lagg asked in mock surprise. "We never use 'em, Gale. We put stock in kindness at this camp."

Tully gathered the reins and swung up. "Let 'er go!" he yelled.

For what seemed a minute, after the ropes were taken from her, the mare stood in her tracks. Tully wished he had his own saddle under him as he sat slick-heeled and clean, waiting for the eruption. It came. All at once he was astride a sweaty-haired cyclone. The mustang left the ground in a cat-back that lifted all four hoofs into the air. She came down again on legs like fence posts. The jar traveled the length of Tully's back, and his eyes all but left their sockets. He managed to keep seat, and to keep his gun in its holster, both accomplishments being es-sential to his survival.

Suddenly the little beast was whipping across the corral, sun-fishing her pliant body, her breath whistling and her head threshing. She beat out a rhythm with her hoofs that she broke irregularly, putting torture in the human frame that could not adjust fast enough. Tully rode it out and was a thought ahead when the horse reared high, attempting a back throw. He knocked her head down with a balled fist. She repaid him with a series of vertical gyrations, pitching in a circle, fence-cornering, pile-driving, showing temper and resourcefulness that made Red look like a worn-out cow horse.

Time lost its meaning. All Tully knew was that he had climbed aboard the toughest horse in his experience. It made him yearn for the relative quietude of Red's back. He could feel saliva run across his chin and had a feeling that his ears were bleeding. Sometimes he was driving against his gun in a way that made him fear the weapon would pierce his side. But he had to keep hold of the gun, and he had to finish the ride.

He caught blurred, swirling glimpses of the mustangers, sensed the cruel relish in them. Lagg was slow-witted but no fool. He knew what was in a wild horse of top quality. He wouldn't offer one as a gift, if a man could ride it, without confidence that the ride could not be accomplished. Tully had seen men die in the saddle.

At long last Tully sensed a weakening in the mare. It was time to unwind and line her out. He yelled — "Open the gate!" — at the mustangers.

He had come full circle before he realized that they weren't going to obey him. They meant to hold him in the killing ride, giving the bronco the full advantage. He clenched his teeth and rode on. But he was winning. The mare was weakening, slowing. Then, after what seemed more hours, she quit as abruptly as Lagg had left the fight. Her head hung, barrel heaving, bloody foam dripping from her nose.

"You call that a ride, Sugar?" Tully managed to yell.

"Hell, no!" Lagg bawled. "Them was just openers!"

Tully slid off the horse, hardly able to stand. The mustang was beat, and any man but Lagg would have admitted it. Tully's whipping anger was like an injection of new strength. He held onto the reins. He started toward the gate, pulling the mare along behind him. She had been worked with the halter and obeyed him. He brought up his preciously preserved gun and yelled at the mustangers.

"Open that gate! Me and Blue are coming through!"

He could hardly see the men who stared at him but hoped they didn't realize it. His insides roiled with sickness. He feared that at any minute he would keel over. But he saw the poles of the gate drop down. He walked out, drawing his new horse behind him.

He got the red. For the first time Lagg looked uncertain. He glanced at the blue, his thick lips mumbling silently.

"That's my saddle, Gale," he said finally.

"Settle with you sometime, Sugar," Tully said, "and I *mean* settle." He started out on a clearly marked trail leading southward. He hoped it was the trail to Banca Basin.

He walked for what seemed an hour, constantly fearful of what might come upon him from behind, but the warning he had given Lagg, as to the wisdom of letting him return to Splinter Rock unmolested seemed to have taken root. He knew by then that the trail would lead him to the basin, and he kept going.

He had had enough of tramping the hot earth in his worn, high-heeled boots. The red was as easy to lead as a plow horse now, and his docility had a quieting influence on the blue. Tully kept talking to the two mustangs, his manner easy and reassuring. Once he felt himself safely away from the horse camp, he halted and tied the red to a shrub. Once more he climbed aboard the blue, but she only pitched a little and lined

269

out. When she had run out her remaining rebellion, Tully went back and got the red.

Twilight was dropping upon the brakes, and, although it actually grew no cooler, the disappearing sun made the going more pleasant. He began to cheer up. He had a homestead, and now he had a fine pair of mustangs, both hard won. It was the start of a horse ranch and a different outcome to what he had expected from his trip into the *malpais.* But he did not find it displeasing. . . .

When Ed Handel saw who it was that, an hour before daylight, had thumped so loudly on the livery barn door, he planted his fists on his hips and stood silently, staring.

"Matter, Ed?" Tully said. "Don't tell me you ain't had your breakfast."

"Where's my horse?" Ed demanded.

Tully laughed. "Ain't it odd? I left on a flea-bitten bag of bones and look what a vacation done to it. Changed color completely and she's sure full of ginger. In fact, she even changed sex."

"You swap off my horse?" Ed thundered.

Tully swung down tiredly. "Lost him, Ed. And had to leave your saddle. Sugar Lagg will find it, so you can have the one on the blue and all I owe you is for the horse."

"Back up," Ed said, "and try it again. I don't get you."

Tully explained more carefully, concluding: "I brought back the caps, but there's the dynamite and camp stuff. I'll square up with you."

"The devil with that," Ed said. "If you've learned a lesson, it's worth the price to me. And I'm glad you got back. Clyde Colby was in town looking for you. He was some exercised."

"Clyde was?" Tully asked, staring at Ed hard. "Say what he wanted?"

"To see you," Ed said. "Boy, how many women do you have to have in your string? Clyde said I was to tell you Louise Bentham's honing to see you again."

Tully said: "Help me switch saddles on the blue." He forgot Ed and everything else but Clyde and Louise and his own damned fool dawdling. Presently he was fogging it along the basin road, still leading the red behind him.

He reached Sam McNulty's at noon and by then had a subdued horse between his legs, the blue mare. Sam was outdoors.

Tully yelled: "Can I borrow Bess? These plugs are played out, and I've got to go to Two Hump!"

Sam shook his head. "Aurora's got Bess.

271

And why've you got to go to Two Hump?"

"Louise wants me! Lord A'mighty, Sam
. . . !"

"Now, take it easy," Sam drawled. "And
light down. You need rest. Clyde was here,
and I told him you went to town. When he
couldn't find you there, he come back. Told
me about it. Him and Daimler had a ruckus.
Daimler fired him, but Louise hired him
back. It brought on a fight between Daimler
and Louise. Clyde's scared. So's Louise.
And so are you, it looks like."

"I've got to go over there, Sam," Tully
insisted.

"Aurora went over," Sam said. "That's
where she is, and there's no sense in you
busting in. Go on in the house and rest
while I tend to these imps you brung home
with you."

Tully swung down. He was bone-tired,
dizzy, and beaten, but still sick with concern
about Louise. He let Sam off saddle and
turn the horses into the corral. He washed
at the water trough, feeling 100 years old.
He sat down in the house, and, before he
knew it, Sam was there putting food on the
table.

"Been peaceable," he reported while Tully
ate. "Vines is still holding on. Johnny Babbage and his boys ain't had any trouble with

Two Hump. They found plenty of water and the grazing's good. Two Hump's acting like it come down with blind staggers and can't see a thing. I don't like the looks of that."

Tully agreed. Two Hump would have given up the fight the way rattlesnakes would back off from a rabbit invading their den. Daimler and Lagg had been obliged to plot new strategy, that was all. When their next move came, it would be aggressive and final. Tully told Sam where he had been, and how little he had accomplished beyond recovering the red and acquiring the blue.

"But when you take the long view of it," he concluded, "that could have been the turning point of my life. Give them horses time, and they'll stock a horse ranch for me."

"If you live long enough," Sam agreed, "and there's no misfires. Let me give you some advice. You ought to spend some time on the improvements you've got to make to that claim to prove up on it. What about a house and barn, since you've already got the required water?"

Tully nodded, sobering. "Know it, Sam. I'm catching onto the fact that I'm too given to frittering. That come to me in the *malpais* when it looked like I was finished. I'm going to dig in and get that homestead going."

He didn't want to do it, but it was a matter of going to sleep in the chair, or of piling into a bunk. He chose the bunk and dropped off instantly in spite of the fact that the soddy was like a furnace. But worry disturbed his rest, concern for Louise and his wonder if she had confronted Daimler with her suspicions. If she had, it was hard to tell what Daimler would do. The whole scheme had hinged upon her remaining ignorant and trusting. Daimler would know who had turned her otherwise and he wouldn't like that a bit.

Tully awakened from a groggy half slumber to realize that a horse had come into the yard. He shoved up and by the time he stood sleepily in the doorway, Aurora had dismounted from Sam's old Bess. She looked intently at Tully.

"Well, it's nice to see you back. Louise is going to be wanting to know."

"I'll see she knows," Tully retorted. "Why'd she want to see me?"

"Do you have to ask?" Aurora inquired. Then she smiled again. "It's Daimler, no less. You go and find out for yourself."

"Does Daimler know she's onto him?" Tully thundered.

Aurora came on into the soddy, nodding. "He does. While pretending not to. He still has hopes of bringing her around to his viewpoint apparently. Tully, when do you want to meet Louise? We'll have to get word to her, and the only way I know to do it is to take it myself."

"What was Clyde's trouble with Daimler?" Tully asked.

"Daimler accused him of a double-cross. He fired Clyde, and Louise hired him back. Clyde is now Louise's private cook and houseboy. In high heels and spurs. He's good-looking, Tully."

"She can have him."

Aurora frowned. "That would mean his having her, too, you know."

"That's right," Tully reflected. "I reckon I'll meet her. Whenever and wherever she says."

The frown left Aurora's face.

Sam helped Tully doctor the saddle galls on Red's back. Afterward Tully saddled Blue and rode over to his homestead, leading the red. The camp was as he had left it, for no one from Two Hump would prowl with a heavily manned cow camp so near. When he rode onto his claim, a sense of ownership came up in him. Sam figured he had better get busy on the improvements required by law, and Sam was right.

It wasn't shiftlessness that had caused him to avoid thinking about that. For one thing he had been busy. For another, there was something final about a man's starting to build for himself. *Cut just one log and you're stuck for keeps,* he warned himself. The reasoning part of his mind was ready for that step, but something deep in his spirit still stirred in a rebellion against it. Yet he knew that he had to obey his head, take an axe, and start for the timber on the upper side of the claim.

He neck-looped the two mustangs on the grass. He was still worn out, and he went into the tent to sleep some more. When he came out of the tent, it was night. He wondered if anybody was still up at the cow camp, and wanted to talk with the basiners. It was only a short distance over there, and he decided to walk.

This took him past the artesian pond where he halted, wondering if Daimler's saddle was still safely hidden in its depths and what he had ought to do about it. He found a pole and began to fish around and soon had worked the saddle to the edge of the water. He hauled it onto the bank and hunkered beside it. He had a notion to turn it over to Clyde Colby, now that there had been an open break between the cow-puncher and his ramrod. If worse came to worse, Clyde could use it as he saw fit, giving him a lever against Daimler.

Tully was certain now that Clyde was a man to tie to. He was considering the advisability of Louise's firing Daimler, as she had once threatened, putting Clyde in his job. But Clyde himself had said that a large part of the crew followed Daimler, out of resentment of Louise's inheritance and in concern for their jobs. Yet that might not hold true if a respected member of the crew was promoted to Daimler's place. It was at least something to discuss with Louise, when he saw her. He tossed the saddle into the pond again and went on toward the cow camp.

Men still sat about the fire. Even before he came clear up, Johnny Babbage's cheery voice called: "Howdy, Gale! We been wondering if you'd been thrown in jail."

"How's business, Johnny?" Tully asked as he walked on in.

"It's come off so easy we're scared to death."

"That's the smart attitude," Tully agreed. He told them about Daimler and Lagg meeting in Valen's. He reported how Vines had sent for him, making an offer and finally divulging the whole plot against Two Hump.

"Vines is sure that Daimler will hit you with everything he's got. And that Lagg will rustle Two Hump before, during, or after that. They aim to buy Two Hump from Louise and pay her off with her own coin."

"Like they thirsted our steers half dead, then offered to take 'em off our hands," Johnny commented. "Give them two their way, and they'd get ahead in the world."

"We've got to be set for two things," Tully said. "A strike at your camp and a pass at the Two Hump herd."

"Why do we care about the Two Hump herd?"

Tully grinned. "On account of a girl who I've got to keep richer than sin. Even when I'd rather see her starving and my bed and board her only hope."

"So it's that way," Johnny said. "All right, Gale. We not only got to fight Two Hump, but we got to protect it, to boot."

X

Tully slept late the next morning, his weariness demanding that he rest. Rising refreshed, he explored his whiskery face with contemplative fingers. He was hungry, but even more than his breakfast he wanted to clean up. He dug a change of clothes from his war bag, got towel, soap, and razor, and headed for the pond.

He had planned to bathe, shave, and wash out his dirty clothes. He was bathing when the sound of fast travel came to him. He waded out of the pond and began toweling hurriedly. But he was only partly dressed when Nick Daimler rode up to him.

Daimler swung from the saddle to stare at Tully, who ignored him while he finished dressing. The ramrod was excited, pleased with himself, and, while he tried to keep it hidden, the excitement showed through. Tully thought about that, not liking the looks of it. Babbage's invasion of Bentham

279

Valley had set the schemers back on their tails. But Daimler had had time to recover and plan steps of his own. Whatever they were, they pleased him.

When Daimler spoke, he showed the brooding single-mindedness that had marked their other meetings. "The saddle, Gale," he said. "You don't seem to understand that I want it back."

Tully gave him a look of mock surprise. "I can understand your wanting it, mister. Was I in your boots, I would, too. But that's no sign you'll get it."

Daimler frowned. "I'll get it. *Now.*"

"Let's not have threats, Nick," Tully warned. "I told you what I'll do if you bother Louise."

"You told me what you'd try," Daimler contradicted. "But it happens I ain't talking about her. I know Clyde Colby done me dirt. It was him who told you that saddle's mine. It wouldn't upset me if something should happen to Clyde. It's his fault you latched onto that saddle. You could fish him out of the soup by giving it back."

Although he still managed to look relaxed, Tully had turned cold. He had been afraid of that. Daimler's threat to Louise had been mostly a bluff, since he needed her alive to realize his ambitions. But Clyde was another matter. Something could happen to him, and it wouldn't interfere with Daimler's plans a bit. Tully knew that Daimler had beaten him. The good the saddle could do him wasn't worth the risk to Clyde's life.

"You win, Daimler," Tully said. "You can have your fancy hull. It's out there in the pond. Just fish it out."

Daimler turned to stare at the water. "I'll be blamed," he breathed.

They both stiffened to listen. Another horse was coming, in the distance, from the direction of the cow camp.

Hoping to delay Daimler until it was too late to get the saddle, Tully said: "But you're playing the fool, Nick. You've got sense enough to see that the little greenhorn girl isn't fooled. You've taken steps that're mighty dangerous to you. Climb aboard that saddle and ride out of this country. Promise me that and I'll jump in and get it for you."

Daimler smiled. "You've still got the saddle, but I know where to get it. You'll leave it where it is till I do. Because I've got an alibi for the night Sam McNulty was shot. I've got men who'll swear Colby took my saddle that night and rode it some-wheres. Try to make something of it, Gale, and Clyde'll be in trouble . . . not me."

"So you've talked your 'punchers into lying for you," Tully reflected.

"My men are behind me." The assurance in Daimler was completely restored. "And nobody's trying to fool Louise Bentham any more. She'll sell and be glad to. Why do you care, Gale? She never done anything to deserve Two Hump. Her being Cass Bentham's heir was an accident. In fact, Cass was going to will that spread to us boys but he never got around to it. Figured he'd live forever, I guess."

"I don't believe that," Tully snapped.

"She don't deserve it," Daimler repeated vehemently. "Me and the boys have froze and roasted and worked ourselves half dead for Two Hump. We helped make Cass rich. We're the ones who should have got it, and not a chit of a filly."

"That's your bunkhouse harangue, anyhow," Tully responded. Vines had envied Cass Bentham and had planned that Daimler, and apparently the bulk of Two Hump's crew, felt resentment at Louise's good fortune and considered it to be at their expense. That was Daimler's hold on his men, and Tully was astute enough to realize the strength of that appeal.

"Louise and me have had it out," Daimler resumed. "She told me how you filled her with hot air about me meaning to fleece her.

But she knows now that I'm ready to pay the going price for the spread."

"After you've whittled down its assets," Tully retorted.

Daimler glanced at him sharply. "You're guessing wild. It ain't hard to see how you hope to cook my goose and take over Two Hump and the girl to boot."

The horseman had appeared from the direction of the cow camp, and Tully saw it was Johnny Babbage. Johnny appeared to recognize Daimler from the distance. He straightened, lifting the speed of his horse. His face was black as he rode in to them.

Staring at Two Hump's tall ramrod, he blazed: "You're sure smart, Daimler! I hand it to you for that!"

Daimler grinned at him. "Figure you were the only one in this country who knew how to play checkers, Johnny?"

"All right!" Johnny grated. "We moved and you moved, and now somebody's got to jump."

"You figure to jump your cows outta their pickle?" Daimler intoned. "It's a long leap, Johnny. They'll never make it. But don't let them come down on Two Hump grass when they miss."

"What is this?" Tully cut in, staring at Johnny who was deeply disturbed.

Johnny gave him a sour smile. "Some homesteaders moved in and took up three of the sections we've used getting back and forth to the government graze. There's a half dozen tough-looking customers, armed to the teeth and sticking together. The first thing they done was serve notice we can't trespass on 'em. Moved in behind and they've got our herd trapped out in the valley."

"No," Tully gasped.

"What's more," Johnny went on, "they say Two Hump's promised to help keep us from crossing their boundary lines trying to get back to your claim."

"What's more," Daimler mocked, "Two Hump'll see that you stay off its own land. Nice morning, huh, Gale? Seems to me you're the one who'd better saddle and ride."

"God damn you, Daimler," Johnny raged, "there's no water out there! We've got to get them critters in! We got to cross you or them fake nesters to do it!"

"Should have thought of that before you put 'em out there," Daimler snapped. He walked to his horse and swung up. He grinned at Babbage, then flickered his cool gaze to Tully. Without farewell he swung his horse and rode off.

"I heard," Tully told Johnny, "that Lagg's been hiring saddle tramps. This is one reason why."

Johnny's face was tight with anger. "They sure out-foxed us. Me, that is, anyway. Tully, how're we going to get our steers in to water, and what'll we do for grass after that? They've sure trimmed our wick. How does it tie in? If trouble between Two Hump and the basin was what Daimler wanted, he could have hit us any time. He had an excuse already."

"He expects to own Two Hump," Tully reflected. "He don't want it chopped up by squatters. The men he's hired will light out when he's done with 'em. But he's got to keep us from working farther into the valley, and that's how he done it. One thing's certain, it don't leave you any choice. You've got to get your herd out of there. They know it, and they're set for it, too."

Johnny muttered to himself, turned to his horse, and swung up. He rode off, swearing to himself.

Tully shaved, then went down to his camp, started a fire, and began to cook his breakfast. Daimler had appeared to be confident, and it was clear that he had a right to be. There had always been the danger of his hiring squatters to take up the remaining open land in Bentham Valley and hold it until the quarrel was settled. But his timing it so as to catch the basin herd in the valley without water was something no one had foreseen. It forced a showdown, compelling the basiners to make a bona-fide trespass on Two Hump property in order to extract their cattle.

Tully was eating when something drew his attention to the west. He glanced that way to see Sam's little bunch top the rise and crowd toward the break in the fence. Aurora followed, riding as easily as any man ever set a saddle. Tully grinned.

He had finished his meal and was scratching his head when Aurora rode up to the camp.

"What's the trouble?" she asked, studying his face.

"Just wondering," Tully said thoughtfully, "if these dishes would stand another meal or if I'd ought to bury them."

"If that's a hint," Aurora answered, "you can wash your own dishes. Or get you a wife."

"You don't consider it decent to wash a man's dishes unless you're married to him?" Tully inquired.

"Somebody else would like to wash yours," Aurora replied. "She'll meet you at noon, Tully. If you'll ride south along the ridge, you'll come to her. You'll recognize her by her snow-white skin, she's that scared."

"What of?" Tully asked quickly.

"That you'll ride off, one of these days, and leave her stranded."

"You sure crowd me, Missus Meade," Tully reflected.

Aurora smiled at him. "You crossed wills with me voluntarily, Tully Gale. Don't disappoint me by begging off."

"What do you mean by that?"

She looked toward the pond. "I see my steers have finished drinking. Good bye." She gigged old Bess and rode away, leaving him both suspicious and worried.

She took the cattle back over the hill, and he finished the camp chores. The prospect of seeing Louise again had been in his mind ever since Aurora agreed to arrange a meeting. Now it troubled him. He wished he could see what there was between them as simply as she did.

He took a look at the red stallion. Its back was nearly healed, but the horse needed more rest. He saddled the blue, rose to the saddle, and was repaid by a display of pitching. Tully found that the mare was putting less heart into this formality.

When he had her lined out, he turned along the Two Hump fence, following it through the thin timber of the ridge between Bentham Valley and the basin. The day was serene, its heat less oppressive in the heights, where there was even a gentle wind to riffle the pine. Unconsciously his mind noted trees that, felled and trimmed, would make logs for the walls of a house and barn. It would take a lot of them for he wanted a big house and an even bigger barn. But he would have plenty of time to build them, if he waited for red and blue horses to stock his range.

Half an hour's riding and he saw Louise coming toward him. She was on a good horse, and he was surprised at how well she sat the saddle. Moving along through the pines, she was small and appealing, and he hurried the blue. Then he received the impression that Aurora had exaggerated Louise's emotions. The girl regarded him with cool caution as they met.

Tully touched his hat, smiling. When she failed to respond, he said: "What's got into you?" He dismounted and walked toward her, but she disdained his help and came down lightly. He secured their horses, wondering what had turned her against him so unexpectedly.

Then, in a rushing breath, she said: "Tully, I'm going to sell Two Hump to Daimler. Don't you try to talk me out of it!"

He halted in his tracks with a sense of having been poked in the stomach. "Whoa," he breathed. "Say that again and plainer."

"You heard me," she returned. "I'm closing the deal today. I promised to tell you before I did, and now you're told."

"What happened?" Tully thundered. "What's eating you, anyhow?"

"I don't want the place. Daimler does. Therefore, we should make a deal."

Tully put his hands on her shoulders and nearly shook her. She met his eyes and he saw that she was serious about it.

"So he finally scared you into it," he muttered.

"He did not. I don't want Two Hump for private reasons. I have no will to fight for it. Who would, for something he doesn't even want? Show me something I do want, and I'll show you a fight."

"Aurora put you up to this," Tully came back.

"She helped straighten out my thinking," Louise admitted. "Since your pride's in our way, she says, it's up to me to go broke voluntarily. Therefore, Daimler and I see eye to eye at last."

"You told him so?"

"I promised to tell you first."

"By damn," Tully murmured. "Aurora really sold you on it, didn't she? Damn her hide, I'll fix her plenty."

"So you want to keep a barrier between us," Louise retorted.

Anger was churning in Tully. Louise had something in mind that was less ingenuous than she made it sound. It was more than trying to corner him and get a bit in his mouth. He pushed back his hat and stared at her.

"What're you after," he demanded, "besides a wedding ring?"

"It also happens," she admitted, "that, if I sell Two Hump to Daimler, peace will come back to this country. He's promised that. He says that, if I'll deal with him, he'll give a written guarantee to help the basin through its trouble. If I won't sell, he's going to clean the basiners out of the valley and keep them cleaned out and you know what that means."

"Why didn't you say so in the first place?" he asked, relieved that she was not as weak as she had appeared.

"Because you'd have tried to talk me out of it."

"Did Daimler tell you that you'll get what

he feels like paying you?"

"Two cents would be ample," Louise said. "The way I feel."

"Just listen to that!" he snorted. "Two Hump's worth two cents because you've found out troubles come with it. So you'll let the man take over and laugh up his sleeve. You'll make Cass Bentham turn over in his grave if you tuck your tail and run. I reckon the Two Hump boys are right in one respect. You don't deserve the ranch. You fell into it, and you can't handle it."

"But, Tully. . . ."

"You heard what I said."

Louise turned slowly and walked to her horse. She loosened the reins and swung up. She stared down at Tully and there was pained bewilderment in her eyes. Without a word she started the horse, pulling it around, going back the way she had come. Tully nearly called to stop her but couldn't bring himself to it.

He took time to ride to a headland that lay south of his claim and that would give him a sweeping look into Bentham Valley. He didn't like what he saw. Far to the south Louise's horse had come down out of the foothills with a small, forlorn figure in the saddle. To the northeast, and farther out, he could detect the dotted shapes that were the drought cattle from Banca Basin. Short of them, he could make out what he knew to be a wagon, used by Daimler's squatters to bring in camp equipment. The cattle out there were pinned down where they were, unless they were driven across squatter claims or Two Hump's own range. Thirst would make it mandatory for them to be brought to water soon. Perhaps Daimler meant to use that as a bargaining point, or maybe he had only seen a chance to discomfit his enemies. Studying the terrain below him, Tully began to wonder what chance there would be to swing the cattle around the new claims, across Two Hump's unguarded range, and on to the Sam McNulty's graze. The right kind of diversion to pin down interference might make that possible. His eyes began to glimmer.

Johnny Babbage was at the cow camp when Tully reached there. Johnny was sourfaced, depressed, and angry. "We've got it figured out, Gale," he reported. "We're going to tie kites to them steers and fly 'em out on the next good wind. You got any string?"

"Look," Tully said, "you feel like a good fracas?"

"Nothing I'd like better, right now," Johnny admitted. "But why should we

292

tangle?"

"After supper," Tully told him, "you take a few boys and go see them squatters. Beg, pray, and try to bribe 'em. The longer you keep it up the better. When that don't work, tie into 'em for a good rumpus. How many men are with the steers?"

"Two."

"Then give me a couple more," Tully said. "If you keep the squatters tied up long enough, maybe I can bend the herd around their claims and onto Sam's place."

Johnny stared. "Run 'em across Two Hump?"

"Who else has got real estate in that neighborhood?"

"We'll do it," Johnny breathed. "If it works, all we've got to worry about is a new supply of grass."

"You've still got fair grass on your own spreads," Tully reminded him. "What you're short of there is mainly water."

"It ain't going to rain, Gale. We'll still be short."

"Maybe the creek'll come up," Tully said vaguely. He wasn't going to say anything about the *malpais* reservoir as yet. He'd talked big to Ed Handel about what he meant to do about it, and had ridden back from the *malpais* with his ears knocked down. Moreover, if he revealed that information with the situation as tight as it had become, Johnny would fog into the badlands himself, leading an army of furious men. "Send me a couple of boys when you're ready to go visit the squatters," he concluded.

He went back to his own camp, started a fire under the coffee pot, and waited for it to heat. He knew that the sally he had proposed for the night might itself start a bloodletting. But the drought herd had to be sprung out of its trap, and that was the only way he knew to do it.

The day was growing hot, and it was still early afternoon. He had his coffee, with a couple of cigarettes. He couldn't keep his mind away from Louise and the fact that he had turned her against him forever. He had figured that best all along.

XI

He had finished his supper and was sitting disconsolately in a star-blazed night when two riders came in from the cow camp. They both showed high spirits.

"Throw on your saddle, Gale!" one of them called. "We're all set."

He recognized them as George Taft and Slim Trawn. Taft was stocky, bearded, with a button on his lip. But Trawn had an easy manner and ready tongue.

"Johnny's allowed us an hour to get out to the herd," Trawn reported. "By that time he'll be at the squatter camp with some of the boys. They guarantee to keep the squatters interested for another hour. You reckon that'll give us enough time?"

"Ought to," Tully reflected. "All we got is a little hazing chore."

"How do you figure to cut it?" Trawn asked.

Tully was saddling the blue. He didn't

295

reply until they were riding south, then he briefly told them of the plan he had developed. "We'll swing the herd south toward Two Hump headquarters. They'd expect us to use the other side of the squatter claims because it's wilder. Down south we can lose ourselves in the foothills quicker, then kite in toward Sam's. If Johnny keeps the squatters from catching on, there won't be much to it. If he can't, there'll be basin steers all over Bentham Valley. The skunks'll stampede them if they get wise."

"Sounds good," Trawn said. "Except for one thing. If the squatters don't have a man watching the herd, Two Hump has."

"Naturally," Tully acknowledged.

They clung to the ends of the small spurs thrusting into Bentham Valley along the west boundary. There was more moonlight than Tully would have liked, although that might help as well as hamper them. A vast quiet hung over the plain below, so that the sound of their own travel was loud. Tully meant to gain as much distance from the squatter camp as the time Johnny had allotted would permit. Well south of the claim he swung his horse outward, the others turning with him.

They were quiet, each man searching the night for sounds or vague sights that would

296

tell them that they were being watched. Tully felt sure that they were, but little could be done about it. Yet there was nothing to disturb the deep serenity, so far. They began to swing back toward the drought herd and presently could see it shaping itself in the moonlit forward terrain.

"Might draw a pot shot," Trawn reflected. "The boys're apt to take us for Two Humpers."

Yet they drew near the lower end of the herd without seeing anyone. The riders who had been caught with it in Daimler's surprise blockade had chanced to be at other positions or were not riding circle. The newcomers put their horses to the right, quietly moving along the eastern edge of the herd. Then two riders appeared ahead, and a voice called a sharp challenge.

"Gale and some friends!" Tully yelled at them.

"If you brung grub, come ahead," a gruff voice responded.

"You'll have to earn your supper," Tully said as the two groups joined. "We're going to grease this herd and skid it over to the foothills real fast. Sign of anybody keeping tabs on you?"

"If we'd seen anybody, we'd've blowed a hole in the cuss," the cowpuncher returned.

"Pegging us down in the middle of nowhere without any grub. Boys, if you come to help move this herd in, let's get at it."

Tully told them off, assigning two men to the point, two to the flank, and saving the dusty drag for himself. He gave the men their final instructions: "We'll maintain peace and quiet as long as they let us. If trouble shows, we'll goose the steers as fast as they'll travel and still hold together. The idea is to reach the foothills as soon as possible, then swing north to Sam's. Let's drag it."

They all helped get the partly bedded herd to its feet and moving, swinging their horses back and forth, popping out with the ends of their catch ropes. By the time the movement was started, Tully felt pretty certain that Johnny had had time to get himself set at the squatter camp.

The big drought cut began to move, fanned back from a point and hazed gently. There was nothing to mark the boundary lines, but presently Tully felt certain they had passed off the Public Domain and entered Two Hump graze. Tension began to build in him. After having given warning, Two Hump would have grounds for calling this a flagrant trespass and contesting the crossing.

Fifteen minutes passed with nothing disturbing the even tenor of the night beyond the scuffing of massed hoofs and the cowpunchers' occasional soft voices. Tully figured they had drifted two miles south of the squatter claims. The danger lay in look-outs having been posted against such an attempt.

More time slipped by, and it seemed that the distance to the base of the western hills had increased by a dozen miles. Yet they had less than four miles to cover altogether, which at this pace should take no more than an hour. That could be cut down plenty if the herd was lifted to full speed. His eyes kept searching the benighted plain to the north.

He sensed danger before he knew what faculty had detected it. Suddenly he pulled down his horse and kept still for a moment. He could see very little in the northward night. He could hear nothing above the low racket of the moving cattle. But he swung the blue to the right, moving up the flank of the herd.

Presently he fell in beside Slim Trawn and said: "You boys can handle it from here on. I'm going to outride you. If I scare up trouble, I'll make a racket. That'll be your orders to roll their tails into the hills." He reined over and headed north.

When he was safely away from the herd, he lifted the blue to top speed, pointing toward the darker reaches along the base of the foothills. Presently he rose in the stirrups, his gaze straining forward. He saw them then, two riders poking along quietly, keeping themselves covered in the dark background of the hills. Tully cut his horse on a slant, driving toward them at a hard pound.

When the other horses lined out, Tully was sure they were ridden by enemies. He pulled his gun and fired twice into the air to warn the men with the herd. Still out of pistol range, the oncomers kept riding. He sent a shot singing over their heads for the moral effect. It only peeled the others apart, causing them to swing over farther to the hills. They kept driving on toward the fleeing herd, trying to cut around him.

He didn't want a gunfight and doubted that Two Hump would want that at this point. They were trying to get close enough to the herd to scatter it. Hauling his horse around, he could make out the vague outlines of the herd. At this distance, it seemed scarcely to crawl but he knew that the boys were pushing it hard. He spoke to the blue, digging in his heels, streaking toward the oncoming riders.

They were shooting now, toward the herd, screaming like banshees, wanting racket. Still wide of them, Tully pulled abreast, then a little ahead. He began to fire across their line of travel, forcing them to slow down. One of them snapped a shot at him, but it went high and harmless. He cut in upon their line of progress, again and again, sending a bullet across it, not knowing when they were going to start playing for keeps.

The drought herd had been lifted to a surging speed and was now thundering headlong for the foothills. He angled his horse harder upon the other riders, making them turn out. The daring of his course shunted the others off. His gamble that they were not yet ready for bloodshed paid off. They kept shooting and yelling but it was meant for the herd. The cattle thundered on, and now a rider was streaking this way from the herd, shooting as he came. The hecklers whipped about then, breaking off. They went back the way they had come, and at the same hard pound.

"Them two were just look-outs," Tully told Trawn presently. "We're too far away for them to hear at the squatter camp. But when them two get in with the news, Johnny won't be able to keep the others pinned down. You boys can make out now. I'm heading north." He wheeled his horse and started riding.

The wiry little blue gradually closed the gap between him and the fleeing riders ahead. If they thought it was vengeance in pursuit of them, they meant to give it a wide berth. They kept crowding their horses. But Tully realized they had turned back only to get help, hoping yet to raise hob with the trespassing cattle.

Then one of the forward riders emptied his gun into the air, pulling Tully's nerves tight. They were close enough now that it would serve as a warning to the squatter camp. Whatever had started there would be broken off summarily. His mouth went dry. He slacked the blue, knowing the futility of going on.

It seemed only minutes until, in what was now a fair quiet, he heard the drumming of bunched hoofs. They were coming out from the squatter camp. He thought a moment, then swung his horse. He struck out on a hard, driving line for the spur of the nearest hills. He could see nothing now of the thundering herd, which apparently had gained the hills. Everything, thereafter, depended on its herders' ability to swing it north again through the ravines, letting it slow as it climbed and bringing it to a full stop on Sam's ground. Two Hump would have to break off if that was accomplished.

The oncoming riders racketed past him as he cut into the ravine. Tully picked his way up a long draw and over the top. Thereafter, he clung to a ridge, working to the southwest. Presently he halted, keening the night with a close interest. He could hear nothing yet of the steers but had come to a place where he figured he would be able to intercept them. The quiet seemed to indicate that they had been allowed to slow in the rough going and were coming on in good order. But he had to ride on for nearly a half mile before he was sure of that. Finally he sat his horse, grinning, watching a long file of cattle moving doggedly up the draw below him. He let it pass, then dropped down into the drag behind it.

Slim Trawn yelled: "It was sure fast while it lasted! And I thought it was going to last forever!"

"Big bunch of Two Humpers on your back trail!" Tully called back. "If they got close enough to see where you come in, they'll be along! Let's you and me wait here while the boys go on with the steers! If Two Hump comes along, we'll make them bring tickets!"

They sat their horses in the bottom of the draw. Presently the sound of moving cattle was lost above them. Yet at the end of a half hour nothing disturbing had appeared below. The oppressors had not cared to come into the hills in pursuit. *But what did we gain?* Tully asked himself. *Out there we had grass and no water. Now we got water, and no grass.*

The liberated herd was milled to a stop on Sam's range. Johnny Babbage and his men rode in, all of them upright on their horses and looking sound. Johnny grinned sourly because he, too, realized that this victory, although essential, did little to solve their problem.

"They were too suspicious of us," Johnny reported. "And when some ginzo shot off his gun, they fogged for their horses. They had no mood for a dog fight. But it worked and we got our steers, and where do we go from here?"

"You can use my grass as long as it lasts," Tully said. "That'll take care of you for a few days. Meanwhile, I got an angle I aim to look into that might help some, too."

Johnny stared at him. "Everybody ain't that generous with his grass, Gale."

"More'll grow by the time I need it."

The guard on the herd had been doubled.

The rest returned to the cow camp and sat about, having coffee, drawing what comfort they could from their escape from Daimler's trap. But they were tense and worried men, with their entire future in the balance. In this touchy mood, a man's sneeze might start trouble. Tully was about to leave for his own camp when a cowpuncher spoke up sharply.

"On your feet, boys. We're all accounted for, and somebody's coming from down the valley."

It grew evident that the oncoming party, several fast-moving horses, was not headed for the herd. Every man in the cow camp was on his feet and staring sullenly when Nick Daimler rode in at the head of a half dozen hard-eyed men.

Daimler pulled up at the edge of the firelight and let his gaze travel slowly until it found Babbage.

"Johnny," he snapped, "you've finally breached Two Hump range. So I'm warning you to take your stinky, diseased herd out of here. I won't risk having that happen again."

"The herd's on McNulty's land, Daimler," Babbage answered. "And it ain't diseased. It ain't even breechy. We drove it across your range and you know why."

"He's got more on his mind, boys," Tully drawled. "What else have you got to say, Nick?"

"That I'm giving Johnny forty-eight hours to get this herd out of here."

"See?" Tully asked the others. "He calls it diseased, and he'll stand on that to justify them running it off."

"If it's around in another forty-eight hours," Daimler said slowly, "it'll sure get run."

"You know it'll be here, Daimler," Tully shot back. "So you're only building up to your big play."

Daimler's gaze slapped him. "Who cut you a piece of it, Gale? I'm giving Johnny Babbage his warning. It stands." The man still seemed confident that he was top dog. He moved out, slack in the saddle, his men swinging their horses to follow.

Babbage stared at Tully. "He sounded like he meant it."

"He did."

Tully rode over to his own camp, unsaddled the blue, watered and neck-looped it. His spirits were as low as they had ever been in his life, with Louise angry, the basiners denied their vital grass, and Daimler so self-confident he could hardly hold it. Forty-eight hours. Tully doubted that it would give him time to do any good in the *malpais*. But the water in the *malpais* was the only hope now, and he had to see Ed about it once more.

He turned in, still beat out from the hard pace of recent days. He didn't know how long he had been asleep when a low voice roused him.

"Gale!"

Tully sat upright in bed, his heart slamming as he recognized the voice of Clyde Colby. He shoved out of bed and moved to the tent flaps unclad, worry running through him.

"Trouble, Clyde?" he asked tightly.

"What would you call it?" Clyde drawled. "But right now I figure I know something you should. Lagg sent a man over to see Daimler today. Our cook . . . he's a friend of mine Daimler don't suspect . . . heard 'em talk. Lagg wants Nick to meet him in town tomorrow night for a conflab."

"Then I'm going to town tomorrow for certain," Tully reflected.

"Figured so," Clyde said. "Daimler's talking up a strike at the cow camp. He's got the boys hot on it. I can't figure out how Lagg comes in, though."

"I can," Tully said. "Louise hasn't made a deal with Daimler, has she?"

Clyde's laugh was short and sour. "Says she aims to build the biggest, toughest cattle outfit this country ever seen. You should hear her talking, Gale, save for one thing. She says she loathes you. That's the word she used. It's a dandy, ain't it? She loathes and is going to show you."

"That's music to my ears," Tully grunted. "Thanks, fellow."

But the cowpuncher had already turned and was fading into the night.

Tully crawled back into bed. He had hoped his rebuke might cure Louise of her itch to get rid of Two Hump. But he hadn't wanted it cured to a point where she had nothing for him but loathing.

He rose early, had his breakfast, and saddled the blue. "Don't look so jealous, Red," he told the stallion. "Your sores are about well. If I come back in one piece, you can get back in business." He had a lot of sympathy for Red, caught between two worlds, rejected by his own kind and ignored by the man who had mastered him.

It was a hot, clear morning. Tully reached Sam McNulty's before Aurora had ridden out on her ranch chores, and he turned down an invitation for a second breakfast. He told Sam of recent events, concluding: "I aim to see if Ed Handel's found a way to get Lagg's dam opened by the law. If not, it's got to be opened anyhow."

"How'd you make out with Louise yesterday?" Aurora inquired innocently.

"She tried to blackmail me, the way you put her up to."

Aurora smiled brazenly. "Did it work?"

"Like a firecracker," Tully told her. "It went off in her pretty face. Anything you want me to bring you from town, Missus Meade?"

She shook her head. "But get yourself a set of brains, if you see any."

Tully took his time on the ride to Splinter Rock, for the meeting between Lagg and Daimler wasn't to be held until evening. He reached town in mid-afternoon and went at once to the livery stable.

Ed listened with interest to a report of recent developments and pricked up his ears at the meeting scheduled between Daimler and Lagg. "You'll play hob eavesdropping on 'em, though," he commented. "You let me handle that. I know men who could sashay into Valen's and get close enough to hear things. And you'd best not show yourself around town. That'd tip 'em off."

"What can I do?" Tully asked.

Ed grinned. "You could go to the Paine House. Or, if you had sense, you could turn in on my bunk and get some rest."

Tully glanced at him sharply. Ed's mind was not smutty and a remark like that didn't fit. Tully was on the point of demanding an explanation but thought better of it. Instead, he said: "Got anything new on Lagg's dam?"

Ed shook his head. "Nothing short of lawing will fix that permanent. But there's a temporary way, and a better one than the notion you keep getting of trying to blow it out. Pin something real crooked on Sugar, and he'll be glad to blow it out himself."

"Like catching him rustling?"

"That ought to do it," Ed said.

Tully helped him put up the horse. With people coming and going, he knew he hadn't ought to hang around in plain sight. He went into the tack room finally, and stretched out on Ed's bunk. He wasn't sleepy and knew the hours ahead would drag. But when he woke up, it was pitch dark.

All he could hear in the barn was the stomping of a horse somewhere. He lay for a while wondering why Ed had it in for Maggie. He wanted to see her again, and would have time, for Ed wouldn't have anything to report on Lagg and Daimler before morning. He rose, yawning and stretching, then stepped out into the barn.

Ed had hung up his lantern, and the doors were still open, but the stableman wasn't around. Tully took a look along the street. The town was still active, but he judged that it was getting late. He went through the back of the barn, not wanting to show himself but set on checking in at the Paine House for the rest of the night.

The lobby of the hotel was deserted when he entered, and Maggie wasn't in evidence. He started to lift the hand bell, then put it down. Turning to the stairs, he climbed them boldly. Her door at the end of the hallway was closed, but light showed beneath it. He rapped.

Surprise mounted on Maggie's face when she opened the door. Then she gave him a quick smile. "Tully Gale, and he needs a bath and shave again."

"Don't bother tonight," he told her. "Just give me a room. I'll know by which one I get if you're still mad at me."

She glanced at him sharply. "I wasn't angry, Tully. Disappointed is more the word. I'm not as strait-laced as most women let on to be. But all women want to be respected until they've given reason to be regarded otherwise."

"Then I get the same room?"

She shook her head. "Too late again. Nick

Daimler's used that room for years, starting back in my husband's day. And Nick got here first tonight. Come on in, Tully. I'm glad to see you again."

He stepped into the room and watched her close the door. A lamp burned low on a marble-topped table, and he saw that she had been sewing. He caught her making a quick search of his face as if seeking signs of irritation because of Daimler's priority. Realizing she had been caught at it, she made a quick smile.

"How are you getting along with Louise?" she asked.

The question surprised him. "We're on the outs. How come you wondered?"

"Nick says you're ambitious to marry her and Two Hump."

"That mouthy son," Tully snapped. Yet something drew his mind away from his crowding antipathy toward Daimler, the fact that he sensed jealousy in Maggie about Louise.

"I don't blame you," she commented. "She's a lovely girl."

"You don't have to take a back seat to her or any other woman," he retorted.

"Thank you. But you don't mean it."

Yet a smile had broken the passing severity of her mouth, and he saw her breasts lift in a deep breath. He remembered the night she had told him of a beautiful sister who had made her seem the ugly duckling of the family and of her conviction that she was plain and would always be. It dawned on him, then, that this was a canker in her heart, mind, and soul, a nagging distrust of her appeal to men.

"I've wanted you," he said bluntly, "from the moment I laid eyes on you."

Again that lift of full, firm breasts, the parting lips and preoccupied smile.

"More than you've wanted her, Tully?"

"I'm here, and for no other reason than to see you."

He watched her savor that and draw from it a feeling of triumph over the rich and appealing girl in Bentham Valley. He knew then that he had the key to Maggie, and the surging, aggressive urge rose up in him to use it. Men were her constant need, not because of body longing but because she needed a steady reassurance of her power to attract them, and he saw rising in her a mental passion to match that flaming through his own flesh.

"Say it again," she breathed.

"I've never wanted anything more in my life."

He found himself being drawn into the

awesome hypnotism enfolding her. He watched a weird, subtle satisfaction come and go in her face and eyes, the two of them still standing apart and only regarding each other. He was beyond his depth but powerless not to play her game with her, and he waited to see if her mind's arousal would translate into the physical. But she only stood there, watching and gratified and passive.

"In spite of the gossip," she whispered.

"What gossip?"

"You must have heard it. The way you've acted shows it."

"Daimler?" he asked. "Call that jealousy."

"Not Daimler. The gossip, as far as I know, is all about Mark Paine. The drunkard. Haven't you heard what they say about that? That he drank himself to death because of me?"

"I've heard no such thing!" Tully rapped. "Why would he?"

"I didn't say he did. They say it."

"Well, it's got nothing to do with now."

But he sensed that she had already passed on through what he sought, the rise to delight, the fall. She seemed, also, to have gained some sort of reassurance from his denials. That left him in an awkward corner, and suddenly he was anxious to make it plain that he was speaking only of this night and what he wanted it to be. He found it impossible to crowd her, for it was obvious that she had already gained what she needed. He knew then that no man had ever possessed her actually, that no man ever would. It was over with her as soon as she had gained evidence of her power. Anger rowelled him, and suddenly he was determined to take away from her what she had realized from him.

"If Paine dug his grave with a bottle," he said, "it was because he couldn't get to you."

"What do you mean?"

"It's only your head that wants a man."

She studied him closely, then said: "That's true of most women. What's wrong with it?"

"With a real one it eventually reaches the body."

Her shoulders lifted, her head came back, and he watched color slowly stain her cheeks. "So, after all, I'm not all there."

"I wouldn't know. Outside, yes. Inside . . . maybe Mark Paine knew, I don't."

"Are you trying to sulk me into sleeping with you?"

As swiftly as they had been drawn to each other, they were furious. He knew that he had stung her more intensely than he had gratified her, while her taunt had too much truth in it to be shrugged off.

"Hell, no," he snapped. "You asked a question. I answered it. And now, if you'll give me a room, I'll take my aching back to bed."

"You can go to the Commercial House!" she cried. "I don't even want you in my hotel!"

He reached the door before she stopped him. He heard the swift, soft fall of her slippered feet, then her hand laid itself on his arm.

"I'm sorry, Tully," she said quietly. "But I didn't think I'd given you reason to tie into me, like that. I wasn't standing you off, was I?"

He turned. Again her eyes were lambent, her lips parted, because again she was exerting her appeal upon him. He had so shrewdly sought this response that for an instant he was disturbed by it rather than lifted. When he kept his hand on the doorknob, she caught his free hand.

"Come on."

She blew out the lamp as they passed it, going to the inner doorway.

He knew as soon as it was over that he was going to make some excuse and leave, that he did not want to spend the night as he had so long yearned to do. He had all

316

but forced his way into a world that was strange and frightening to him, a world of unhealthy desire and of sordid satisfaction. He knew now that all along he had been the object of a twisted woman, one whose natural impulses had been channeled into self-regard and self-eroticism. Even in his abandon to the delights of her person, he had been aware that her own gratification came from triumph, not only over him but over the woman she believed she had defeated in that victory. It had loosened her tongue, so that over and over again she had whispered: "Now what do you think? Am I all woman? Could she be any better?"

He lay on his side, against the wall, her hair touching his face. He searched his mind for some way to extricate himself without too much embarrassment to them both. He was more than physically spent for his mind was wholly deflated, his vanity with it, in his realization that he had served her only as a mirror for herself. But she was not done with him for, as if she sensed his sudden weariness, her hands still clasped his sides.

He raised onto an elbow and thought she had misunderstood his intentions when she pressed quickly to him, tugging him down. Then he caught her barely audible whisper: "Oh, God. . . ."

317

He heard the other sound finally, that of weight on the gallery porch. Somebody came up to the screen door of this room and tried it quietly. When the door did not give, a whisper came into the room.

"Maggie?"

In a slow, unbreathing way she pulled the cover up over Tully's head. He lay there in flaming embarrassment, which rapidly gave way to discernment and a heedless fury. In spite of her denial, the man beyond the screen was accustomed to visit this room, and, without seeing him, he knew that the man was Daimler.

Maggie, trapped, did not answer the man and Tully could feel the slamming beat of her heart.

"Maggie," Daimler called again, lifting his voice slightly.

It seemed an hour to Tully before he heard the man go away. Fearing that he would speak, Maggie clasped a hand over his mouth. Suddenly her unclad flesh was abhorrent, and he moved over her and to the floor. By then there was no one outside the screen door, and he dressed hastily. Maggie lay, unmoving and quiet. Ready to leave, he bent down to her.

"That why Mark hit the bottle?" he whispered. A man's voice spun him around.

"I figured it would be you, Gale," said Nick Daimler. "Sooner or later."

I figured it would be you, Gale," said
Nick Daimler. "Sooner or later."

XII

Tully heard the latch give as Daimler
wrenched open the screen. Maggie emitted
a protesting cry when he came on through.
But nothing she could say or do could
change the look of things and, aware of that,
she resorted to anger.

"You get out of here, Nick Daimler!"

The man laughed. "When I've thrown
Gale out, maybe. That's the way I take a
thing like this. I don't hit the bottle, the way
Mark did. Gale, it's kind of funny we should
have our showdown over her."

"You've got no right!" Maggie cried.

"No more than Mark had?" Daimler
taunted. "Gale, she two-timed him with me,
and I knew it was in the cards she'd two-
time me with somebody else. There ain't
any satisfying her. She don't want a man.
She wants men . . . men . . . men . . . a
string of 'em that never ends. It ain't that
she's a bitch. She's a cannibal."

320

"Daimler, shut up," Tully rapped.

"So you're still fooled by the way she strings you along till she's ready to hang your scalp on her belt. Gale, I'll do you the favor of breaking your neck before she breaks your heart. She would. Sure as hell there'd be a man along who'd beat your time. Turnin' you wild . . . into a drunk like Mark . . . or a crook like me."

Unabashed by the bareness of her body, Maggie got out of bed. She said: "All right, I'm a slut. But don't make a scene, Nick . . . not here." She began to dress.

Tully felt pity for her suddenly. Maybe she couldn't help being the way she was. He had seen enough of life to know that people got hurt in ways that changed not only their subsequent life but their very natures. In honesty he had to admit that she had sought to keep this hour from coming upon them, that he had forced it more than she had coaxed it along. He had no kick, and now he had Daimler to handle.

He said: "She's right, Nick. This is no place to settle it."

"It's the place," Daimler retorted. "And time she got what's coming to her, instead of being protected the way Mark done. I got a lot of sympathy for that man. We was friends till she begun to show me little

321

come-ons that made me lose my head. Time she was exposed to the whole damned town, instead of keeping it guessin'."

Daimler swung, driving at Tully, using the bitter run of his words to gain surprise. Tully halfway expected it but still was not fully prepared. Daimler didn't come in fighting. Instead, he caught Tully in a powerful grasp and lifted him bodily across his shoulder. He swung in the same movement, driving Tully's head against the wall, dazing him. Reluctance to turn Maggie's place into an uproar had been Tully's undoing.

He went limp as his head slammed the boards, but it didn't save him. His brain seemed to explode in a flash of white light. Daimler lunged to the doorway, went through, and onto the gallery, Tully growing dimly aware of his intentions of hurling him off into empty space. The danger made its impact, clearing away the fog, and, reaching out, Tully managed to catch hold of the door jamb. He wrenched himself, kicking savagely, and managed to peel loose and drop to the floor.

Scrambling up, he saw that he had knocked Daimler back against the balcony railing. He drove at the man, determined to feed him his own medicine, but Daimler danced aside. Still woozy, Tully managed narrowly to keep from pitching himself into space. He skidded around, and they came at each other, each driving haymakers with both fists. Impetus behind him, he managed to nail Daimler against the wall. But Daimler brought up a foot, kicking him hard in the belly, lifting him off his feet. Sliding along the wall, Daimler held back as again Tully staggered to his feet.

Once more they came together with hammering fists. Tully lost consciousness of everything but his flaming desire to destroy the man. It was more than Daimler's catching him like a raccoon in a hen coop. There was Louise and Two Hump, the suffering cattle, the worried basin ranchers. Again he drove the man into the wall and held him there for seconds by the sheer impact of his sledging fists.

Abruptly Daimler drove stiffened fingers at Tully's eyes. Jerking his head, Tully escaped it, but his arching back presented his belly as an exposed target that the man hit hard. Nausea boiled up in Tully, together with the realization that he had a smarter, dirtier fight on his hands than he had had with Sugar Lagg. Daimler was not easy to fool, was faster than the mustanger.

Somewhere beyond Maggie's rooms fists were thumping on the door. A man bawled:

"What the hell's going on in there? You all right, Missus Paine?" Tully heard her near scream tell them to go away. Once he caught sight of her in the obscurity of the interior, dressed now, watching the fight in terror, whether for Daimler, for him, or for her own destroyed reputation. If Daimler wanted revenge against her, too, in this fight, he was getting it.

Sparring until his stomach quit retching, Tully managed to hold the man away. He opened an abrupt barrage that drove them down past the door of the second room. But Daimler was too canny to be caught by the railing that ran at right angles at the end of the balcony and stood fast, hammering Tully to a standstill. Then he tried another lashing drive with his foot.

Tully was onto that trick by then. Using both hands at lightning speed, he caught Daimler's foot and ankle and gave a sharp twist to the foot. It threw Daimler hard on his side. Tully was on him instantly, sailing and coming down flat. Astride the man, he seized his hair and began slamming his head against the gallery floor. Daimler let out a long, cursing groan. He rolled onto his belly, reared up, lifting Tully with his back.

Tully let go, but Daimler had him by the legs. Hanging, Tully felt himself being spun, aware that Daimler again meant to hurl him off the balcony. He managed to catch the railing with his hands and jerk loose, coming down hard again. Gasping as he sucked air, Daimler hauled around, off balance but reaching back. On his back now, Tully kicked out with both legs. His boots hit Daimler fully in the belly, blasting an anguished — "Ugh!" — from the man.

Daimler flailed back against the wall, slid down to a sitting position. Tully tried to get up but, dizzy from the spinning, flattened on his belly. Daimler's lashing boot heel caught him in the face, seeming to macerate the nose. Blood gushed. Afterward, neither could do more than stare at the other, both sobbing as they drew breath.

By then shouting within the hotel revealed that the whole place had been aroused. But Maggie kept them locked out. As he scrambled up with Daimler, Tully saw her in the door to her bedroom, her hand to her mouth. Daimler caught him in that second's distraction, belting him about, driving him toward the gallery rail again and the long drop to the yard. Tully put up both hands, trying to shove Daimler back. For the first time expression showed on Daimler's sweating, bloody face — a glint of triumph.

Tully grabbed him, jerking to regain balance and swing away from the dangerous rail. Daimler struck again, and now Tully went back but he drew the man with him. He felt his weight break over the rail, then they fell, free and together. Tully had the instinct to roll himself limply, the way he would take a fall from a horse. Then something slammed violently against him, and he lay still, sinking into the deepest blackness of his life. . . .

When he opened his eyes, he realized he had been carried to the back porch of the hotel. He was drenched with water, which somebody had sloshed over his head and face. The kitchen lamp had been lighted, and he could see half-dressed men standing about. They were hotel guests, roused by the fight, and guilt flamed in Tully as he climbed groggily to his feet. His nose had quit bleeding but felt like pulp, and he hurt all over his body.

"Better take it easy," a man warned. "You had a mean spill. Me, I got to the side yard in time to see it. You hit rollin' or you'd have got a busted neck."

"Where's Daimler?" Tully gasped.

"He lit his shuck. That lucky son-of-a-bitch made a full turn and come down on his feet with bent knees. Jumped out of a lot of upstairs windows, I reckon. Only had to dust hisself off."

Tully looked around. Maggie wasn't in evidence. He found his gun where it had spilled into the yard and wondered if he should go up to her room for his hat. Something rose in him that made him prefer to buy a new one. He went into the yard, rounded the hotel, and looked up at the balcony for a moment. Her room was dark.

Five minutes later he knocked on the door of Ed Handel's tack room. Presently the old hostler ambled out and the scowl left his face when he saw the marks on Tully.

He lifted broken fingernails to scratch the whiskery line of his jaw. "So you went and got yourself a ruckus, after all."

"One just come along," Tully said vaguely. "You learn anything at Valen's?"

"You learned something at the Paine House," Ed reflected, "and from Nick Daimler himself. Boy, I'm glad you found out without me having to tell you. I liked Mark Paine. He didn't have much gumption, but he was all right. Don't look at me like that. I seen Daimler a while ago. He was worse-looking than you, and that's what told me all about it. It was an open secret that he was the cause of Mark's drinking, and no secret you two would lock horns over the same woman. She's a man-eater, that 'un."

"If you're ready to get down to business," Tully said angrily, "what did you learn about their plans?"

"Nothing," Ed said. "This time they talked where nobody could hear them. But I seen something a while ago that speaks for itself. Daimler rode out with Lagg and his bronco twisters. Lagg was waiting for him at the town corral."

"They've decided on sudden action," Tully reflected. "Daimler had aimed to stay all night in town. He must have come to the hotel to tell her he'd changed his mind. Ed, Daimler gave Johnny Babbage forty-eight hours to get out of that country with the drought herd. The time is up tonight. If Daimler and Lagg are in a sweat, it's about that. How long have they been gone?"

"They hit the basin trail," Ed agreed somberly. "And only a few minutes before you come along."

"Daimler's going to attack the cow camp," Tully decided. "Lagg'll do his rustling while Two Hump's crew is tied up with that."

"Wait a minute," Ed cut in. "Somebody's coming to town, and coming fast."

A horse had whipped in from the basin

road. It pulled down before the livery on balled hoofs. A man called: "Ed, you seen that man, Gale?"

"Varmint's right here," Ed said. "But beat up too bad to recognize."

The newcomer was Matt Beer, Tully saw, from the cow camp in Bentham Valley. Belatedly recognizing the battered Tully, Beer rapped: "Gale, I got to talk to you."

"Ed knows all about it," Tully said. "What's up now?"

Beer swung down from his horse, which was lathered from the long hard ride. "I seen Colby," he reported. "He's learned more since he seen you at your camp. Daimler's put the heat on that Bentham girl again. She can sell to him or be responsible for what's coming. He told her what's coming, and she won't want to be responsible for it. Clyde's scared she'll sell, and you're the only one who might talk her out of it. You better get out there, Gale, if you figure to stop her. Daimler gave her less time than he gave us to make up her mind."

Tully groaned. To Ed he said: "You get hold of the sheriff and tell him, Ed. But we don't want him poking around out there too early. Tell him to stand by for word I'll send as soon as I'm sure Lagg's rustled. That's the best hope of nailing them two.

Now, let's try and cinch a saddle on my blue mare."

Matt Beer swapped horses and, fifteen minutes later, was thundering out the basin road with Tully. The man was tired, and this seemed to have settled in his tongue. Tully was grateful for the silence. He was so drained by his fight with Daimler that he could barely stick the saddle. He knew Beer was curious as to his physical condition, but, as Tully offered nothing, Beer asked no questions. They rode at a swift and steady gait.

Tully had no idea as to time beyond the feeling that daylight was not far away. The moon hung, full and bright, in the sky and the steady beat of their horses' hoofs was the only sound. He recalled that Daimler and party had ridden out not far ahead of them, but Beer had not met them. That indicated that they had turned off toward Lagg's horse camp in the *malpais.* If so, Daimler would be late in getting back to Two Hump. Before then Tully had to see Louise and talk her out of giving in to Daimler.

He had other things to accomplish before then. He wanted the rustling to go forward with nothing happening to scare it off. But he didn't want a real fight between the

330

basiners and the Two Hump crew. In addition to seeing Louise, he wanted to talk to Clyde. The crew didn't know what all was going on. With enough inducement, they might be persuaded to enter into a truce with the basiners without warning Lagg and letting him be caught red-handed at rustling. If Daimler's full scheme was made clear to his men, they might see the whole quarrel in a different light.

Dawn caught Tully and Beer at the Splinter Creek ford, and Beer left him at McNulty's turn off. Tully paused a moment for a final word. "You tell the boys to keep their eyes open but not to hunt trouble. As soon as I've been to Two Hump, I'll come over with what I hope's a sensible way to tackle this thing."

"You take it easy," Beer warned.

"Never do things any other way, Matt," Tully said, and he rode on toward the pass to Bentham Valley.

Near the end of the Two Hump road, where he could see the willow corrals, Tully realized that he had judged the situation with accuracy. The day corral was filled, the unsaddled horses stirring in penned-up restlessness. If Two Hump was on routine for the day, most of them would have been ridden out by now on the day's work. If, on the other hand, there was a slack season in the work, the saddle band would have been left in the horse pasture. So it was expected that mounts would be needed. They were being kept ready, the cowpunchers waiting for fighting orders from Daimler.

As he came to headquarters, little knots of men scattered idly about lent validity to Tully's supposition. His appearance went unnoticed for a moment. He decided against going directly to the big house to see Louise and turned into the main compound. Then he saw interest stir and watched men swing about to stare at him.

Tully's mouth was dry, and a hard tension pulled back his shoulders. Without betraying his uneasiness, he let his gaze cast about in search of Clyde Colby. He spotted the man in a group standing outside the cook shack but had no wish to incriminate Clyde by seeking him openly. Tully rode across to a little office building, before which a half dozen cowpunchers draped themselves on a tie rack.

Except for Clyde and Daimler, the crew was strange to Tully, although he had seen a few of them with Daimler the night the ramrod had come to give Johnny Babbage the ultimatum. None of these was in the group before him, which he studied. Nothing about it marked it as in any way unique. They were rough-looking men of assorted bulk and age, some decent enough in mien and others of the breed that rode the back trails. Tully halted his horse under their steady regard and knew that the tension in their faces came not from him but from the prospect ahead of them.

"Howdy," he said in a matter-of-fact tone. "Daimler around?"

A sour-looking man with a heavy moustache said: "He ain't."

"Expect him soon?" Tully inquired casually.

"Could be. Clarkson's the *segundo,* if you're hunting work. That's him yonder at the cook shack." The man's glance drifted over Tully's beat-up face.

Tully swung his horse, glad of a casual excuse to approach Clyde Colby. He rode across the wide yard, seeing a stony preoccupation on Clyde's face. He gave the man no greeting beyond a glance in passing.

"Who's Clarkson?" he asked the group at large.

A young, stocky man with a bristle of yellow beard said: "Me."

"I'm Gale. The squatter you're all on the prod about."

Every man before him pulled straight.

333

Clarkson's eyes showed quick anger. "Thought I seen you at Babbage's camp. The jigger with the gall, huh?" The man stuck his thumbs under his belt, his shoulders pulled high. "What in hell are you doing here, squatter?"

"Come to see if you boys will listen to reason," Tully said. "I run into Nick Daimler in town and I happen to know what you've got up your sleeves."

"If you run into Daimler," Clarkson growled, "he done a proper job on you." He cupped his hands to his mouth and called: "Boys, here's that stinkin' land-grabber! Rode right in to take his medicine!"

The men who swung about and came plunging across the yard sent a wave of cold fear through Tully. He knew he was defying the lightning, that there was little chance that they would listen to what he wanted to say. He wasn't a man easily frightened but the rush of human flesh toward him sobered him considerably.

He looked about as they formed a half circle that pinned him against the cook shack. Their nearness and emotion made the blue mustang prance nervously. Tully knew that, if he had to, he could drive the animal through, although somebody would probably retaliate by shooting him out of the saddle.

He knew that Clyde must have done everything possible to restrain his saddlemates, getting nowhere, for Clyde's tension was patently equal to his own. Wanting to trap Lagg in a clear case of rustling, Tully dared not tell them fully of the scheme because somebody might deem it advisable to relay it on to Lagg. Yet he had to stop bloodshed between the basin and this crew, which mainly was motivated by loyalty to its spread. The only thing he could think of was an appeal to their better judgment. Clyde must have tried that, too.

Despair ran through Tully but doggedly he said: "You boys are waiting for fighting orders from Daimler. From the looks of it, you expect them any minute. Don't know as I blame you. I'd feel the same if I knew no more about that man's intentions and crooked use of you than you men do."

"We don't want any preaching, Gale," Clarkson said harshly. "We had enough of that from Colby. We don't want tricks, either. If you're trying to beg off, it's too late. You people asked for trouble. You've got it coming to you."

"What I want to know," Tully retorted, "is whether you boys are working for Two Hump or for Nick Daimler?"

Clarkson's answer was prompt. "We work for Two Hump. Daimler runs it."

"But Louise Bentham owns it," Tully pointed out. "Would you follow her orders if they ran contrary to Daimler's?"

Clarkson spat. "She don't know anything about the cattle business. Maybe she owns this outfit, but it's our living. Let her have the run of it, and we'd be ruined along with her and no jobs to be had anywhere else. We heard how you can wrap her around your finger, Gale. Maybe you can fool her, but if you figure you can fool us, too, you're crazy."

Tully shrugged. "That's all I wanted to know." He started to swing the blue but a man grabbed its bridle. Tully was on the point of pulling his gun when the mustang took over. Rearing, it struck out with its front hoofs, and they pulled back fast. The blue drove through.

Clyde's voice rapped out: "You boys leave him go! I'll plug the son-of-a-bitch who tries to shoot him!"

Regret of that necessity ran through Tully. He had forced Clyde to take an open stand against his saddlemates. Regardless of Louise's friendship, Clyde's days on Two Hump were numbered unless she won out fully. But Tully had learned what he had needed to know, that there was no swinging this big crew behind Louise, that they were Daimler's men, his pawns in what was coming.

At the end of the compound Tully swung his mount left, down the lane that led on to the big house in the poplar grove at the edge of the lake. He dismounted at the porch, securing the blue to the tie ring at the bottom step. He crossed the porch and thumped solidly on the door.

When it swung open, Louise stared at him wordlessly, then ran forward into his arms. Her anger was gone. She was only frightened now, needing him. He kissed her, then held her arms and stepped back from her, angered that the love between them had always to flare up when it was so utterly impossible. He said: "What's worrying you, girl? Daimler can't make you sell. That's your decision. You're not responsible for what's happened or for what he means to make happen. He is, and don't let him make you think otherwise."

"I've been so afraid for you," Louise breathed. Her eyes searched his fight-marked face. "Somebody's tried to hurt you already."

"Got bucked into a cactus," Tully told her. "You can help me a lot by promising to hold onto the ranch."

"I knew you'd say that," she said in a despairing note. "But Clyde says the boys will follow Daimler to the bitter end. Clyde's nearly got himself beaten up trying to talk them out of it. But I think I could stop that fight, Tully."

"Not by selling to Daimler."

She shook her head. "Something else. The men won't take my orders, but I don't think many of them would want to see me killed, either. They've been kind and considerate to me. It's just that they don't like me owning Two Hump. So I'm going to take steps, Tully. I'll join your side. I'll move over to that cow camp, and, if my men attack it, they'll have to risk killing me."

"Now, wait a minute," Tully gasped. He lifted the flat of his hand to his cheek and stood in deep thought. "Dag-nab it, you're talking sense, at that. But it's too dangerous."

"Tully," Louise cried, "I'd give anything to stop more shooting and killing. I'd sell Two Hump right now if you'd let me. You made me see something the other day, and Daimler and the boys are right about one thing, too. I've never lifted a hand for Two Hump. It came to me on a platter. I'll never know as much about the cattle business as the poorest 'puncher on the payroll. I'm dependent on the work and knowledge and the loyalty of others. But I do know one thing. I'm responsible for Two Hump. I want to meet that responsibility."

"Good girl," Tully breathed. "Let's go indoors."

With the door closed behind them, Tully gave her a long and careful inspection. Something had come to her since their meeting on the ridge, resulting perhaps from his angry lecturing. There was a settled look beneath the obvious strain on her face. There was strength and determination in her mouth and jaw. She saw Two Hump now as more than a source of revenue, as more than a barrier between them. Two Hump was responsible for the men that made it go, to its neighborhood and the country that made possible its being. The last frivolity was gone from Louise, a becoming humility taking its place. All the love he had ever felt for her welled up in him, and in that moment he forgot Maggie forever.

He said: "We figure Daimler will attack Babbage's camp mainly to tie up your boys while a bigger caper takes place. There's reason to think Lagg is set to pull a terrific rustling job on you to make you look broke when the time comes to sell. Lagg will handle that end, and we want to catch him at it. So we've got to let Daimler lead the boys against the cow camp. And trust that you can stop a fight."

"It's worth the risk, Tully," she insisted. "I'll do it. I'll ask for a horse and poke off like I'm only going for a ride. I often do that. Then I'll swing around to your place."

"Do it, then," Tully agreed. "It's two to one the big play will come tonight. So get away as soon as you can. Tell Clyde what you're up to, so the boys will be sure to know you're in that camp. And make double sure you yell your head off if shooting starts, anyhow. I won't be around, I've got my eye on Lagg."

He started to turn, but she said: "Kiss me good bye, Tully. I don't care if you are determined to have nothing to do with me. This is special. Something might happen to you."

Or to you, Tully thought with a sobering start. Aloud he said: "I'm not trying to act big and noble, Louise. This change in your life has put you where it just couldn't pay off for us. Me, I'm loose-footed and don't have much ambition. I've got none at all for a nest that my wife had to feather for me. I'd go wild, and it would be worse than if

I'd never tried. So . . . I just don't aim to try."

Louise smiled. "I understand, Tully. And I won't throw myself at you any more."

He couldn't let it go at that, and maybe she knew he couldn't. He stepped forward, Louise meeting him again with a small, relieved cry. For a long moment they stood there, pressing hard against each other, happy in being together. Tully broke away and walked out blindly, and, when he rode out of the yard, he dared not look back.

XIII

Tully cut a loop around the lake and struck for home, following the course he had ridden the night he had visited Louise. Now, in full daylight, he could see parts of Two Hump's vast herd, grazing north of ranch headquarters. Experience had told him that the *malpais* lay farther on. A sweep by fast-moving, well-organized rustlers would be easy, provided Two Hump's own riders were pinned down at a safe distance. Every instinct told Tully that he was guessing correctly. Lagg would come out of that wasteland tonight, to make a big, crippling cut on Bentham cattle.

When Tully reached his land claim, he found Babbage had kept the drought cut there in close herd because of the lingering danger of Two Hump's trying to stampede it. Half a dozen alert riders herded the big bunch. The other men were at the cow camp, tired-looking yet keyed-up and sullen.

He swung down at the campfire, helped himself to coffee, and rolled a cigarette. He saw from the watching men that they were waiting for him to explain his hammered, swollen face and the fresh-scabbed abrasions on his knuckles. His eyes surveyed them blankly over the rim of his coffee cup.

Then, removing the cup, he grinned at them. "You're right, boys. I run into Daimler in Splinter Rock. But what we settled was a private matter. So . . . to public business. You know what Two Hump intends to do if it finds you here when the ultimatum expires. Beer must have told you that Daimler saw Lagg last night in town. They rode out together afterward, and Lagg had some hardcases with him. They went to Lagg's horse camp. They're getting set."

"You think we'll catch it from two sides?" Babbage asked worriedly.

Tully shook his head. "Lagg's got another job. He'll go after a cut of Two Hump steers while the frolic's on here. Him and Daimler aim to buy that spread by using some of its own capital. I reckon the time's come to tell you some other things, too." A man had brought him a plate of food. Tully ate hungrily, telling them between bites about

Lagg's dam in the *malpais*. It had the effect he had feared. Except for the threat that they had to meet here, they would have hit the trail to the badlands. Yet, seeing the whole, carefully planned scheme, they were ready to meet it here, letting the next hours decide the outcome for the basin, their families, and themselves.

"Now," Tully concluded, "it's a hard thing to ask, but your main job tonight is to stay out of a fight if you can manage. At best you're pinned down here. Louise Bentham's presence might not do a thing to stop her outfit from attacking. In that case you'll have your fight."

"How about Lagg?" Beer asked. "Who's going to stop him?"

"We don't want him stopped," Tully said. "We want him to pull it off and get caught at it. He'll have plenty of men, and catching them's a job for the law. I told Ed Handel to have the sheriff set and I'd get word to him. No use waiting any longer, now that I'm sure from what I seen at Two Hump that it will come tonight. I'd suggest that you go for him, Matt, and bring him out here after dark. Me, I'll try to keep tabs on Lagg, then help the sheriff when the thing is ripe."

"That'll be risky," Beer said.

"Riding to town, Matt?" Tully taunted. "Hell, a man your age hadn't ought to be scared of that."

He went down to his own camp, washed at the pond, and turned in. He was bone weary, but this kept him wakeful instead of inducing sleep. Yet he was composed in his mind, for the issues were clear at last, and the chips were down. Finally he slept but it was only for an hour or so. He gave it up after that, rose, and went out to take a look at the red. He would want a more trust-worthy horse than the blue under him that night. The red's back seemed healed enough to stand a saddle. He saddled up and headed for Sam McNulty's.

Sam stood framed in the doorway of his barn when Tully rode on across the yard.

"Howdy, young fellow," Tully greeted him. "Feel up to some Indian wrestling?"

"Nope," Sam admitted. "And it looks like you've already had a workout. Boy, I've got some news for you. Light down while I go to press." Sam was curious about his appearance but refrained from asking questions.

Tully dismounted and stepped into the shade. Sam said: "The doc was here this morning. Ellery Vines has cashed his chips."

"No fooling?" Tully said.

Some of his quick depression must have showed, for Sam said: "Don't let it eat on you, boy. He was out to kill you and would have except that luck fell your way."

"It's not that," Tully said, and he motioned dismissingly with his hand. There was no point in divulging Vines's last desperate effort to realize his driving ambitions. Pity touched him, for he had an instinctive respect for the departed. He thought: *Maybe he knows now what a fool he was. I hope so.* He said: "That all the news, Sam?"

Sam shook his head, grinning. "The doc brought out some mail for Aurora. She got a letter from her husband. He's chafing over her staying so long, so she's going home. In case you don't catch on, she's willing to go alone."

"Bless her heart," Tully said. "I knew she'd come through, Sam. You've got a girl there."

"I know it," Sam admitted. "I feel like a skunk but I couldn't pack up and go with her. But I'm going to write her. I'll answer that letter I got from her last winter."

Tully straightened, staring toward the corral. "What's that horse doing in there?" he demanded.

Sam looked guilty. "What horse?"

"That Two Hump horse."

"Oh, that one," Sam reflected. "Why don't

you go ask Aurora?"

Tully was halfway across the yard when he heard Louise's laugh from the soddy. He halted outside the door, staring in at the girl who was at the table with Aurora.

"What're you doing here?" he demanded.

"Helping to eat a pie. It's apple. Want a piece?"

"Thanks," Tully said. "I've seen Two Hump's cook."

"I baked it myself," Louise retorted. "And I decided to leave before Daimler got back. I came around by the road with a basket on my arm and it was easy. But what are you doing here? You're supposed to be catching rustlers."

"Smelled pie," Tully told her. "If it's your'n, I'll take what's left. And I wanted to see if Sam had a hat I could borrow." He stepped in, smiling at Aurora. "Heard something nice about you, ma'am. Come to say that if you don't mind whispers, I'd like to kiss you."

"You look like a whipped bear," Aurora retorted, but she caught on and was pleased. He had feared she would rowel him for fighting, but she said nothing more about it.

He took a seat and accepted the pie that Louise served him, along with a cup of coffee. It struck him that it was the first time they had shared food. Her pie was good, sweeter and flakier than a cook-shack product. He eyed her with a new respect. But there had been poverty in her life, he remembered; she had learned to be useful. In more ways than one she was all any man could want in a wife. He shook his head so violently that both women looked at him in wonder.

"Sleepy," he said.

"Well, I like that," Louise breathed. "In the middle of a piece of my pie."

"She tells me you were bucked into a cactus, Tully," Aurora said unexpectedly. "Did it have gray temples and jet-black eyes?"

"Yes, ma'am," Tully admitted.

"Tully Gale, I love you, too," Aurora said. "You've all but redeemed yourself with me."

"You and me both, ma'am. It's a shame you're already married."

Relaxation was coming over Tully and he was finally growing sleepy. He wanted that because he figured he had a hard night ahead when he would need sharp faculties. He walked down to the barn and stretched out in the hay and was soon lost to the world.

When he awakened, the shadows of late

afternoon were deeply in the barn. He got up, stretching, feeling fully restored. He went out to the water trough and scrubbed his hot, swollen face.

Sam came out of the soddy, carrying an old battered hat. "Here, put this on," he said. "It'll give you back your self-confidence." He knew from experience that a cowboy pulled on his hat ahead of his pants when he rolled out of bed.

The women had a meal ready, and Tully went in with Sam to eat. Tension was building in all of them with the fading light, and the gaiety had gone out of the girls. Louise kept her face in repose, but something in her eyes disclosed deep strain. She had volunteered for a task that a man might try to avoid. Afterward, with dusk running in over the countryside, she rode with him toward his homestead claim.

She paused at his private camp a while, dismounting and looking about. "It's beautiful here, Tully," she told him. "Much prettier than the flat where Uncle Cass built his home. I wonder why he picked that place, with country like this up here?"

Tully laughed. "A cowman's main interest is the grass and water it takes to put beef on a steer. What's pretty doesn't mean much, save maybe in horses and women."

"In that order," Louise said.

"Depends entirely on the woman," Tully rejoined. "Let's go on and meet the boys."

The cow camp's anxiety was equally apparent. The time that Daimler had allowed it to clear out of the country had nearly run out. A man challenged them, as they rode in, and let them pass on only to come upon others equally vigilant. There was no fire. The group at the cow camp came to its feet when one of the newcomers was seen to be a woman.

Johnny Babbage said — "Howdy, Miss Bentham." — and touched his hat. "Ma'am, we're grateful for your sympathy and help. And we'll try to sit on our hands unless Daimler is able to move his boys against you. Which he might be, and you should know it. What we've been up to would rile any good cowpoke. I'm willing to admit even Two Hump's got a few good ones on its payroll."

"Help her down and take care of her horse, Johnny," Tully said. "I got a chore to tend to." He touched his hat to Louise and turned his mount quickly, not daring to look at her too closely. He rode away from the camp, heading north.

Night was coming in fast. He remembered a place that he had noticed the night he rode the uplands making his first visit to Two Hump. Up there was a wide rim break. All day he had tried to put himself in Lagg's place, recalling what he had learned of the man's character. Lagg was blunt, direct, without subtlety. He lacked the capacity to adjust to sudden change.

Reviewing what he knew of the *malpais* and of Two Hump's layout, Tully had a hunch that Lagg would bring his rustling party through that escarpment break and return the same way with his cut of stolen cattle. If a man stationed himself at the break, he could see everything and fall in behind when they left the valley. He could trail them far enough to ascertain where they were taking the cattle. In the darkness, trailing would be difficult, dangerous.

The flats and badlands were linked by plateaus within a fringe of low, rolling foothills. The slants were gouged by arroyos and draws, with here and there an infrequent meadow. The low knolls were barren, save for scattered juniper and the ever-present rabbit brush and sage. As he rode north, he passed frequent outcrops of scab rock and volcanic cones.

Out in the lonely distance he saw Two Hump cattle, the vast, loose herd segregated into the small bunches in which range stock instinctively divided itself. Sometimes the animals were near him, but they disappeared as his elevation varied. The mountain enclosures of Bentham Valley grew ever nearer. The destination he had chosen loomed at last, the vaulting portals of the badlands that he was certain Sugar Lagg would use. Tully was gambling everything upon it, a night's hard effort and a night's full danger.

The air was warm and still, the moon wane beyond the heat haze still painting a star-dusted sky. Scents, because of lack of breeze, hung in eddies where the heat rendered them, so that he passed through a changing stimulation telling him much about his surroundings. Without wind, the only sound was that scraped up by his horse on the sandy soil and rock. Although usually these impressions were a cowpuncher's pleasure, tonight they were forbidding.

As he neared the escarpment break, he paused, choosing the side he would take for his long watch. The moonlight would serve him better from the right, he decided, and he struck out across the bottom toward that shoulder. Reaching the long talus, he climbed until he found a rock cluster that would hide his horse. Dismounting, he secured the reins and went on afoot.

The bench was high and bare, warm as

flesh to his feet. He came to the standpoint he wanted and dropped flat. He hoped that he would see them enter the valley and be warned. The task he had set himself was to determine, for sure, that a raid had been undertaken and to gain an inkling as to the direction of the drive inside the *malpais*. A quick, surprise challenge by the sheriff, within hours of the event, would be more certain of success than an attack made after Lagg was set and watchful.

He was annoyed when, in the quiet, the accumulated fatigue of recent days rose up in him. His torpor grew, and once he had to rise and walk a while to rouse himself. He knew the experience well, the jadedness that could come at the very moment a man needed his powers, because he had already made too heavy a demand on them. He cursed the dullness and finally, when he jerked up his head with a feeling that he had been asleep, he thought: *They could steal Sam's hat off my head and I'd never know it.*

He rose for another walk and at that instant was fully alerted. It seemed to be the result of instinct, for he had heard nothing. Setting himself down again, he cast an anxious glance to the north, scanning the flat, moon-bathed floor of the break. Out of the shadows toward the *malpais,* far off, a party of horsemen rode at a trot. Excitement swirled in him, washing away his weariness and the last of his doubts. It had to be Lagg's bunch, for there was no good reason for anybody else to come out of there at this hour.

They passed below him, undisturbed, moving at a steady, mile-eating gait. The rustlers were too far away to be identified, but there were seven of them. Tully stiffened at that. Lagg had picked up more men than Tully had figured would be with him, and that would make the going tougher. He watched them recede into the lost distance of Bentham Valley, knowing he had more dreary hours of wait. But waiting would be easier, for he was sure, and this had restored a full measure of energy.

When they were well out in the obscurity, Tully rolled a cigarette, carefully concealing the match with which he lighted it and the subsequent glow of the tobacco. The caution made him grin, yet it was wise insurance against the imponderables that might foul him up. He finished his smoke, rose, and walked down the bench. When they came back, they would be moving cattle, or he would have nothing to gain from this. He could hear and see a herd from the point where he had left his horse, and he had a feeling that it might be well to have the red under him when it happened. He went back to the horse.

The wasteland-bred stallion told him, two hours later, that the wearing wait was ended. The horse swung his head to stare south. Seated on the talus, Tully hastily dropped a cigarette and ground it out with his heel. The red kept watching for several minutes before the muted bawling of cattle came through the starlight. Tully rose and stood at the mustang's head, ready to prevent his nickering, although distance and the racket of the drive seemed to be assurance against the rustlers hearing it. The muscles of Tully's heart seemed to tighten, and the heart increased its beat. Then he could see the herd, far out in the valley, making so wide a front that he knew Lagg had cut generously in the gather.

Tully let the great mass drive in through the escarpment break before he stirred. He knew from experience that the declivities of the *malpais* had an east-and-west alignment. Lagg might decide to swing down toward his horse camp, where the terrain was familiar to him and where Tully knew there was a vast lost valley plentifully supplied with water. Yet it seemed reasonable that

Lagg would go the other way, doing what he could to dissociate this foray from his regular operations, especially since the existence of that lost valley was known to others.

The only thing concerning Tully now was the need to ascertain in which direction Lagg really went. He meant only to follow far enough to be sure before streaking out for the claim to bring in the sheriff — provided Matt Beer had brought him. Put directly on the trail, the sheriff would have little difficulty in overtaking Lagg, catching him red-handed.

Dust hung thickly in the break in the bench, which ran for a considerable distance. He held the red to a careful gait, but excitement had come into the horse, a sense of his nearness to familiar haunts or some brute warning of danger. It took a careful rein to hold the red back, and this slowness through the dust-laden air made the going hard. Even then Tully sometimes feared he was getting too close to them.

The shot came so unexpectedly that its shock was like the explosion of dynamite. He wasn't hit, and the sudden bolt of the stallion settled his alarm. He had seen the flame of the gun muzzle, a dirty orange in the dust ahead. He had his own gun out by reflex, and then could see two horses that squarely blocked his way. Despair ran in him, for he knew that something had warned Lagg, that there was going to be no surprise, that once more Tully Gale had let himself into a tight situation.

He fired, causing the red to bolt again because he had had no experience of gunfire from his back. This saved him, for two guns cracked aflame up there. He shot again as the red wheeled around. Ahead he saw a rider and horse come apart, the man throwing out his arms and leaving the saddle in an unbroken tumble. The other horse whipped away, and Tully dug heels, driving the red behind. He knew he was doing a foolish thing, that the riders with the herd would be drawn back by the shooting. But something had wiped away the meaning of this effort, and the knowledge brought anger boiling out of him.

The man ahead kept going, but twisted in the saddle, and threw a shot that went wild in the turmoil. Tully fired again and caught his breath when the forward horse stumbled and fell, going end over end. The rider flung himself free and was trying to struggle up, dazed and groggy, as the red stallion pounded in. Tully left the saddle in a flying dismount, crashing down upon the man,

exultation singing in him with the awareness that it was Lagg himself.

He kicked the gun from Lagg's loosened
fingers, then, kicking again, drove him back
so hard that he went down again. It dawned
on Tully only after that wild moment of action that he had left the red stallion riderless. The horse would use the occasion to
make another escape into the *malpais,* putting him afoot in a bad spot. For he knew
that Lagg's men would be whipping back at
any moment, once they realized there was
trouble back here.

Lagg tried again to rise, making an animal
whimpering in his frenzy to save himself.
Tully stood over him with the gun and
rasped: "Climb to your feet, Sugar. And take
it easy or I'll kill you."

The mustanger cursed but got up, still
groggy from the spill. "You thought you
were smart, Gale," he panted. "But it looks
like you never rustled. I watch my back
trail."

"So this isn't the first time, huh, Sugar?"

"No. But it's the last time you'll ever spy
on me."

"Right," Tully agreed heartily. "By the
time you're out of the pen, I hope I'm too
old and feeble. Start walking, Sugar. We'll
head for the right talus and go up on top.

Your boys won't be back till they're sure something jumped the track. When they come, you better swallow your tongue or you'll have lead in your belly you never swallowed."

The gun barrel's sharp jab in Lagg's ribs started the mustanger walking. Far down the cañon riderless, running horses drummed up sound. This would warn Lagg's men that all had not gone well. There would be five men left to handle. Tully knew he had only the ghost of a chance to escape detection and keep Lagg in custody.

They reached a point where rubble lay at an angle against the rise of the rim. There was no getting on top at that point. A moment later he realized that there wouldn't be time in any event. Hoof sound was swelling up. Horses were coming toward him. He motioned toward a nest of rocks.

He said: "In there, Sugar. You let out a peep and I'll put one through your head."

"You won't get away with it, Gale," Lagg panted. "You better give up. That way we'll only kill you, and there's things that can be worse."

"Drop onto your belly, Sugar," Tully retorted.

The man hesitated, then obeyed. Tully hadn't wanted to warn him for fear that

Lagg, in his desperation, would put up a fight. With a sudden motion, he swung his gun barrel at Lagg's head. The mustanger tried to jerk aside but the glancing blow caught him. Tully whacked again, and this time the big body relaxed. He straightened, rocking from dizziness brought on by the strain. He crawled out beyond the rocks but kept himself merged with their contours.

The dust of the herd was clearing, and the oncoming horses were near. There were several of them. He meant to let them pass, if possible, and pray that they would be fooled into a long ride back into Bentham Valley. But he was at an elevation to them and in a position to put up a fair defense if he had to do it.

He grew aware that there were two riders but four horses. It dawned on him that, in the construction of the passage, they had been able to catch the escaping mounts. He recognized his red and knew that he would risk anything to get the horse back. He rose, hoping that they would mistake him momentarily for Lagg.

As they came nearer, he waved his hat and yelled: "Here, boys! Some varmint knocked my horse out from under me!" He fired a shot above their heads as they pulled up down below, and in a more natural voice continued: "Don't twitch a muscle. And hold onto them horses you're leading. I want the red." He started down the talus.

A man's blurting voice called: "Where's Sugar?"

"You lose Sugar?" Tully taunted. "Well, never mind. He knows his way on the back trails. If he ain't lit out for the North Pole in his scare, he'll show up." He moved warily toward his horse as he needled them, wanting the red beneath him. He was unwilling to force the rustlers to disarm for fear it would precipitate action. When he had the reins in hand, he said: "You huckleberries light down now. First one to make a funny move will land on his face."

The man farther from him swung his horse in sudden, whirling rebellion. Tully had to shoot, and the man left the saddle. The other man jumped his mount straight toward him, driving him back against the rearing red. He held desperately to the reins, going down. For an instant he thought that the stallion would grind him to pieces with his hoofs. But the animal came down lightly, away from him. Tully rolled over, knowing that his prize no longer harbored the urge to kill him. He turned onto his belly and flung a shot at the fleeing rustler, who bent his full effort to escape.

Tully climbed to his feet. He had accounted for three of them, including Lagg. The stolen herd had moved on steadily. The man he had just shot was dead. Tully mounted the stallion to hunt up the first rustler he had dumped and found the fellow face down, unmoving. The man was hit in the shoulder but his head rolled loosely. The tumble had broken his neck.

There were still four men with the Two Hump cattle, and they were without a leader. If they were like the vanished Lagg, they would stick doggedly to their plan, trying to reach a hiding place as fast as they could get there. They would leave it up to Lagg to join them and press on. Tully didn't want to take Lagg into the cow camp but to leave him here for the sheriff to find, together with the dead rustlers and the copious sign left by the stolen steers. Lagg had been smart enough to watch his back trail, but that very effort had built an incriminating case against him.

Tully went back and used the man's belt to tie him, then stuffed Lagg's handkerchief in his mouth. There was little chance that his men would find him, even if they tried again. A couple of hours more should bring the sheriff to the scene. Tully went back to the red, mounted, and struck out for his claim.

He was on the last stretch, feeling elated over the night's achievements, when the sound of distant gunfire reached him. In the next moment he felt the deepest despair of his life, and the thought rocked him: *They went ahead and hit the cow camp in spite of Louise.* He hit the red with his spurs.

XIV

The stallion had been pounding it, but now he traveled faster. All Tully knew was that Louise was at the cow camp, that her own men had been willing to attack in spite of her, that, now that they had, they would prefer to see her die with the basiners. Maybe the sheriff and party had been caught there, too, if Matt had got back with them. It seemed incredible that Daimler had been able to drive his men to it. But the far-off shooting was ample evidence that he had succeeded well. The sound of the firing grew louder and was heavy, determined.

When he whipped up from the last draw, he couldn't see the drought herd, which had been bunched near the camp. He knew that the gunfire had exploded it, that the night guard would have come in to join the fight. He left his horse, feeling the deepest worry of his life. He penetrated a thicket that would let him down behind Two Hump's near line.

He paused at the edge of the brush to replace the empties in his gun. He could see the camp vaguely, although the flashing gunfire was vivid. Two Hump had formed a spaced-out circle about the camp. An enemy at their rear would be a nuisance. He slipped to his right, the copse helping to conceal him.

Like the hub and broken rim of a wagon wheel, the two factions faced each other, keeping up a steady fire. Two Hump's line was too scattered for him to pick off more than one man very easily. Once he had disclosed his presence, he would be in for plenty of trouble. He selected a point just below him and began to crawl carefully toward it.

He could make out the heavy sound of rifles, which probably were in Two Hump hands. He knew that the cow camp was hard pressed. It indicated that Beer had not got back with the sheriff, and what had seemed the start of triumph had turned to ashes in Tully's mouth. He moved on at a swift crawl, and then he saw a Two Hump man propped on an elbow with a rifle butt against his cheek.

Tully fired and saw rifle and man fall flat. He crawled into the man's position, hoping that the shot would rouse no curiosity on his flanks. When it failed to do so, he crawled to his left again, bent on another stalk. Guns spat a ragged volley all about. Then somebody in the enemy line grew aware of him. A bullet kicked into the ground just ahead of his face. He dropped flat, and a second shot flung dirt on him. It had him at a disadvantage, for he was in the enemy line so that the flash of his gun was a target for his comrades as well as his enemies. Biting his lip, he crawled on, determined to pick off another man or two before one side or the other stopped him.

Ahead, a man shoved to his knees and leveled a rifle at the camp. He never pulled trigger, for, at Tully's shot, he let the gun drop and fell over backward. Tully pressed as flat to the earth as he could get. Then a hidden gun blazed close at hand and he jerked to the impact of a bullet.

It struck him high in the left shoulder, numbing it, sending an unbearable feeling down his arm. He rolled, thereafter lying quietly. But he could still use his gun. In a moment he would go on with his chores, but now he was tired. He rested and, after long moments, threw off the shock to realize that the firing was tapering off.

Most of the present shooting seemed to

come from the cow camp. Daimler's purpose had been to tie up his crew while Lagg got away with the rustled cattle, vengeance against the basiners being only of secondary importance. With resistance mounting against it, Two Hump might be pulling out, with or without Daimler's orders.

Tully yearned to join his friends, and find out about Louise, but knew that, if he moved in closer, he might stop a slug from a basiner. He kept watching the Two Hump positions on either hand, but nothing further came from them. The end was signaled only by a complete halt in the shooting. Men began to shout back and forth at the camp.

Without daring to rise, Tully yelled: "Johnny! It's Gale and I'm coming in!"

A long moment passed before anyone answered: "Come on in, Gale!" It wasn't Babbage's voice that called.

Tully crawled up to the camp, and they let him through. Men were beginning to stand up warily. They had prepared themselves well for the attack, he saw. Numerous rock forts circled the cold fire, and heaped camp equipment completed the barricade.

He got to his feet, hardly able to stand. He gasped: "Louise! Where is she?"

"Daimler's got her, Gale," a man said

reluctantly.

"Daimler?" Tully could only stare at the speaker.

"Yeah, Daimler. That man is smart as a fox. Before the rumpus, he sent a 'puncher in with a white flag. And a threat to plug Clyde Colby unless the girl quit us and come home. Johnny told her to go. She went."

"No," Tully gasped.

The man stared back at him. "What would you have done, Gale?"

"I guess, if I'd been Johnny, I'd've told her to go," Tully admitted numbly. "And, if I'd been Louise, I'd've gone."

There were dead men here. More were hurt, and Johnny Babbage was one of these. Matt Beer hadn't got back with the sheriff, Tully learned. He found that Two Hump had paid a stiff price for its foray, but he had lost his sympathy for them. They had been given every chance to pick their sides, and they had gone far to carry out the fight. But he had little time to think about that now. He had to get to Louise, which meant that he had to go again to Two Hump headquarters. The camp was too pre-occupied to object, and he staggered up the slope toward his horse.

He couldn't stand the strain, he thought,

and this had little to do with his exhaustion and the now flaming pain of his wound. It was because of Louise alone. His mind crawled with anxiety for her. Daimler had crossed his bridge. Now, with the last chips down, it was hard to tell what he would decide to do about her. And with his fear was Tully's knowledge that she had offered him her love and he had turned it down. That now appalled him. What difference did it make what either of them possessed? She had been willing to give up everything for him, without regret. What had he been willing to give up for her? He no longer cared who she was or what she owned, for death was all about them in its full insistence. If she were still alive — dear God, that was all he asked, that she was still alive. . . .

He rode straight for Two Hump, unmindful of the bullet-torn camp behind him, of Lagg and the stolen cattle, of the stampeded basin steers. Finally he saw a horse, far out in the moonlight, and pulled down. The rider came on steadily, bound openly for the cow camp. Tully rode forward again but kept his gun in his hand. He saw the other horseman pull down hesitantly, catching sight of him, then come on.

Presently Tully called and was answered, and he leaped his horse into a full gallop. It was Clyde Colby, hatless, his shirt hanging in tatters, the man holding to the saddle horn for support.

"Gale," Clyde said, and his voice was like torn cloth, "I hoped I could get hold of you."

"Where's Louise?" Tully shouted.

"Dunno," Clyde said tiredly. "That's what I wanted you for. They had me locked up, down there, and it took a fight to get away. But I was where I could tell what was happening. Daimler come back with what's left of the outfit, and he ain't their bright and shining hero now. They're shot up. They got their ears knocked down. And him telling them, all along, that it'd be a breeze."

"Louise," Tully said insistently. "Where's Louise?"

"Off on her own somewheres," Clyde said. "Her throwin' in with the basin forced Daimler into the open. He couldn't get the boys to jump the cow camp with her there. So he had to show her his mean side. He threatened to kill me if she didn't. . . ."

"I know," Tully cut in. "Where is she?"

Clyde rested a moment, then said: "Gone. She cut out on her own. Daimler's got snake tracks to cover up. He took so many chances, it's make or break for him now. So I told her to light out, to get away from

370

there. She wouldn't go till I promised to follow. That took me a while. I've lost track of her."

"Would she have a horse?"

"No," Clyde said. "Cook helped her get started. There was no chance to saddle a horse. She just lit out on her lonesome."

"Maybe she headed for Sam McNulty's," Tully said hopefully.

"Maybe. We got to get hold of her, Gale. Daimler's hunting her himself."

"She'd head for McNulty's," Tully decided. "Clyde, you scout around between here and there. I'm going on to Two Hump."

"They'll kill you, Gale."

"Only one man there really wants to," Tully said tiredly. "Daimler. He'll keep wanting to till one of us is dead." He moved the red on, not wanting to argue the matter. The cold will was in him to end this, and it had become a thing that lay strictly between Daimler and himself.

He halted on the last rise where once before he had sat his saddle to search the hostile area running out below him. Two Hump's structures were dark and looked deserted in the still night. He was on the point of starting his horse again when he pulled straight in the saddle.

The big lake lay between him and Two

371

Hump headquarters, and he saw a rider coming around the east end, riding slowly. The horse was moving close in, and Tully saw it bend on around as it followed the brush-cluttered shore. The rider seemed to be searching the brush, and suddenly Tully understood what for. Whoever it was, the man was figuring more shrewdly than Tully had in the turmoil of his talk with Clyde.

Men with range experience dreaded being caught afoot on the graze. Louise had mentioned her habit of taking frequent, solitary rides. She must have been warned of the danger from ornery cattle, and even from horses, to anyone set down in the open. This man assumed that she had tried to hide in the high grass, cat-tails, and brush that fringed the water, rather than brave the open country without a horse.

Tully knew the man could be figuring it right. He held himself motionless while the distant figure moved squarely across his line of travel, intent on the lake margin. Then the horse stopped, the rider dismounting and entering the high vegetation. Tully held his breath, but the man soon came out to swing up and ride on.

When he had his back to Tully, the latter started the red forward at a careful pace. The man might be satisfied with one turn around the lake, but if he re-circled, Tully meant to confront him. He gained the outer edge of the heavy belt of foliage without interference or alarm. Swinging in the direction the other man was riding, he kept going with a close attention on the brush.

He wanted to call Louise's name and let his voice reassure her, if she was in there. Since his horse had not nickered to the other mount, he decided to risk it. He rode three-quarters of the length of the lake, calling quietly and at regular intervals. He had about decided that both he and the other man were wrong about her when he heard her sharp call.

"Tully!"

He was beyond the place and he jerked the red around. She came out of the thicket and ran toward him. He was about to sweep her up with him when a contradicting thought struck him.

He dismounted, saying: "Do you think you could handle this horse?"

"I don't know," Louise gasped. "I'm not very good."

"It's your best bet. Get aboard and ride, girl. For Sam McNulty's."

Her voice lifted in alarm. "Not without you, Tully. That's Daimler. He only wants to keep me in his grip. He'll kill you. Can't we ride double?"

"Not right now," Tully told her. "I've got business with Daimler."

"Then I'll stay, too."

Tully saw that argument would do no good, and, if Daimler swung around the lake upon them, the horses would betray them. He said: "Then crawl back in where you were hiding."

"What are you going to do?"

"Don't argue so much. Do what I told you."

She obeyed, stepping back into the obscurity of the thicket. Tully remounted, and now he swung his horse the other way, aiming to meet Daimler head-on and make his challenge. He kept the red at a walk and was wholly cool, although his hurt shoulder throbbed with each beat of his heart. He had his gun out, and at this point the moon was in his eyes. But that was a thing he couldn't change.

At the end of the lake his horse swung his head but made no sound at the moment. A few steps later he nickered, and Tully figured this was as good a way as any to throw his warning to Daimler.

He kept riding, canted a little in the saddle to ease the strain on his hurt shoulder. There was no response from Daimler's animal, but it was near or the red would have made no sound. That warning would have put uneasiness in Daimler. It struck Tully that the man might enter the brush and keep his horse quiet while he saw what was coming. Daimler would have no compunctions against shooting from hiding.

Sighing, Tully stopped the red, dismounted, and tied it carefully at the edge of the brush. His throat tightened more and more, and, as he rounded the end of the lake, he put the moon behind him so that he became back-lighted.

It was probably some slight shifting by a horse in the thicket that halted him again. Daimler was watching for a mounted man, waiting for a horse to come along. Tully entered the brush with only the faintest idea of where Daimler was. He moved a few steps and halted to listen but there was no sound. He pressed on, picking a slow way through areas that would let him pass without scraping.

He heard a twig snap a second before he saw his man, and he called: "Daimler!"

The man was at the head of his horse, keeping it quiet but looking out toward the moonlit edge of the brush. He held a gun and swung about, trying to back step into the cover of the animal. It seemed to Tully that he fired after Daimler did, and it was a mild shock to realize that he hadn't been hit again. Daimler's horse hauled back on its reins, leaving the man exposed.

Tully fired again. Daimler's exploding gun put a bullet between Tully's feet. But Daimler swung a hand to his chest, took a faltering step, and went down.

Tully moved forward in a cold numbness. The gun had spilled from Daimler's hand. The man lay still and there was only the sound of the bolting horse as it crashed through the brush. Tully had only to take a short look at its erstwhile rider. If not through the heart, Daimler had been shot so close to it that he was finished.

Tully sighed and walked out of the brush. Like Vines, Daimler was released from his passions. Tully felt no more enmity for either.

He called reassuringly as he rode along the lake's far side. Louise was waiting in the shadows and tried to speak but was too weak to make the words come out. Her arms were uplifted, and he bent on his good side and swung her up to him.

He said: "We're close enough they could hear that down at headquarters. We'll have to pound it."

"Yes," she breathed, settling against him. "Let's pound it. A million miles away. To-night."

He cut out for his claim.

He called a salute to the cow camp as he neared it and was instantly answered. He rode in on a tense, uneasy group that still was alert against a renewed attack from its enemies. A man helped Louise to alight, then Tully swung down.

He said: "I reckon you boys can let down your hackles. I got Daimler. When his horse comes in, his sidewinders will start hunting him. When they find him, they'll know there's no sense in hanging around any longer. Their prospects in this country went with him. I've got a notion Two Hump will be deserted by tomorrow save for a few hands who wouldn't come in on it."

"Tully," Louise cried, "you're hurt! You got blood all over my blouse!"

"Happened a million years ago," Tully told her. He looked groggily about him. "There's one more thing to tend to. I got too bold, and Lagg jumped me in the *malpais*. Left him tied up, but I got to go back and get him."

"Gale," a voice said, "you've chored enough for one day." It was Matt Beer, who Tully had not made out in the dim background.

Tully swung toward him. "Where the hell's the sheriff?"

Beer laughed. "Mind your manners, Gale. He's right here but nailed down till you come back. Boys said you lit out without leaving directions as to where to find Lagg."

A tall man stepped forward, and Tully saw moonlight glint on something on his vest. "Just tell us where to go, Gale," the sheriff said. "I've got a half dozen deputies. We'll take care of Lagg. Whoa, there! Don't knock off work till you've told us where to find him."

Tully held on while he explained how to reach the place where he had left Lagg. He knew that daylight couldn't be far away, and it would be easy to follow the herd from there. He was willing to let the law take over,

When the sheriff and party had ridden out, Tully turned to Louise. "We better go down to my place. There's a cot there and you need rest."

"Tully . . . !"

Her voice seemed to pull off a thousand miles, and he saw the ground swing up at him. . . .

Louise wasn't using the cot in his tent because he was on it himself. Daylight had come, and the camp was quiet. His shoulder had been bandaged, and he had been washed clean of blood and dust. He swung to sit up, pain rocking him, then got to a dizzy stand.

He could smell smoke and looked out through the tent opening to see a woman squatted at the cook fire. He moved quietly to the opening and said: "Howdy, Missus Meade. If you had a blanket over your shoulders, I'd have sworn you were a squaw. This country has sure got you."

Aurora turned her head to frown at him. "You get back into bed, Tully Gale."

"Where's Louise?" he demanded.

"Asleep on a blanket behind the tent. After all, I haven't got you two married yet. But she wouldn't leave and come over to our place. So I had to stay here. Tully, I hope I never put in another such night. I'm going back to my husband old enough to be his grandmother. A good part of it's your fault."

"Where's Sam?" Tully asked.

"Over at the cow camp and mighty happy. The sheriff brought in Lagg's men and the Two Hump cattle. Clyde went down to Two Hump, and there's nobody there but a few old hands. The squatters have vacated their claims. Louise swears she won't pay the taxes on Two Hump and the county will have to take it over. She says she won't set foot on the spread again. Though it didn't do him any good, Daimler succeeded in sickening her on it, the way he wanted."

"She don't mean it," Tully said weakly.

"You should hear her talk."

Tully swallowed. He had feared that the violence would produce that repugnance in Louise, a thing that would be hard to talk out of her.

He found a towel and went down to the

pond to wash. When he got back, Aurora had fixed a plate of food for him and poured a cup of coffee. He had to drink the coffee before he felt like eating. He was slack, drained. He wouldn't argue with Louise any more about holding onto Two Hump. But the thought of her selling and going away took the heart out of him.

The food strengthened him, and he found his hat and went over to the cow camp. The atmosphere was different now, although there was no merriment. Two basiners had died in the fight and there had been four Two Hump dead. Between the two sides there had been a number of wounded, the worst of which had already been taken away to be cared for. The drought herd had been rounded up. There was serenity there, but no air of triumph.

Johnny Babbage was on hand, as was Sam McNulty. Tully stared at the two and broke into a laugh. "You boys want to box hats with me?" he asked. They each had an arm in a sling.

"To my mind," said Johnny, "we ought to retire and move to town before we get hurt. It was some tussle, Gale, and we're obliged for your help. Miss Bentham's promised us all the grass and water we need to get through the drought. So likely it'll rain in a day or so, now that we don't need it. That's a fine girl, Gale. Makes a man sorry he's married."

Tully motioned that aside. "I've had a notion about that dam Lagg built," he said. "Why don't the stockmen's association go on with it. Wouldn't cost much to change it into a permanent affair and give yourselves water the year around."

Babbage stared. "How?"

"Just put in some sluice gates," Tully said. "Pool the winter run-offs, and you'll always have water to waste."

"I'll be blamed," Sam said. "Why don't we, Johnny?"

"A good question," Johnny agreed. "Wait till the boys hear about it!" He went off to talk to the others about it.

"We'll wind up," Sam drawled, "giving Lagg a medal."

Sam returned to the other camp with Tully, whose heart began to pound when he saw Louise at the fire with Aurora. Neither woman paid any attention as the men came in, going on with their work. Sam poured Tully a cup of coffee, then rolled him a cigarette. But Louise still hadn't looked at Tully. It looked like she had it in for him again.

"Tully can finish this," Aurora said to her,

nodding at the cooking. "You ready to go home, Dad? Louise and I are anxious to get started."

Tully nearly jumped. "You mean for Sam's place, I reckon."

She smiled at him. "I mean back East. We're leaving as soon as we can."

Tully swung and stared at Louise. "You can't!" he yelled.

She tossed her head. "And why not? I didn't need your permission to come out here, Tully Gale. I don't need it to leave again."

"Two Hump . . . it'll go to pieces." That sounded pretty weak, but it was the best argument Tully could manage.

"Fine," Louise said heartily.

"Clyde's the man to run it for you," Tully said. "He deserves the chance, too."

Louise shook her head. "I already made the offer, Tully. Clyde says he's happy in a top hand's saddle, and he doesn't want to go any higher. I offered the job to Sam, who says he's got King Pin and that's worry enough. So I'm going to abandon the place and make the county take it over for taxes."

Tully's mouth was dry. "Look," he said desperately, "if I helped you get onto the ropes. . . ."

Louise rose. "That might help, but not much."

Sam waved an impatient hand. "Let me work on the critter, Louise," he said, and he looked at Tully. "I figured out an arrangement that'll save your touchy pride. We could make it a combine, one of them big outfits you hear about. You throw in your claim and me King Pin and Louise can put up Two Hump. You can raise horses, me beef, and Louise young 'uns."

"Done," Louise said promptly, "provided, of course, that the cowboy there's the father."

Tully stroked his jaw while a slow grin spread over his face. "I'm licked," he said. "I'm euchered. It's a deal, and a good one."

He caught a glimpse of Aurora, who was smiling triumphantly. Let her have her victory. His interest was in Louise, who stood smiling and waiting as he moved toward her.

ABOUT THE AUTHOR

Giff Cheshire was born in 1905 on a homestead in Cheshire, Oregon. The county was named for his grandfather who had crossed the plains in 1852 by wagon from Tennessee and the homestead was the same one his grandfather had claimed upon his arrival. Cheshire's early life was colored by the atmosphere of the old West that in the first decade of the century had not yet been modified by the automobile. He attended public schools in Junction City and, following high school, enlisted in the U.S. Marine Corps and saw duty in Central America. In 1929 he came to the Portland area in Oregon and from 1929 to 1943 worked for the U.S. Corps of Engineers. By 1944, after moving to Beaverton, Oregon, he found he could make a living writing Western and North-Western short fiction for the magazine market and presently stories under the byline Giff Cheshire began appearing in

Lariat Story Magazine, Dime Western, and *North-West Romances.* His short story, "Strangers in the Evening", won the Zane Grey Award in 1949. Cheshire's Western fiction was characterized from the beginning by a wider historical panorama of the frontier than just cattle ranching and frequently the settings for his later novels are in his native Oregon. *Thunder on the Mountain* (1960) focuses on Chief Joseph and the Nez Percé war, while *Wenatchie Bend* (1966) and *A Mighty Big River* (1967) are among his best-known titles. However, his novels as Chad Merriman for Fawcett Gold Medal remain among his most popular works, notable for their complex characters, expert pacing, and authentic backgrounds. A first collection of Giff Cheshire's Western stories, *Renegade River,* edited by Bill Pronzini was published in 1998.

The employees of Thorndike Press hope you have enjoyed this Large Print book. All our Thorndike, Wheeler, and Kennebec Large Print titles are designed for easy reading, and all our books are made to last. Other Thorndike Press Large Print books are available at your library, through selected bookstores, or directly from us.

For information about titles, please call:
  (800) 223-1244

or visit our Web site at:
  http://gale.cengage.com/thorndike

To share your comments, please write:
  Publisher
  Thorndike Press
  10 Water St., Suite 310
  Waterville, ME 04901